THE GUNS OF MORGETTE

THE GUNS OF MORGETTE

G. G. Boyer

WALKER AND COMPANY
NEW YORK

CHAPTER 1

DOLF Morgette drew the precious document from the large official envelope. It was the last thing his numerous and bitter enemies ever expected he'd hold in his hands. It was probably also something they prayed most he'd never hold in his hands, next to a six-shooter.

Dolf squinted at the fine print, tilting the page toward the lamp on the warden's desk. The whole thing was like a dream. He had never really expected to set foot outside again for years, not until he was an old man. Now, here was this document signed by President Cleveland.

"I'll be damned," he said, his eyes looking questioningly into those of Warden Bowden.

The warden grinned. "It's real. It's a pardon. You're a citizen again."

"Who?" the natural question formed on his lips.

Bowden pointed his index finger at his own chest.

"Me. I always thought you was railroaded. What you did to Pardeau and his deputies was kill or be killed. You've got a profession now; you're a lawyer. That pardon means you can be admitted to the bar and live a normal life again."

Their eyes locked for a moment, Dolf's still questioning.

"You laid your political reputation on the line for me. Why?"

"You're a helluva man, Dolf. Too good a man to rot in here the best years o' yore life."

Their eyes still held each other in mutual appraisal.

"Any strings?"

The older man hesitated and sighed.

"Nope. I oughta make you promise never to go back to Pinebluff. I'm not gonna."

5

"Why not? If I strapped on my six-guns and went after the skunks that murdered my pa and brothers, it'd ruin you politically."

The old politician smiled and rocked back in his chair.

"I'm about at the end of my string," he mused. "Once I thought I was goin' somewhere. But I didn't play the game. I'm gonna leave Idaho and go someplace a clean sight warmer and raise some chickens. I don't care whether you strap on your guns again or not—kind of hope you will. But on the other hand, I'm kinda countin' on you havin' more sense 'n that."

Dolf didn't say anything for a long while, looking again at the pardon. He grinned crookedly, thinking what it could mean.

"Well?" Bowden said.

Dolf looked up at him, still half-grinning.

"Pinebluff can probably use an honest lawyer. Besides, my kids are growin' up there."

"And your wife—?" Bowden added, knowing what was probably going through Dolf's mind.

"I reckon I never really had a wife," Dolf said.

Bowden sighed wearily. After a long silence he said, "Speakin' of your guns, you'll probably need 'em after you walk outa here in the mornin'. I had Doc bring 'em down."

He pointed to a worn carpetbag on the corner of his desk.

Dolf opened the bag carefully and examined the gleaming blued six-shooters to be sure they were empty, reverently laying each on the desk.

Bowden watched with avid interest as Dolf strapped on the plain black cartridge-filled belts with their matching holsters. The warden suspected he was about to be a spectator to a historical event. The Morgette gun magic was famous.

Dolf expertly slipped the guns in place, hefting them once, then held his arms directly in front of him at shoulder height. With a chain lightning flash, the guns leaped from the polished black holsters and appeared cocked and aimed in the outstretched hands. All Bowden could be sure he saw was a blur of unbelievably fast movement. The deadly blue weapons were steady as rocks.

"My Gawd!" Bowden exclaimed involuntarily. "I heard about that draw. Don't look to me like you slowed down any from lack o' practice."

Dolf fixed him with an amiable stare.

"I made the moves every day. The muscles are still there. And I thought about it. You've got to get the hang of thinkin' about it too."

The guns flashed neatly back into the holsters almost as fast as they had come out.

Morgette grinned. "I'm a little rusty. I'll get the hang of it again."

The irony did not escape Bowden. He grinned. "Sure, Dolf. In the meantime, I hope some clumsy kid out for a rep doesn't knock you over."

It was a couple of miles from the prison to town and the railroad station. Bowden hitched up his buckboard to carry Dolf in personally.

I could get a place like these someday and start over, Dolf thought as they passed by small, neat homesteads. Lawyering didn't really appeal to him.

When he was young, his constant dream had been of a ranch or farm of his own. Raised as they were on the farm, none of the Morgette boys were afraid of work. They'd been helping the old man build the finest cattle spread in the territory when the trouble at Pinebluff broke out.

Now they're all dead but Matt, Dolf thought bitterly.

Matt was the youngest brother now back east at school. He'd been eighteen when the trouble started, twenty when Dolf sent him east just before he himself was railroaded to the pen.

I could send for Matt, he thought, *and we could go away somewhere and be a family again*. Then he remembered that Matt was no longer a kid. He'd be twenty-five, a man.

Probably has plans of his own, Dolf reasoned.

For a while his mind wandered back over the events that had ended up with his being railroaded to the pen. Pinebluff had been the center of a politico-economic feud for control of the rich mining and ranching district. He'd ended up on the wrong side of the political fence. Mark Wheat's star was ascendent as district attorney and political boss of the district, and he'd picked Ed Pardeau, his fair-haired boy, as sheriff. At first Dolf had been Ed's under-sheriff, handling the toughs for him; that had been a little out of Ed's line. Ed's pliant tactics with the riffraff attracted by the rich mines had inevitably led to their final falling out. He'd been fired. Dolf hadn't yet been aware then that the suave sheriff was also after his wife, Theodora. Well, he'd got her. And the Morgette ranch in the bargain, after Dolf's father and brothers were murdered and Dolf had been railroaded to get him out of the way. He'd never been sure if Pardeau, or Wheat—or both—hadn't been behind the killings which they had tried to blame on the Indians. That was one of the things he intended to find out. However, he was sure that Pardeau had come to murder him, rather than arrest him, the night Dolf shot him in his and Theodora's bedroom at the ranch. To prove that fact, he'd needed Theodora's testimony. That's when he'd found out how it was with her and Ed. Her testimony would have kept Dolf out of the pen—and perhaps put Ed in. She had refused to testify against her lover. What a devastating blow realization of the truth had been to him.

His train of thought was interrupted by a well-developed sixth sense that he'd learned to depend on in the past. It seldom misled him.

His keen blue eyes warily swept the roadside ahead, then the bluffs some three hundred yards to their left.

Bowden seemed not to notice his sudden alertness.

It was then that the puff of dust sprang up in the road a few feet ahead of the team. A bullet glanced and ricocheted away into the brush with a whine. The horses shied and danced nervously around the spot. Bowden, a little too slowly if the ambusher was going to shoot again, slashed the ends of the reins across the horses' rumps and yelled at them. They leaped into the harness.

Dolf had jerked a six-shooter and was scanning the bluff in the direction of the sound. No second shot followed. Instead, a horseman broke into view, just spurring his mount into a gallop.

"Pull up!" Dolf yelled. "I can plug his horse at this range with a little luck."

Bowden tried to saw the team down to a stop, but was as uncoordinated as he'd been getting them started. Dolf restrained an impatient thought about the older man's clumsy driving. He leaped nimbly to the road as soon as the rig slowed enough, planted his feet firmly, and got off a steady two-handed shot at the receding horseman. He couldn't tell the result—at least he saw no puff of sand spurt up around horse and rider.

Probably a little high, he thought. *Or else I winged one of 'em.*

By then Bowden had awkwardly stopped his team some fifty yards up the road. The nags were still mighty nervous.

Dolf walked rapidly down to them.

"Damn poor rifle work, whoever he was," Dolf observed to the warden. "Or else he wasn't tryin' to hit anything."

"Think ya hit him?" Bowden asked.

"I doubt it. Pretty long range to hit a moving target. Can't tell."

"Wanna unhitch that big buckskin there and go after him?" Bowden asked.

Dolf had already noticed that the big horse probably had speed and bottom, running seventeen hands high and having the rangy build of a thoroughbred.

He shook his head. "I don't think so. He's headed for town. He'd have that horse out of sight somewhere by the time I got that far. Damn small chance of trackin' him in town. But just for the hell of it, let's drive up there and look at the tracks."

Their assailant had been riding a barefoot mount.

"If that hombre's real dumb, we could probably go uptown and find his horse at a blacksmith shop about now. My bet is he's in a barn. But whoever rode him'll try again. That's my best bet to catch 'im."

"If ya like bein' a clay pigeon," Bowden observed wryly.

They resumed their drive.

A thought was bothering Dolf. "Why did the damn fool ride out where we could see the horse?"

In that country, even kids and women could identify a horse a mile or more away. It was common to hear talk such as "that big roan livery nag," or "the school marm's little bay mare with the white stockings," and "the sheriff's big Roman-nosed black that throws its feet," and so on. In view of this, why would anyone up to no good ride out in plain view unless they had to? Obviously because they wanted to be seen.

"You know that horse?" Dolf asked the warden.

"Can't say as I can place him," Bowden said. "Don't belong to nobody I know. Maybe we'll see it uptown, but I wouldn't bet on it

"Me either," Dolf said.

They were both wrong. It was loose in a small pasture not one hundred yards from the railroad station. Its back was still sweaty. The brand was "P Bar P."

A warning sounded in the back of Dolf's mind.

"Know whose brand that is?" he asked Bowden.

The warden didn't look at him right off. Finally he gave him an unhappy look. He nodded.

"Does that mean you're gonna start it all over?" he asked gloomily. "We ain't even sure Pardeau was ridin' that horse. Could be a coincidence—he mighta sold it—maybe even had it stole from him."

"If Ed Pardeau was ridin' that horse," Dolf stated pointedly, "it'd hardly be me that started it all over again if I did go after him. But I'm bettin' he ain't a big enough fool to have been ridin' that hoss himself."

By then they were at the depot.

Dolf jumped down and picked up his skimpy carpetbag. He hefted it easily, exchanging glances with Bowden.

"Quite an accumulation for thirty-seven years o' honest work. A change of socks and underwear, a picture of my two kids, a shaving mug, and a razor—oh yeh, and a toothbrush, me bein' the refined type of jailbird that's studied law."

He laughed, and only then did Bowden smile since he hadn't been sure of the big gunfighter's mood.

"You're still alive 'n' kickin', Dolf. Besides, you got lots to live for. Them two kids, fer example. And you got a profession to support you."

"Okay, if you say so," Dolf agreed. "Let's go in and get a ticket and ask who belongs to that sweaty strawberry roan."

Dolf stepped up to the ticket window. A little fellow with a mousy mustache and timid eyes grinned out at him.

"Yes sir!" he said. Then he noticed the warden, looked back at Dolf, and the grin faded. It was obvious that Dolf's reputation had preceded him. The papers had made a big story of the impending release of the West's most notorious ex-lawman. Wild stories circulated that he'd killed dozens of men; some said hundreds, including Indians and Mexicans.

"What can I do for you, Mr. Morgette?" the little man quavered.

Dolf suppressed a grin. He could imagine the newspaper reports if he grinned: "Morgette grinned sardonically," or at the very least, "darkly."

"You know who belongs to that strawberry roan over in the next pasture?" Dolf asked.

The other's eyes shifted nervously. It was pretty clear what the answer would be. Everyone knew of the feud between Dolf and Pardeau.

"I hate to say."

"Say anyhow," Dolf ordered coldly.

"Ed Pardeau. He keeps it here for when he comes down to this part of the country."

"Is he down in this part of the country now?" Dolf inquired.

"If he is, I ain't seen 'im," the little man said warily.

Dolf and Bowden exchanged looks.

"You gonna look around town?" the warden asked.

"Nope. If it was Ed, he'll come lookin' again. Okay," Dolf said. "Now I'll have a ticket to Pinebluff."

The agent, obviously relieved, got extra busy over the ticket business.

Dolf saved the grin for Bowden.

"I knew you was goin' back to Pinebluff," Bowden sighed.

Dolf shrugged.

"My kids are back there. Mark Wheat offered me a job in his office and practically promised he'd get me admitted to the bar."

"Wheat?" Bowden said questioningly. "Wheat? I thought he was in cahoots with Pardeau."

" 'Was' is the word," Dolf said. "As I get it, relations have cooled a whole lot in the past couple of years. In fact, I ain't too sure that what Mark Wheat wants isn't a bodyguard instead of a partner. Be that as it may, beggars can't be choosers. I'll play along."

Bowden whistled. "Well, I'll be damned." He paused, thinking the proposition over.

"Well," he finally allowed, "like you say, play along. But watch your back. If Mark Wheat is backin' you, though, you're a lead-pipe cinch to pass the bar. He's a big stick in politics. Territorial delegate, a shoo-in fer senator if we get statehood. You could do worse." He paused again. "But I still wonder what his game is."

"So do I," Dolf said. "Maybe I'll find out."

"If you live," Bowden said. "Watch your back in Pinebluff."

"Do you know something I ought to?" Dolf asked bluntly.

Their eyes met firmly.

"Nope," Bowden said. "Just a hunch."

There was a parting handshake. Dolf swung lightly aboard.

Bowden watched the chuffing engine snake the cars rapidly out of sight around a bend in the track.

He shook his head as he walked back to the buckboard.

"I'm glad I knew 'im, whatever else ya say about Dolf. There's somethin' about 'im." Had Bowden been a schooled man, he'd have been able to say what it was. Scholars would have called it "a history-book quality."

CHAPTER 2

DOLF Morgette took the precaution of cruising the three-car train to see if, by chance, any suspicious-looking characters were on it. There was a sprinkling of the usual immigrants, salesmen, farm and ranch people, and travelers, but no one that had "hired gun" written on him. If Ed Pardeau had been riding his own strawberry roan that morning, Dolf certainly didn't expect to find *him* on board. Nonetheless, he cautiously took the rear seat in the last car, where he could see everyone who might come his way. He settled down to get as comfortable as possible for the long eight-hour pull north to Pinebluff Junction, the last thirty miles by stage.

The sky looked somewhat as though a late snow might be in the offing, and Dolf thought longingly of his buffalo overcoat stored with Doc Hennessey in Pinebluff. Pinebluff's local joke about its weather was, "We got only two seasons: winter and Fourth of July."

It might sound like the Fourth when I hit town, Dolf thought ruefully. *Depends on how many old friends like that one this morning are on hand as a reception committee.*

He hoped none. He'd had five years to think over the past and his own violent ways. All he wanted was to be let alone. Revenge schemes to get even for the wrongs done to him and his family had gradually left his mind. He had mellowed, and wanted only to live as normal and peaceful a life as a man with his past could hope to.

If only they'll let me, he thought. *Especially the peaceful part.*

The railroad followed the river for the first twenty miles or so, then crept up onto the plateau that extended for a hundred

14

miles north, broken only by one river valley. Trees gave way to powdery reddish soil and sagebrush.

Dolf recalled an old farmer's remark: "Land'll grow sage, it'll grow anything if a man can only get water on it."

Maybe someday they will, Dolf thought, *and this'll all be covered with pretty little farms like back in Missouri.*

He remembered how this land looked the first time he'd seen it.

Twenty years, he said to himself. *Where did they go?*

There had been no railroad then. They'd all headed west right after Pa and his older brothers, Jack and Henry, got back from the war. There were still a lot of hard feelings in Missouri, which had divided over the issue, not that the Morgettes were the kind who dodged out over threats.

If we were, Dolf thought, *we'd sure as hell never have stuck at Pinebluff. Maybe we should've got out. Stickin' only got Pa and the boys early graves. Today they're already beginning to call folks that came in like we did 'pioneers.' You'd think we was Daniel Boone or someone.*

Then he grinned as a funny thing came to mind. "We even had a tall Shanghai rooster like Sweet Betsy from Pike," he said to himself. "In fact two of 'em, and a dozen of Ma's laying hens—and the dogs Jim and Harley."

Jim was found dead with Dolf's dad and brother Jack when they got theirs. Jim was old by then, but he'd been a fighter. They found a chunk of one of the killers and a piece of his shirt still in old Jim's mouth, even though someone had beat his head almost to a pulp. He died game. At the remembrance, Dolf swallowed down an involuntary lump in his throat. Jim had been his pup and his special sidekick. He'd have to get another dog when he settled down, one like old Jim, a fighter when he had to be, but most of all a good faithful pal.

The train stopped for water and coal at Carbon. Dolf got off and stretched his legs with a short walk, then bought a hard-boiled egg and a cup of coffee at the railroad lunch room before he boarded again. All the while, he was on the alert for any signs of renewed danger. The bum shooting that morning still struck him as strange, perhaps more of a warning than a serious attempt on his life, but you never knew. No one who knew him would be fool enough to think an attempt like that would scare him off.

I don't know any old-timers dumb enough to send a poor shot after me, he reasoned, *and Pardeau himself, whatever else you say about him, is a damn good shot. But he's too well known to be sashayin' around the country butcherin' his own meat. Besides, I sent him word I ain't bearin' grudges, if he's only got sense enough to believe me.*

It was in this frame of mind that Dolf reboarded the train. He carefully surveyed the crowd while he made his way through the cars without having his suspicions aroused. It was when he stepped back into his own car that he spotted what could be his man. Small chilly warnings traveled up his spine at the sight of the newcomer who may have found his chance to slip in after Dolf left. He was now occupying the other rear seat directly across from the one in which Dolf had left his own carpetbag. The other eyed him coolly and speculatively as he moved down the car. He looked like a product of the range except for a too-careful and self-assured look about his level gray eyes. He had a closely trimmed mustache above a firm mouth and determined jaw. His eyes never once left Dolf's. The sense of danger stayed with him. His eyes flicked over the stranger to see where he might carry a weapon. He could spot nothing—not a cartridge belt or the telltale bulge that would denote a belt weapon or shoulder holster.

The other nodded to him, perhaps sensing that his over-long appraisal might be taken as a warning—or an insult, depending on the circumstances.

Dolf edged into his seat without turning his back on the man, then moved his carpetbag so he could sit by the window. He kept himself in position to eye the stranger and detect any false move he might make. He noticed the fellow look his way several times. When he did it again, Dolf looked directly at him.

"Don't I know you?" the stranger said. "You're Dolf Morgette, ain't you?"

"You got the handle right, pardner," Dolf stated, carefully watching for some move.

The stranger seemed to sense the situation. He grinned.

"Sorry to be lookin' yuh over so close, but I figgered I knew yuh. I'm Joe Lane. I repped with yore outfit one year up on the Quarter Lien before I got into the law business."

He extended a hand in a friendly fashion.

Dolf relaxed and shook the proffered hand. The face came back to him now; it had seemed remotely familiar.

"I remember," he said. "Was a couple of years before we had all our trouble up at Pinebluff. You was ridin' the roughest string of wildcats I ever saw, especially that big buckskin."

"Yah," Lane said, appearing embarrassed and not knowing quite what to say next. "That was some string." Then he paused. "The way we got it over our way, that wasn't trouble of yer own making." He went on quickly to cover his embarrassment. "I heard yuh was pardoned. I'm glad of it. Anything I can do to get your feet back on the ground, just say the word. I'm sheriff of Bison County—could always use a good deputy. I'm so short-handed I had to herd a bunch of galoots back east to the pen at Joliet myself; we got a contract with Illinois since we ain't got a pen of our own yet over across the line."

Then he seemed to recognize what he was saying.

"No offense mentionin' the pen, you realize. I really could use a deputy too if you need a job."

Dolf grinned. "No offense," he assured Lane, "an' much obliged fer the job offer. But I've had my bellyful of lawin'. I'm headed home to Pinebluff. Aim to be a lawyer—studied it in the pen. If they'll let me, I'm ready to forget the past."

Joe Lane inclined his head, then shook it sadly. He looked at Dolf seriously.

"It won't be easy. The big part is that 'if'—*if* they'll let yuh. I've seen a lot of 'em try. Never seen one make it yet. The ones that think you owe 'em one'll have it all augered around in their heads that they owe you one instead so's they don't have to live with knowin' what that smell is right around where they are. It's human nature. I hope it don't work out that way for you."

Dolf thanked him, then settled back to his own thoughts, watching the country glide past while the sheriff got out a *Leslie's Weekly* and got interested in it.

Dolf's first thought was, *Am I gonna have my heart jumping in my mouth the rest of my life every time I spot a hard-lookin' galoot like Joe over there?*

It would be a helluva way to go on living. Yet there was plenty of reason to suspect that at least Pardeau, and maybe some others, could have a warm interest in seeing him pushing up the daisies.

Joe Lane got off at Redrock where the stage route branched west over the state line to his bailiwick.

He bid Dolf a cordial good-bye with a firm handshake and a steady earnest look.

"I meant what I said. If the old home ain't what it used to was I got a job for you so long as I'm sheriff. Got a pretty fair cattle spread back in the hills too if you hanker for somewhere to git scarce. And good luck. Watch yor back, Dolf."

Dolf watched Lane's solid figure navigate down the car with his awkward rider's gait, leaving behind a warm feeling around Dolf's gizzard. Here was a real old-time Westerner; he had hardly known Dolf but was willing to get him back on his feet. Not only that, but he practically guaranteed him a hideout if he ever needed it, which was going some for a sheriff.

Even told me to watch my back, Dolf mused. *I wonder if everybody knows something I don't, or if they just know people? At least there's some straight ones left. Joe Lane there and Warden Bowden, fer example. And I just might even have misjudged Mark Wheat. At least he offered me a job and help gettin' admitted to the bar. That's more'n a lot that I thought were my friends offered to do.*

He scouted away from that notion, not liking the feeling of the old bitterness.

From Redrock, the first distant snowy peaks of the mountains showed their heads beyond the high desert. They seemed to grow out of the ground, but soon, he knew, the train would crest the divide and start down toward the Mustang River. Then the distant foothills, climbing bench after bench, ridge after blue ridge, would come into sight. He could almost smell their piney fragrance in his imagination.

One vexing thought entered his mind, however. Theodora. He'd tried to put off thinking of her. Lovely, wild, willful Theodora. When he had married her, they had been twenty and eighteen respectively, and he'd thought she was the only woman alive. While their love lasted, that had never changed. And it had lasted till Ed Pardeau came on the scene, although it took Dolf another two years to find that out.

He couldn't find it in him to blame Theodora. He probably understood her as well as she did herself. As a beautiful woman, she deserved attention. As a slightly selfish and spoiled one, she demanded more than he could provide. To make the situation impossible, he was naturally undemonstrative.

But Theodora wasn't his direct concern. It was their two children: Amy, now twelve—once the cuddly little apple of his eye—and Dolf Jr., seventeen. Whether, and under what circumstances, he could see the children he loved, depended on Theodora. He wasn't at all confident that the children themselves wanted to see him, at least Amy.

After faithfully answering his letters for a few years, Amy had sent him one final terrible letter, a typical questioning letter from a child with principles, a letter that convinced him she was being systematically poisoned against him at home. She wanted to know what sort of man her father thought he was, having done the terrible things he did. Childlike, she hadn't asked if he had really done them. It was his saddest time in prison. Apparently the potent Pardeau charm had even extended to eleven-year-old stepdaughters. And, after all, Amy's charming new stepfather had almost been killed by her real father. It was one of the main reasons Dolf had received a twenty-five-year sentence; he'd almost killed the sheriff. Everyone knew that Pardeau's two deputies who were killed in the attempt to "arrest" Dolf were hired gunmen. Killing them may have weighed in his favor in a community like Pinebluff. Plenty of people, despite the famous Pardeau charm, thought the whole affair had been just what it was: part of a scheme to get Dolf out of the way. After all, Theodora hadn't actually divorced him until he was behind bars. Then Ed married Theodora, and with her came the Morgette Ranch, which Dolf had turned over to her for child support despite her refusal to give the testimony against her lover that perhaps would have sent him, rather than Dolf, to prison. In any event, it would have kept the father of her children out of prison. It was a cruel awakening for him. This twist of the knife he could not forgive.

Dolf Jr. was a different proposition. He had been old enough to know what was going on. He was a chip off the old block. At twelve, he had already been a pretty fair hand all around, dependable and determined. Like his father, he had little to say, and what little he said was right straight to the point. The sparseness of his letters was not due to defection, his father suspected, but due to a dislike for writing letters, coupled with a secure knowledge that his father knew how *he* felt—that he wouldn't change, and it didn't need saying more than once or twice a year. Consequently, Dolf felt pretty confident as to why he hadn't heard from his son for over six months. Next year the boy would be of age. It wouldn't matter anymore that the court had placed him in his mother's custody. Maybe then it would be time to think of going away with at least part of a family and starting over.

But the thought of losing Amy always caused a cruel hurt somehow near his heart. He remembered the warm, trusting chubby arms squeezing his neck, and the small soft cheek on his, especially after her bath and just before bedtime when she wanted a story. After the story, the warm rosebud lips would kiss his cheek, with another huge unrestrained childish hug thrown in. Then he'd carry her to bed with her fervently saying to his good-night kiss, "I love you, Pa. I do."

Dolf felt the sting of tears that misted his eyes. Almost aloud, he answered his own remembrance: "I love you too, honey, I do."

Then he thought, *Killers aren't supposed to have any tears. Funny. Nobody needs them more—their own and everyone else's.*

He recalled some of his prisonmates whom he'd heard sobbing like big unhappy children at night when no one was supposed to hear. There was no tragedy to match lost hopes or chances hopelessly lost. Maybe they wept for a mother, or a sweetheart, a wife or children—maybe only for themselves. He turned to look out and perhaps shake off his unhappy thoughts.

In this somber frame of mind, he stepped down from the train and went through the futile motions of gathering his short coat around him to keep out the sharp evening chill.

His carpetbag swung in his left hand. He kept the right always free. One of his six-shooters was conveniently beneath his belt out of sight under the coat at the left. It was less obtrusive than wearing a belt and holster. Hick constables sometimes got officious about conspicuous hardware. He was headed for the small log hotel that served as a stagecoach depot, anxious to get to its warmth. The thought occurred that if it still had the same proprietor, he could borrow a blanket for the thirty-mile stagecoach ride.

"Hey Dolf."

The unexpected greeting startled him. Then he recognized the voice. He turned to greet Doc Hennessey, who had been waiting, unobtrusively seated on a baggage cart between the depot and an adjoining log shed.

"What brings you down here, Doc?"

"You."

"How'd you know what train I'd be on?"

"I'm a good guesser—especially with the help of the

telegraph and Al Bowden. If you got a stage ticket, you won't be needin' it. As the feller says, I done brung us a couple o' hosses."

"It'll be cold ridin', Doc. What's up?"

"It might be a damn sight hotter ride on that stage—maybe too hot. And I also 'brung' yer overcoat. I'll tell you about it while we ride. I think it might be a good idea to slope fast before too many people see us, especially that gabby stage driver, Hen Beeler."

Doc and Dolf had developed an unquestioning faith in one another during the two real bad years that constituted the Pinebluff War. The last few months of it could have been called Dolf Morgette's Vendetta. From confident habit, Dolf didn't question Doc's judgment now. He followed him quietly to the horses he had tethered behind the depot, slipped into his familiar old buffalo overcoat with the exterior pistol pockets, and quickly mounted, following Doc out of the little village at a rapid trot.

"Anybody taken a shot at you on the way up here?" Doc inquired.

"Before I got to town from the pen," Dolf told him. "They could hardly wait. Guess whose horse he was ridin'?"

Doc was silent, thinking. "Coulda been almost anybody's. I'll bite."

"Ed Pardeau's. Did you give him my message?"

Doc whistled. "I'll be damned," he said. "Ed's the last guy I'd figger to go after you. He was so glad to hear you wasn't on the warpath he almost kissed my hand. But he's tricky."

"Agreed. But I don't think Ed was ridin' that hoss. Too obvious. I think someone who'd like me to go after good old Ed for 'em was on it. I think someone was shootin' close enough to maybe get me interested in doin' their chore for 'em. They left the nag still sweaty in a little pasture right down by the depot where I'd be sure to see Ed's brand on it. The whole deal 'sounded' to me."

The two old partners were riding shoulder to shoulder just like the old days.

"It 'sounds' to me too. This whole country is restless. Somethin's gonna happen. I can't tell what just yet, but I think yore comin' home has stirred up some kind o' hornet's nest. Too many people figure you owe 'em something. But I think it reminded 'em they may owe each other somethin' too. That's why I thought I'd get you off that shootin' gallery you was fixin' to ride to town on. Besides, I got a little party of my own planned. We need to talk."

He led the way into the forest and up the ridge, leaving the road at a rocky spot where there were none of the few remaining patches of snow left.

This careful choice of a trail didn't escape Dolf.

"Anybody follow you, Doc?" he asked.

"Dunno. Wouldn't be surprised. If they did, they're somebody to worry about—I couldn't catch 'em at it."

With that they rode in silence. Dolf suspected from their direction where Doc had his little welcoming party planned to come off. It pleased him.

He surrendered himself to the welcome feel of the surging strength of a horse under him again, the tangy fragrance of balsam, and the sight of a million stars coming out with no bars to mar the view.

I'll be gimpy in the legs tomorrow, Dolf thought. But it was a trivial worry compared to the rest of the load he'd been carrying that seemed suddenly to have sloughed off of him.

For the first time he felt really free again. He recalled an old saying: "There's something about the outside of a horse that's good for the inside of a rider."

CHAPTER 3

DOC was undoubtedly leading the way to the old Morgette line cabin on Spruce Creek. Dolf was quiet, content to follow and be a part of whatever plan Doc had in mind. Besides, he was pervaded by a feeling of contentment at the thought of seeing again the place where he'd once spent so many happy hours. He used to bring the old hounds Jim and Harley up here, pack in a supply of grub for them all, and just loaf around the place, giving the excuse of hunting.

Because of its ties to his heart, the cabin was the one piece of Morgette property to which he'd retained personal title. Matt still owned an undivided half of the home ranch, but Matt didn't give a rap about the West or ranching anymore from what Dolf could learn from his few letters.

Dolf doubted that anyone knew he'd ever homesteaded this place, or that he still owned it.

After full dark settled across the forest, Doc pulled in his mount.

"Let's mosey off the trail and have us a look and listen," he suggested.

Doc had chosen a spot where a narrow ravine, almost obscured by overhanging bows, cut into the trail from the downwind side. He pushed beneath the branches, Dolf following, brushing springy limbs aside. They tethered the horses securely out of scent and hearing of the horses of anyone trailing them. Then, as soundlessly as possible, they worked back to where they could conveniently spy.

There was a soft soughing in the upper branches of the forest giants that dotted the hills, towering over their younger kin that were more densely spread everywhere. Occasionally

24

the wind would pick up, becoming a steady rush like the sound of a rapids. At other times it died completely so that the sound of his own breathing seemed excessively loud to Dolf. During these hushes, there was no other audible sound. For at least a half hour they waited patiently, Dolf's thoughts ranging far away to tomorrow and to yesterday.

The two were rewarded at last by the sound of something sharply striking a rock. It was not repeated.

"Elk maybe," Doc whispered close to Dolf's ear.

He nodded. *Maybe not too,* he thought.

This suggestion of pursuit put his nerves back on edge, as when he'd spotted Joe Lane in the railroad car.

The next sound, nearer but still distant, was of a dislodged rock rolling down the hill. It was followed by a curse, as though perhaps someone's mount had slipped off the trail. Coming as it did during one of the stillnesses, the sound was alarmingly clear.

"Fer crissakes, don't make so much noise," a voice cautioned, the low tone carrying clearly all the way to the two hidden listeners.

Doc whispered, "Can't trail us in this light and probably don't know the country."

The two old friends waited another half hour or so, hearing their unknown pursuers moving away.

"If they knew the country," Doc said in a low voice, "they'd guess we were headed for your old line cabin. 'Course they could be hunters trying to find their way back to camp—but why would that feller be so particular about keeping quiet if that was the case?"

"Let's find out in the morning," Dolf suggested. "They'll probably pick up our trail by then. Maybe we'd oughta interview 'em like in the old days."

"Yah," Doc said, savoring the memories. "If they come sniffin' down our trail, let's interview those hairpins *like in the old days.*" He grinned in the dark, sardonically. *I can hardly wait,* he was thinking.

With that he led the way back to the horses. They pushed on toward the cabin, Dolf becoming more anxious by the minute to reenter those familiar surroundings.

He knew, by the lay of the starlit land, exactly where they were. One more ridge would bring them to Spruce Creek Valley. Before they were skylighted there, Doc pulled up and dismounted. He handed the reins of his horse to Dolf.

"Got to announce us," he explained.

Within a few steps the darkness engulfed him. Two or three minutes passed.

Then the great silence was shattered by the startling, full-throated baying of a timber wolf. The horses spooked at the sound, dancing skittishly. Dolf didn't blame them. He'd been expecting the sound; he knew it was Doc's calling card—still, it caused him to jump and raised the hair on his neck.

Doc hasn't lost his touch, he chuckled inwardly, but his heart still pounded a little.

After perhaps a couple of minutes passed, Dolf's keen hearing picked up the answering sound of an owl hooting.

Before long, Doc materialized out of the surrounding gloom.

"Sounds like you rounded up some of the old gang," Dolf said.

"Some of the young gang would be more like it," Doc responded, grunting as he remounted. "I'm the old gang."

They set off again, the horses carefully picking their way down among the rocks and deadfalls. By the stars Dolf could discern the spruce-dotted meadow below the cabin. Soon the cabin itself loomed up in the night. All was dark and still, but the inviting aroma of pine logs burning in the fireplace suggested that someone was around or had been recently.

"You galoots can come outa your holes now," Doc announced. "I brought him."

A figure detached itself from the deeper shadow inside the stable doorway.

"Bring the horses in," a voice said.

Dolf was both startled and thrilled at the recognition of that voice.

"Matt?" he questioned.

His younger brother leaned a rifle against the stable and advanced. Dolf leaped off his mount, and the two embraced like a couple of dancing bears, finally drawing apart.

"You're the last person I expected to find here. I thought you'd turned dude," Dolf said.

"Hardly," Matt observed dryly. "But I'd bet I'm not really the last person you expected to find here."

As though on cue, a second rifleman stood up on the low stable roof.

"Looky up yonder," Matt motioned.

"Who the devil's that?" Dolf asked.

No one answered for a moment.

"It's me, Pa," a voice finally answered from the roof—a surprisingly deep voice.

"Junior?" Dolf said the one questioning word.

"You betcha," Matt said. "And growed up some too. Here, kid, throw me your Winchester and jump down here where yore pa kin get a gander at yuh."

No one seemed to notice that Matt, supposedly easternized, had begun to slip back into the careless western way of talking.

Both Dolf and his son were the same unemotional sort outwardly; displays of affection embarrassed them. But this was a once-in-a-lifetime reunion. Both threw restraint out the window, hugging each other wildly just like the two brothers had a moment before. Dolf felt tears well to his eyes. He'd lived this reunion in his mind many lonely nights in prison. Of course, he'd always pictured his son just like the boy he'd left behind. He was all the happier to find a young man almost as big as his father.

Doc and Matt had unsaddled and stabled the horses.

Coming out of the little barn, Doc said, "You galoots go on in and git the talk outa your systems. I'm gonna drift back up yonder just in case that crew we heard got lucky and struck our trail."

"What's that about?" Matt asked urgently.

Noting the tone, Dolf teased, "I didn't think you'd be that anxious over your older brother's skin."

Matt laughed. "It's my skin too now."

Doc answered the question. "We might have picked up a couple of shadows back at the junction. We'll know for sure in the A.M. when they can pick up our trail."

With that he dissolved out of sight.

Inside the cabin, Matt lit a lamp. Dolf's eyes went involuntarily to his son. Junior caught himself doing the same thing; both he and his father sizing up one another. Caught in the act, both grinned. Dolf cuffed the young man playfully on the shoulder

"By gum, I believe you're doomed to be almost as handsome as your pa," Dolf teased.

Seeing that the remark embarrassed his son a trifle, Dolf turned his eyes on the rest of their surroundings.

The reason no light had been visible outside was that the window shutters were closed and barred. This had still been Indian country when Dolf put up the cabin—still was occasionally when "friendlies" passed through. The term "friendlies" was usually intended sarcastically. The shutters were heavy enough to turn anything but a high-caliber rifle bullet at point-blank range. The logs themselves were massive and chinked between with moss, mud, and heavy batten strips both inside and out. The same rationale—defense—had prompted this method of construction. Above was an attic under pole rafters, a plank roof with cedar shakes, and on top of it all a layer of creek-bank sod for fire protection. Beneath the cabin was a root cellar, reached through a trapdoor.

The single room was about eighteen by thirty feet, with a lean-to woodshed across one end. The plank ceiling lay on peeled beams almost as massive as the wall logs. The floor was made of the same sturdy planking. Out back there was a sawpit that explained how these materials got almost to the head of a rough, crooked creek valley. They grew there.

Dolf sadly remembered another feature of the place. Out back on the ridge, there was a small mound with a stone at its head. After burying Pa and his older brothers, saddened and harried as he'd been, Dolf had packed his old hound Jim over here and tenderly buried him. Later he'd had a native rock inscribed for Jim, reading: "My Pal."

Thinking back on these affairs, Dolf looked the place over carefully. It was spruced up as though he'd just left it. Canned goods stood neatly on the shelves. Sacks of spuds and onions ranged along the wall. A big granite coffeepot simmered on the stove. A large iron kettle hung on the hook over the fireplace; judging from the smell, it held a stew. Someone had packed in or made some woven thong chairs that had blankets draped comfortably over them, and the four bunks were neatly made with rolled-up buffalo robes.

"Well, boys," Dolf observed admiringly, "you've fixed this place up first-rate. Was this in my honor?"

"Me and Matt been livin' here," Junior blurted out. Matt stood silently by, listening and watching.

A thought occurred to Dolf from the defiant way the young man put his answer.

"Your ma know you're here?" Dolf asked.

"Nope," Junior admitted.

"What happened?" Dolf asked.

"Old Pardeau was always on my neck."

"Over what?"

"I wasn't respectful enough, he said. And I argued with Ma over the way she let him git away with tellin' Amy all that baloney about you."

This, at least, confirmed Dolf's suspicion about Amy's letters. He didn't press his son for details.

"So what happend then?"

"Well, old Ed gave me one cuff too many one night at the supper table. He'd been drinkin'. I cuffed him back before I stopped to think. He jumped up, hoppin' mad, sayin' he was gonna take a gun to me. I grabbed him, and he tried to slug me. I ended up whippin' the daylights out o' him."

Matt was laughing delightedly, although he'd heard it before.

Dolf tried to suppress a grin and had a hard time of it.

"I wasn't sure I could lick him, but I thought I could. Shucks, he was easy. He's soft. Never does any work. Too lazy even to split kindling. You shoulda seen it—him bellerin', Ma yellin', the cat on top of the cupboard, Amy cryin', the dogs barkin', and me whalin' away at old Ed until he couldn't get back up again. When he did, he still said he'd take a gun to me, so I lit out so's I wouldn't have to kill him."

"Where'd you go?"

"Down to Doc's first, but good old Ed came down an' said he'd have me put away as a delinquent if I didn't come home where I belonged with Ma. She prob'ly sent him. I told him to go to hell. He reached fer his hogleg, but Doc threw down on him with his old double-barrel Greener an' ya shoulda seen him crawfish. That's when I lit a shuck fer up here. I knowed Matt was batchin' up here. Figgered the two of us could handle Pardeau an' any o' his gunslingin' hands if they come nosin' around. None showed up so far. That's been almost a month, so they prob'ly won't."

This raised the question of Matt's presence.

"How long you been batchin' here, Matt?" Dolf inquired.

"All winter. Finished school and felt the old home range callin'. Besides, I ain't the marryin' kind, so I took the coward's way out with a real nice lady. Said I'd have to go up home an' think it out. I'm still thinkin'."

"Think you'll stay?"

"I reckon."

"Glad ta hear it. We'll make a family yet."

Matt didn't have to be told what Dolf meant. His older brother had lost two families; he'd only lost one.

Their ma died of a clear case of heartbreak less than a year after their pa was killed. Matt would have gone on the revenge trail alone long before if Dolf's friends hadn't talked like Dutch uncles to convince him what that would do to Dolf's chances of ever getting a pardon.

But the pardon came, Dolf thought. *And Matt may have got wind of it beforehand. I wonder—*

He knew his younger brother's hot temper well. He'd had to whip some sense into him a dozen times a year when Matt started to grow up. The same went for Jack and Henry, who took over when Dolf wasn't around.

"What're your plans?" Dolf asked Matt cautiously.

By now they were all comfortably sprawled out in the rawhide chairs.

Before Matt could answer, Doc thumped to be let in. Junior unbarred the door.

"Cloudin' up ta snow," Doc announced. "Be a damn shame if it wipes out our tracks. I was lookin' forward to interviewin' them dudes."

"There's still hope," Dolf reassured him. "I was just askin' Matt about his plans."

Before he answered, Matt produced a box of Dolf's favorite Perfectos. All four lit up and settled back; Dolf watched with restrained amusement as his son attempted to handle a cigar like an old hand. It was probably the kid's first cigar.

"Well," Matt started. "It may shock all and sundry to know that Granny is plannin' to move out to Pinebluff since Gramp died. Wants to be near her only livin' kin, she said."

"Lord, she's almost eighty!" Dolf exploded. "That's no age to be pullin' up stakes, especially for a frail old lady."

Matt eyed his brother indulgently. "You seen Granny lately?"

"Not in twenty years," Dolf admitted.

"Well, save your worryin'. I'd bet on her against any of us in a wood choppin' or hay pitchin' contest. And you'd better remember she's a tender seventy-seven, not eighty, unless you want your ears boxed. Anyhow, I thought Granny and me could put a cabin up over on the home ranch so she could get her licks in on good old Ed."

Everyone laughed.

"Sounds like a great old gal," Doc allowed. "Let's get her out here and run her fer sheriff against Tobe Mulveen. She sounds like she'd beat him all hollow."

"So Tobe is sheriff," Dolf mused. "He's a good man for it in a place like Pinebluff—brave as a bull and dumb as an ox."

"You wanted the job once," Doc gently kidded him.

"I was young and green then. Wouldn't have it on a stick now, not that they're apt to run me fer the job." He looked around, pleased.

"There's somethin' missin'," he suggested obliquely, as though he couldn't quite place what it was.

"Only out of sight," Doc said.

He fished a quart bottle from his overcoat pocket.

"I thought you hung that coat up pretty careful," Dolf said.

Matt got out four cups, casually passing Junior one along with the rest. Doc poured a big slug all around.

"It's your party, Doc," Dolf suggested.

Doc raised his cup in a toast. His eyes engaged Dolf's steadily.

"To old times, true friends, and better days ahead," he saluted.

They all drank. Dolf was glad to see that Junior didn't show an unbecoming familiarity with hard liquor. The kid choked over it, coughed, his eyes watered, and he gasped for breath. Doc gave him a couple of hard thumps on his back.

"Jeez!" Junior gasped when he got his breath.

"You'll get used to it," Matt assured him.

"Not likely," Junior stated.

"Yore first drink, son?" Dolf asked kindly.

"Yup—an' my last if I have my way about it."

"That's what we all said," Matt kidded him.

"I hope you stick to that, son," Dolf interrupted. "This stuff's killed a lot of good men, mixed up with women and gunpowder. I never take more than one."

Junior looked at his dad with still-teary eyes from the effects of the raw straight shot. "How about one and a half, just once, for me?"

He offered him the balance in his cup. Dolf grinned, took the cup, held it up, looking around at the other three one by one, and proposed another toast.

"Well, almost never," he said, paraphrasing the then-popular Gilbert and Sullivan *Pinafore*, and tossing off the rest of his son's whiskey.

He looked over at Doc.

"I got the notion you had something on your mind regarding my health, Doc."

"Yup," Doc said. "And not in a medical sense exactly. I told you things were all stirred up over you comin' home. Nothing I could put my finger on, exactly—just a feelin' in my bones. So, to quote the immortal Robert E. Lee, I thought we'd go over to the offensive. The first rule is surprise. Everyone expected you in on that stage. I'd say our surprise was a handsome success so far. Old Hen Beeler prob'ly nigh killed them mules tryin' ta get back to Pinebluff an' tell everyone you didn't show up, fergittin' they'd know anyhow as soon as he showed up without you on board. It almost killed him in the first place decidin' whether he'd git sick, so he wouldn't be in any danger of gittin' killed in case they came after you on the stage, or whether he'd go fer somethin' to brag about to his grandkids by bringin' you in. Braggin' won. I won a two-dollar bet on it too. But as fer world-rattling news—I ain't got any. Just thought it'd be a plumb good idea to throw off anyone that might have plans.

"Somethin's a-brewin' in Pinebluff country though. I can feel it in my bones. There's a new big stick blew in over a year ago. Alby Gould. Seems to have more money'n he knows what to do with. He's startin' to crowd Wheat and Pardeau fer head hog at the trough. It'd be funny since he's playin' their old game on them. Bad part is there's such a good chance the country might blow up again.

"Gould has some tough-lookin' specimens workin' fer him.

Started a freight line, runs a big livery corral, opened a general store, bought the old Carson spread, an' bought out a bunch o' them hoe men down around the junction. Seems like he'd have enough to keep him hoppin', but he's crowdin' for more range. Been rumors of a couple of shootin's between his hardcase and the Wheat-Pardeau crowd up in the hills, but nothin's showed up so far for me to work on in my eminent official capacity as coroner."

"History repeats itself, they say," Dolf observed. Then he fell silent.

He was wondering if this was the kind of situation for him to come back into, especially where people remembered his past so well. Sooner or later they'd expect him to take sides. Sure as people were ornery, one side or the other would try to hire his special talent. He shrugged inwardly, determined not to run out without giving it a chance.

We'll see, he thought.

They were all watching him, waiting to see what his reaction might be to the developing situation.

"What next?" he asked, avoiding the issue. He was perfectly content to leave his next few days' itinerary in Doc's competent hands.

"I suggest we set out on the ridge in the A.M. and see who, if anyone, was followin' us. After that, in accordance with Marse Robert's precepts, I suggest ya do the next thing they won't expect. Go back to the junction an' ketch tomorrow's stage to town because by now everybody'll know I pulled out today leadin' an extra hoss an' figure out why. They'll expect ya to come in on hossback now. Keep 'em off balance. Come in by stage. Besides, it'll kill Hen tryin' to figure out how to beat himself to town so's he can tell everyone you're a-comin'."

That much settled, they all tied into the stew and shortly turned in, full as ticks.

As he did, Dolf was thinking that for the rest he'd take it day by day as it came. He lay awake a long while, staring at the fire and listening to the wind searching around the eaves and stirring some low branch against the roof occasionally. His last recollection was of the pungent smell of burning logs and the flickering sight of them slowly burning down.

The threatening snow still held off. Doc bustled about looking cheerful as he got everyone up to set up his ambush. It must have been 10 A.M. before the expected visitors showed up, blundering along the tracks left by Dolf and Doc the preceding night. It had been a numbing five-hour wait.

"Just like the Fetterman Massacre," Doc muttered under his breath, watching two unsuspecting riders in city garb laboriously following the trail, never once looking around to see who or what else might be abroad.

"What geese," Doc snorted to Dolf in a low voice.

They were now nearing the top of the ridge behind which Doc had spread out his little posse.

Doc stepped into the trail cradling his Greener in the crook of his arm.

"Mornin', gents," he greeted them.

Both almost jumped out of their skins, judging from their startled looks.

"The restaurant's back thataway."

Doc indicated their back trail with a long gloved finger.

"On the other hand, adventure lies ahead. Which'll it be?"

The two horsemen exchanged dumbfounded looks. Then one of them got his voice working.

"Who the hell are you?" was his surly response.

"I thought o' that question first," Doc replied amiably, "an' I got the shotgun."

To emphasize the point, he raised it and covered them for the first time.

"Git down," he ordered them.

Neither responded very quickly.

Doc eared back the twin hammers with an ominous double click. That got better results.

"Now," he addressed them, "tie them two nags to a tree and we'll palaver."

They did as told—this time with a happier look. Palaver

was better than buckshot.

"Now," Doc said again, "suppose you two cough out what the hell yore doin' on my back trail."

He looked from one to the other. His two prisoners exchanged a weak look.

"By way of encouragement," Doc said, "let me tell you two it's mighty easy to hide a corpse up here. Two is only a little more trouble."

That didn't elicit anything either.

"Something tells me," Doc observed, "that you two figure if ya was to tell me the truth, that'd be more apt to git yer hides perforated then bein' quiet. Guess again. Shuck them coats an' don't make any funny moves. There's also three rifles coverin' you dudes. Uh huh—just as I suspected, sneaky guns. One at a time, startin' with you, podner." He indicated the scaredest-looking of the two. "Fish them pea shooters out o' them shoulder rigs an' drop 'em real slow an' careful."

The more determined of the two made his play at that point, jerking a six-shooter. A shot crashed to Doc's left and the six-shooter went spinning from the man's hand. He grabbed the hand with his other, blood running from several small punctures where the bullet that spun his pistol away had splintered and gouged his hand.

Dolf stepped into sight, his six-shooter still smoking.

The wounded party began to bluster.

"What is this, a robbery?" But his dodge didn't sound convincing, even to him.

His partner had dropped his six-shooter as ordered. Sizing him up as the weaker one of the two, Dolf stepped up to him.

"Do you know who I am?" Dolf inquired.

The other shook his head in the negative, his face pallid with fear by now. Dolf was pretty sure from that alone that they knew who he was.

"Don't lie to me. I don't intend to spend the rest of my life with dogs like you sniffin' my tracks day and night."

He was dead serious about that and more than half-angry over the whole idea.

"Don't twitch a muscle," he ordered.

He stepped behind the fellow and fished his wallet from a back pocket.

"Hey, Matt, come here and go through this guy's papers."

Matt stepped out and took the wallet.

The old wolfish mood was back on Dolf, the sense of power that came from desperation. All he wanted was to be left alone. Here, on his first day home, were two men hounding him who didn't even know him, so far as he could tell.

He shoved a six-shooter firmly against the back of his man's head.

"You sure you don't know me?" he demanded again.

"Yes, sir," the other quavered.

"Did I ever do anything to hurt you?"

"No, sir," this time even more shook.

"Do you know any prayers?"

"I got a wife an' kid," the other managed to chatter out. "Please. They won't have anyone to look out for 'em. The kid is sick."

"Oh hell," Dolf muttered in disgust.

He took the pistol away.

"This guy's some kind of detective," Matt said just then.

"I might have known," Dolf said. "Who's your friend?" he asked. "Speak up and we might spare your lousy hide."

"He's a Pinkerton," the badly frightened man blurted out. "I only got a little agency in Portland."

"Shut up!" the Pinkerton told him, rightly suspecting that they were up against nothing more than a strong bluff.

To Dolf he said, "We're onto you. You don't want to go back to the pen." With that he let the cat out of the bag—they knew Dolf. "That's where you'll go if we don't come back," he blustered some more. "There's plenty people know what we're doin'. They'll hound you to your grave if you bump us off."

"That's better," Dolf said. "I figured you were after me. What for? I paid my bill. All I want is to settle down and forget the past, make a living and start over. Why are you coyotes snappin' at my heels?"

The Pinkerton grinned.

"Don't you know, Mr. Morgette?"

Then it hit him. They thought he'd really pulled the train robbery that had been Sheriff Ed Pardeau's dodge to come after him all nice and legal with a warrant and try to murder him while serving it. One hundred thousand dollars had been lost in that robbery. As far as anyone knew, it had never turned up. They thought he had it hidden.

Dolf laughed in sudden relief.

"You dummies really believe I heisted that train?"

The Pinkerton nodded.

Dolf exchanged looks with Matt. His younger brother didn't appear to have much stomach for this sort of work; he appeared nervous, almost embarrassed. In a way it surprised him, Matt looking uncomfortable over a mild piece of work like this, but at the same time it pleased Dolf. Maybe Matt'd avoid following in his older brother's path. He glanced to see how his son was taking it. Dolf Jr. stood by, solid as a rock and poker-faced but alert, holding his Winchester ready. Dolf grinned.

"Me at seventeen," he thought. "Chip off the old block."

He had mixed feelings about it.

Turning back to the two detectives, he said, "I'm offerin' you both an invitation to stick right around the rest of my natural days. No need to be sneaky about it. I'll even board ya for the right price. If I lead you to any hidden treasure, it's all yours."

"You'll never spend any of it," the Pinkerton predicted darkly, ignoring the import of Dolf's offer.

His meek friend said something unexpectedly sensible.

"Shut up!" he growled.

"I'm beginnin' ta like this one's style," Doc said. "Let's let him go. I like the other one's boots, though. I wanna look over the make of 'em."

"That's grand larceny," the Pinkerton protested. "I've already got you for assault with deadly weapons."

"How killing!" Doc said. "Who's got who fer what? Start

shuckin' them boots. What's more, grand larceny starts at a hundred bucks. Those're ten-buck cheapies if I ever saw a pair."

"I know who you are too," the Pinkerton grumbled to Doc.

"Then you know I'd shoot you just fer the fun of it. Shuck them boots."

Dolf watched, grinning.

"You," he told the meek one, "put on your coat, fork your bronc an' git. Your pard may be delayed a little while. Why don't you just take his nag and overcoat with you?"

"Keep him," the meek one muttered as he jerked his nag's head around downtrail.

"Hurry up," Doc ordered, prodding the Pinkerton with his Greener. "I killed plenty o' your kind in my day just ta improve the country."

Somehow that must have made sense to Mr. Pinkerton. He got his boots off, bleeding hand and all, in jig time.

"Now git," Doc ordered, giving him a poke in the behind with the Greener by way of encouragement.

The Pinkerton left in his stocking feet, and Doc tossed the boots and two pistols into the brush.

"Let's go git breakfast," he suggested. "His friend looked like he had enough sense to wait down the trail on him, so likely he won't freeze."

They returned to the welcome warmth of the cabin.

Stretched out on his bunk Dolf observed, "I think I'll play hookey an extra day. Tomorrow is just as good a time to catch the stage as today. Besides, I might run into our two friends, and the lippy one just might try to cause trouble."

"Why not?" Doc agreed.

CHAPTER 4

DOC'S scheme to engender surprise couldn't have been more successful. Unfortunately, his spiriting Dolf away backfired. The surprise was twin-edged. Only Dolf's close relatives and his closest friend, both of whom might logically lie to keep him from returning to the pen, could vouch for his whereabouts for the better part of two days.

Hen Beeler was certainly the picture of surprise when Dolf showed up at the junction exactly two nights after he'd first dropped off the train there. Dolf and Doc walked together into the lamplit hotel lobby that also served as the stage company's waiting room.

Hen spotted Doc first. Then his head snapped to Dolf coming behind, and his jaw dropped. He pointed a finger at Dolf.

"Sheriff's lookin' fer you," he blurted out like a gloating little boy glad he knows the teacher aims to whale someone else.

Dolf felt a sick sensation at the pit of his stomach. He'd felt the same tenseness there every morning in court during his trial. The memory of what prison had been like didn't do anything to cure it. Sooner or later, jailbirds came to expect only the worst whenever officials wanted to see them. Even a man as strong-willed as Dolf was not immune to this dread.

He merely raised his eyebrows expectantly, masking his true feelings.

"He'll see me soon enough if you don't run off the mountain in the dark," Dolf responded.

Doc was instantly suspicious.

"What the hell does that dummy Mulveen want?" he demanded of Hen.

Beeler's face took on a confused look of caution plus a regretful suspicion he'd just put his foot in his big mouth.

"I reckon I shouldn't oughta say," he gulped mulishly.

Doc gave him a look that promised trouble. Everyone knew Doc had made his share of corpses in the wild old days.

Beeler edged toward the door.

"I gotta see ta the hosses now," he pleaded. "It ain't nuthin'."

"Good," Doc said. "I'll step out with you and help."

He had his hand in the breast of his coat, where everyone in that country knew he always kept a .41 Colt self-cocker.

"But on the other hand," Doc went on smoothly, "why get frosted up till we have to? Now why don't you get talkative and answer my first question, Hen?"

Hen's eyes darted around the room desperately, looking for some help. Only the three of them were there just then. He saw no hope in Dolf's eyes and expected none. He directed his answer to Dolf.

"They think yuh stuck up that train down-country since you didn't git here when you was expected the night it was stuck up."

Dolf exchanged a knowing look with Doc.

Doc turned to Hen. "Don't try to tell me a snoop like you didn't see me meet Dolf at the train night before last."

"Nope," Hen insisted miserably. "I ain't a-gonna lie about it. I seen you an' them two hosses, but if he got off the train I never seen Dolf. I was maybe out back."

Knowing what a craven Hen was, Doc had to believe him. The man had neither the courage nor the cupidity to tell a lie of this sort. Doc grasped the hopeless situation in a flash. He didn't know what foul coincidence had put Dolf in this kind of a fix, but he knew what was needed to get him out of it.

He jerked out the wicked little .41, grabbing Hen at the same time and sticking it in his ear, making certain he heard it clicking as he drew the hammer back.

"Yer gonna learn ta lie then real fast if you wasn't doin' it just then!"

Hen looked like he could see the clods landing on his coffin lid already.

"I cain't," he squealed. "I areddy done told the sheriff the truth."

Doc cursed under his breath.

"Let him alone, Doc. He can't help us," Dolf said.

Hen shot a grateful look at Dolf—the look of a condemned man who'd just been pardoned.

Doc reholstered the self-cocker.

"You gonna stick or run, Dolf?" Doc asked earnestly, looking a little sick.

"Stick," Dolf said. "I've done enough runnin'. We'll go up to Pinebluff and let 'em turn loose their wolf."

Hen's uncontrollable mouth got away from him again.

"Not only that—" Then he caught himself, saw he'd already said too much, and plunged on.

"Yuh got my stagecoach riddled fer me too, Dolf. I ain't blamin' yuh fer it," he added hastily. "Lucky no one was in it. Only passenger was up top with me."

Dolf was instantly alert to the implication of that.

"What happened?" he asked.

"Musta been two or three at least, with rifles; plumb sieved the coach the other night. I figure they thought you was on it. Everybody knowed yuh was supposed to git in on that run."

It was that information that was turning over in Dolf's mind on the cold ride into Pinebluff. He sat up top with Hen Beeler, partly because he wasn't certain that Hen mightn't jump off and cut and run for it, but also to pump him.

Doc had ridden on ahead.

"Yer gonna need a lawyer," were Doc's last words to Dolf. "I'll get Wheat. He's the best in the territory," and as an afterthought added, "and likely the crookedest. That might be the best kind in the fix you're in."

The two or three riflemen that shot up the stage puzzled Dolf greatly. There were a lot more than two or three people who might like to see him out of the way. There'd been a lot of tough men mixed up on both sides of the Pinebluff War. The trouble was that he couldn't think of any two that hadn't had their own falling out since then. He'd been able to keep good tabs on the home range, even in prison. In addition to his letters—which, as far as he could tell, Bowden had never censored—the prisoners' grapevine was a wonderful news agency. That had been the means of his learning that relations were cooling between Pardeau and Wheat.

It sure as hell wouldn't have been them two, he thought. *Coulda been hired-done though.*

There were always enough of that kind around. The unsettled country beyond the divide of the Quarter Lien Range was practically a Robbers Roost.

Then another thought occurred to him.

Everyone in the country knew I was supposed to be on that stage. Suppose just a couple of 'em knew I wasn't? Someone coulda seen Doc headed out leading a horse and put two and two together. Could even have followed.

He remembered the clumsy miss in the first attempt on him in Bowden's buckboard.

Maybe, he speculated, *someone's tryin' to secure my services free. I wonder who? Who wants Pardeau out o' the way 'specially bad? 'Cause that's who it's logical fer me to suspect is tryin' to beef me, provided I'm dumber than somebody thinks. Or is Pardeau smarter'n I think?*

We'll see about that, was his last thought before turning to speculate on his current problem with the sheriff.

He'd pumped Beeler for all the details he knew about the train robbery he had supposedly pulled off. Apparently it had been the next train running twelve hours behind the one he'd come on.

Beeler, by that time getting confidential, explained, "It's knowed ya was seen on the train ya was expected here on but only as fur as Carbon. Sheriff figures ya dropped off there to conduct a little business."

"Speakin' fer yoreself," Dolf asked, "how d'ya figure I got up here 150 miles since then—flew?"

"Coulda hopped a freight," Hen suggested innocently. "If'n

'twas me, I'd stay off'n a passenger under them conditions fer fear o' bein' identified."

Dolf grinned. It was obvious that Hen had already tried and convicted him of the stickup. He was comforted by the thought of his ace in the hole: Joe Lane. Joe had seen him as far as Redrock. That alone should be alibi enough. Maybe someone else could be found, in time, who would recall he'd been on the train all the way into Pinebluff Junction. But, as anxious as everyone seemed to be to wish him hard luck, it wouldn't surprise him that they'd figure a way around that too.

"Where and when was that stickup again?" Dolf asked Hen.

He could sense the other's attitude, though he couldn't see his face in the dark. It was: *Why ask me? You know more'n I do about it—an' ya ain't foolin' me by playin' innocent.*

Nonetheless Hen answered him. He didn't see that he had any choice.

"Right outside of Carbon around midnight."

Well, Dolf thought, *a man could make it from Redrock to Carbon in the time I'd a' had by just about killin' a hoss. I sure hope we turn up someone from that train that remembered I got off at the junction because this country ain't about to believe Doc and my own family. Probably the conductor is my best bet.*

He almost changed his mind about facing the music. It would be a bitter pill to go back behind bars, which was sure as hell straight where he was headed. It was just three nights ago, about this time, that he'd been reading his pardon in Bowden's office. He spontaneously checked now to see that it was still in his inside coat pocket.

I thought my luck had changed, he mused.

It would be simple to cut out a couple of the stage mules and head up into the high peaks, riding them in relays. It wasn't likely a posse would overtake him before he got clear. Not many lawmen, and practically no possemen, would be anxious to be prodding around up there. Dolf was confident he could find plenty of hospitality up that way. For that matter, there was also Joe Lane's ranch. No one would expect him to make a break that way. He could circle back to the railroad and catch the midnight freight to Redrock, then hoof it west out of the territory.

Do I want to spend my life as a fugitive?

The thought of Central or South America crossed his mind. Then he remembered his responsibility for young Amy and Dolf Jr. That settled it. He was going to have to face it through. He made that decision just as the last hope of carrying through any other was denied him. As they rounded a sharp bend in the road, they were confronted with a blockade of horsemen. Hen hauled back on the reins and set the brake, pulling to an abrupt halt. A number of previously shrouded Bullseye lanterns' beams were thrown onto the coach, temporarily blinding them.

"Reach for the sky, Morgette," a voice he recognized as Sheriff Tobe Mulveen's roared. "I got a ten-gauge trained on yore gizzard."

This wasn't the place to be a hero. He recognized that someone had telegraphed news of his coming from the junction. Mulveen was taking no chances of his changing his mind, as he had actually debated doing. Dolf raised his hands.

"Git his guns, Hen," Mulveen directed.

Hen wasn't any too anxious to get in front of that shotgun.

"Do as I say, man!" Mulveen shouted, his own nerves tense over the possibilities of the situation.

"Go ahead, Hen," Dolf said quietly. "Just don't drop 'em. I may get 'em back someday."

Someone guffawed.

"Fat chance," chimed in a voice that was somehow remotely familiar.

Dolf heard another suggestion that foretold worse to come.

"Let's string 'im up. That express messenger died this mornin'. Everybody knows he's a killer. No tellin' who'll be next if he comes back."

"What fool said that?" Mulveen rapped out.

No one answered, but there was a general approving mutter.

"Let's git 'im now. We don't need another range war," a voice shouted, hoarse and angry.

Mulveen swung his horse beside the coach and stepped up on the box over the wheel.

"Gimme them six-shooters, Hen," he said.

He shoved them in his belt, having trouble keeping his balance and hanging onto his shotgun.

By then someone had produced a rope and was trying to swing it over a heavy enough limb to get their work started.

"All right, you pinheads," the sheriff roared. "First man tries to lay a hand on Morgette gits ta eat blue whistlers. I ain't foolin'. We're gonna take Dolf ta town and jug him. Cross me an' I'll give 'im back his six-shooters. Now git them mules movin', Hen," he ordered. "Anybody gits in the way, run over 'im!"

Horsemen tried to crowd in and prevent them from moving. Hoarse, frantic voices clashed with each other. Hands were reaching toward them. The tension was so heavy it could almost be felt in the air. Humanity was surrendering to its brute nature.

"Grab 'em!"

"Pull 'em off there."

"There's only two of 'em."

"Yuh move, Hen, an' we'll string you up too," a voice threatened.

The timid stage driver was frozen with fear and indecision. Mulveen gave him a brutal kick and shoved him off onto the road, grabbing the reins as he went.

"Here, Dolf, take this Greener. I'll drive."

He grabbed the whip from its socket and swung it in a mighty arc, cutting at horses and riders alike as well as the stage mules. There were several yelps of pain.

Someone warned, "He gave Morgette the shotgun!"

The mules surged mightily into the harness just then, stung

into swift motion by Mulveen's frantic efforts with the bull-whip.

Riders and horses crashed into one another, scrambling out of the way. The mob knew that Morgette with a gun in his hands could mean sudden death. Now it was mob spirit in reverse, frantic to get away.

Dolf had been icy calm, a calm of desperation. If they succeeded in overpowering the sheriff, Dolf planned to grab his own six-shooters and take a lot of them with him if he went.

Now it looked as though maybe they'd be able to break clear. A gun exploded somewhere behind them, then another.

"The damn crazy fools!" Mulveen swore, laying on the leather.

Someone shouted after them, "Slack off, boys. We'll get 'im outa jail later."

No more shots followed.

Mulveen kept the mules at a dead run, the coach careening wildly in the ruts and over bumps and rocks, leaping high in the air.

"I'm puttin' yuh on your honor, Dolf, ta stay captured till I git these crazy reindeer to town," Mulveen gasped raggedly.

"Hell fire, Tobe," Dolf yelled back, "if you hadn't got impatient I'd a'come in peaceful by myself."

"I couldn't count on that," Tobe threw back.

Apparently the notion of Dolf and a shotgun didn't appeal to that posse. Not a single one tried to escort them a foot beyond where the parting shots were fired.

"Some posse," Dolf observed.

"I'm gonna kick hell outa each and every mother's son of 'em," Tobe promised, jerking the words out between bumps and lurches.

After a couple of swift miles, he pulled the animals down to a fast ground-eating trot.

"I knew there'd be trouble if you came back," Tobe complained. "What the hell for did yuh do a dumb thing like pull another stickup the day you got out?"

"I didn't," Dolf said.

"Yore gonna have a chance ta tell that to the judge," Tobe shot back.

It was the last conversation until they reached Pinebluff. Late as that was by local standards, there were a lot of people still on the streets.

Wait'n ta see the freak—me, Dolf thought wryly.

"Here's your shotgun back," Dolf said, shoving it over to Mulveen. "Might not look good, me carryin' it if you're planning ta git reelected."

"Thanks," Mulveen grunted.

He drove the stagecoach straight to the courthouse where the jail was located. Seeing this, a crowd began to gather and stream after them. Dolf didn't care for the idea of facing another potential lynching. Apparently Tobe Mulveen didn't either.

"Jump down quick, and we'll make a run for the jail. I got some special deputies waitin' that ain't all damn fools."

"I didn't think I'd be so happy to be safe behind bars so soon again," Dolf told Mulveen as the sheriff locked him in.

Mulveen grinned wolfishly.

"Let's hope I kin keep you safe. I'm goin' outside ta see what mood that crowd is in."

Dolf sprawled out on the bunk. He was bone-weary from the tension and the past couple days of unaccustomed activity.

When Mulveen returned to reassure Dolf that everything seemed under control, he was snoring peacefully.

"I'll be damned," the sheriff said. "C'mere an' look at this," he called to a deputy.

"Cool as ice," Mulveen pronounced.

"Yah," the deputy said. "I wish I had nerve like that."

Meanwhile, after he'd left Dolf, Doc had run directly into Mulveen and his posse.

"Where d'ya think yer headed?" Mulveen inquired.

Doc told him. "Dolf's comin' in on the stage of his own free will. He don't need you and an army to show him the way. He's been with me up in the hills the past two days."

"Figgers you'd say that," Mulveen retorted.

"Same goes fer you," Doc said.

"Sure ya wasn't with him somewhere else before then?" someone chimed in.

"Shut up!" Mulveen said curtly. "I seen Doc in town myself the evenin' before the stickup. No way he coulda got ta Carbon that night."

"But he coulda met Morgette somewhere with a hoss the next day. Say his old pal dropped off a freight somewhere an' they had it fixed ahead of time?" someone chipped in nearby.

"Is that you, Abe Brown?" Doc inquired. "You git so much as a hangnail from now on, and I'm amputatin' the next chance I git." He turned his attention back to Mulveen. "Dolf ain't runnin'. All he wants is a chance to clear himself an' settle down to make an honest livin'. I figgered he'd be needin' a lawyer so I was headin' up to town to git 'im one. Now are you boys gonna let me do it or are ya gonna go two hundred miles fer a sawbones the next time ya need one?"

That got results.

"Let 'im through," Mulveen ordered.

If Doc had had the slightest inkling of the posse's mood, he'd have tried to circle back and get Dolf to cut and run.

As it was, he got a hold of Mark Wheat as soon as he hit town.

Wheat lived in a three-story brick mansion with turrets and a mansard roof, surrounded by a wrought iron fence around a couple of acres of formal grounds. The place reeked of money. So did Wheat. Neither one were what a traveler would have expected to find in this out-of-the-way community. But the Pinebluff bonanza had produced a good many unexpected wonders up here in the hills.

Mark Wheat had been a member of the Confederate States' Congress. The war had ruined him, and the death of his wife had shattered him. With his young daughter, Victoria, he had headed west to forget and to start over. The new start had been a cracking success. He was, at the moment Doc found him at his home, the most influential politician and the most successful lawyer in the territory. This was a more notable achievement than might be suspected since the many bonanza towns had attracted an impressive array of talent to a relatively isolated area.

Doc told him the story in as few words as possible.

"You say you, his brother, and his son were with Dolf the past two days? The sheriff will never believe that. A jury might. We'll see. The fact that he's comin' in of his own free will weighs in his favor. I'll go down and see Judge Porter. We can at least get him bail. I had plans for him," he concluded ruefully.

I'll bet, Doc thought. He'd never really liked Wheat, but he gave him credit where it was due. He was the man Dolf needed now.

After Doc left, Wheat called up the stairs to Victoria. "I'll be out for a short while. Something has come up."

His daughter, now twenty-two, was the center of his life. She came to the head of the stairs, an open book still in her hand and a long delicate finger marking her place. Lamplight from the library, where she'd been reading, softly haloed her figure. She had the natural carriage of a queen, though she was not tall. The light burnished her honey-brown hair to a glowing gold. She smiled down, wonderfully even teeth showing between generous symmetrical lips. Her nose was a little short but classically molded, the chin soft but firm.

Her father feasted his eyes on this classic beauty he'd sired.

"Don't read too long by lamplight," he cautioned. "It isn't good for your eyes."

She laughed. "Neither is whiskey," she retorted. Then, more seriously, "Is there trouble?"

He shook his head unconvincingly.

She came partway down the stairs.

"You're not very good at fooling your daughter," she chided. "She knows you too well. Something is worrying you."

He sighed deeply.

"It's Morgette. He's coming in on the stage."

Her eyes widened, mirroring surprise. "I thought he'd be running for the hills."

"So did I. Doc Hennessey was just here. Claims he's been with Morgette up in the hills the past two days. Says he came in on the train we all expected him on, and he met him with a horse so he wouldn't be a sitting duck on the stage."

He paused.

"Good thing he did if it's true. We know what happened to the stage."

Father," Victoria said—she seemed to be gathering her thoughts—"just why did you offer Dolf Morgette, of all people, a job?"

Wheat was reflectively silent for quite awhile.

"Honey, why ask me that?" he said, trying to evade her.

"Because I want to know."

He was quiet again. "I'm not sure, I guess. I thought I might need him. Trouble is coming, I think. I may need his kind of man with me, but not as a law partner." He turned and opened the outside door, then blew her a kiss. "Good night, honey. Don't wait up. I may be late."

Victoria slowly and thoughtfully ascended the stairs. Resuming her seat in the library, she laid the book down and leaned back with her hands laced behind her head. As she did, she was conscious of her high, firm breasts sitting up proudly. She was a woman, and she knew what she wanted. It was not in Pinebluff—at least not until now.

Victoria thought back to the last time she'd seen Dolf Morgette. It had been at the height of the Pinebluff War. He had unexpectedly led a group of his men into town, the stronghold of his enemies then. He sat high and cool on his big dancing bay horse, his deep-set eyes not missing a thing as he had continually turned his head from side to side, alert as a hunted animal. Men were all around who would have liked to kill him if they dared. But something about him stayed everyone's hand. He came, transacted his business, and left in the same fearless, haughty, half-contemptuous manner. She never forgot the impact of the heavy, electric tension his presence and his complete domination of the situation had laid on everyone who had witnessed this cool show of force.

Treachery laid him low, she thought.

She also remembered the first time she'd seen him. She had been a pigtailed twelve-year-old and had been allowed to go, heavily chaperoned with some other young girls, to her first dance.

It had all been exciting. Then there was a little bustle of extra activity around the door. A tall, handsome young man with a beautiful dark lady on his arm had swept in. A crowd of the young blades swarmed around them both. Every woman in the room tried not to appear to be looking that way.

"Hey Dolf, Theodora," the voices were calling, "now the party can start. We thought maybe you couldn't make it."

There was a lot of laughing and chatter.

They were both smiling broadly, nodding, speaking to old friends, accepting handshakes.

Victoria had thought this tall, broad-shouldered, narrow-waisted man with the lean and ruddy tanned face set off by coal-black hair and white flashing teeth was the handsomest knight she'd ever seen. She never forgot that evening. She had watched him dance dashingly with the beautiful lady. When she had learned that Theodora was his wife, Victoria had been crushed.

She smiled at the remembrance.

I hated her, she reminded herself. *I wonder if he does now. I wonder what he looks like. I should have made a scene so Papa would have let me come along.*

Later she looked long at her body in the peer glass before she slipped into her nightgown.

She was smiling as she blew out the lamp.

"I want to see what he looks like now," she said aloud.

CHAPTER 5

OBADIAH Peuke was almost an ideal detective. He had a degree of bulldog tenacity coupled with cunning. While not a fool for bravery, as his encounter with Doc had shown, neither was he a coward. He'd been in the agency's service for fifteen years, had made quite a little reputation to date, and wasn't about to have it tarnished. His outlook on people was that most of them belonged in a jail or asylum. He also believed that, in the former case, it was simply a matter of time before he fulfilled his destiny and put another one where he belonged. This was rapidly becoming an obsession in the case of Dolf Morgette, especially since Obadiah's handful of lead slivers had started to swell and throb with pain.

He was now standing with the hand in a basin of hot water in his room at the little hotel at Pinebluff Junction. He had drafted his timid temporary partner, Leverett Peeples, to run a relay of teakettles of hot water up from the kitchen. He held Peeples in deep contempt, not only for what he considered his craven conduct before Doc's shotgun and Dolf's six-shooter, but because Peeples thought they should provide Morgette with an alibi by telling the truth.

Three days had passed since their encounter with Doc's posse. Normally, by this time Oby (as everyone at Pinkerton's called him behind his back) would have been up to Pinebluff yelling to the sheriff for Doc's skin. He'd been forestalled by learning of the downstate train robbery as soon as he and Peeples had returned to the junction. Now he smelled new game. That required him to wire Chicago for instructions at once. The first instructions were to lay low, wait until he was physically fit for action, and then pursue his original assignment.

53

He almost had a seizure when he discovered Doc and Dolf had been under the same roof the previous night. By then it was also known locally that Dolf was a prime suspect in the robbery and that he was now in jail at Pinebluff.

Peuke sent an encoded wire, bringing the home office up to date on that. He requested permission to transfer operations to Pinebluff proper. The encoded reply advised him not to alibi Morgette but to use that as a potential bargaining ploy to deal for recovery of the hundred thousand he was after. Permission was also granted to transfer to Pinebluff.

"Is there a good doc up at Pinebluff?" he had asked Hen Beeler as he came out to board the stage.

"Best in the territory if you don't scare easy," Hen had assured him. "He's Dolf Morgette's old sidekick, Doc Hennessey."

In the dark, Beeler missed the facial expression that information elicited. He thought, however, that he heard someone unsuccessfully suppress a guffaw and was puzzled by that fact.

"He the only one?" Peuke inquired sourly.

"Yep. Only one fer a hunnert mile, I should guess."

This time Peeples couldn't restrain a snort.

"Shut up!" Peuke snapped.

Peeples was becoming less and less happy with his subcontract to Pinkerton's, and Obadiah was the whole reason.

"I still don't think it's right to let a fella rot in jail when he jist got out—especially when he's innocent," Peeples told Obadiah for the tenth time.

Oby eyed him hostilely.

"Yer powerful soft on jailbirds. You ain't been one yerself by any chance?"

Leverett returned Oby's poisonous look with interest. Neither could see the other's looks in the dark, which was just as well for business relations.

"Happens I have."

He could imagine the gloating I-knew-it look developing on Peuke's fat face and savored the wiping-off job.

"Spent almost two years in Andersonville after I was captured at Gettysburg."

He let that sink in, then turned the knife. "Where were you during the war?"

Peuke turned sulkily away and looked out the stagecoach window into the night. He was silent the rest of the way into Pinebluff, to the intense gratification of Peeples.

A lot had been happening there since Dolf had been jailed. Mulveen's posse straggled back into town, showing evidence of there having been several bottles among them. They still had "get Morgette" on their minds. A dozen or more tied their mounts at the Bonanza Saloon and made for the bar with a lot of loud talk. Their leading spirit seemed to be Stud Foley, bronc peeler for Pardeau's P Bar P.

"Let's get a coupla scatter-guns ourselves an' go over an' give old Mulveen a taste of his own medicine," he suggested, after tossing down his first shot of raw whiskey at the bar.

"I brought a couple," an unexpected voice announced from the back of the saloon.

The mob swung around to see Mulveen backed by a determined-looking deputy with a scatter-gun.

"All you gotta do if ya want a scatter-gun is take his," the sheriff told Foley. "The other 'n is at the front door." He pointed to a second deputy standing inside the front door and just to one side, where he couldn't be taken from the rear.

"Come to papa," the sheriff motioned to Foley.

Foley's eyes got round with surprise. Mulveen was almost as big as a bear. He had a well-earned reputation as a brawler.

"C'mere," Tobe motioned again. "I owe you some fer that fool play at the stagecoach."

"No," Foley protested. "Yer supposed to keep the law."

"So were you, as a member of my posse," Tobe told him.

He cornered Foley neatly where the bar met the wall, being fast on his feet despite his size. Several others shied out of his path or slipped away rapidly when Foley tried to duck behind them.

"Put up your dukes, Foley."

Foley frantically tried to cover himself, but a huge fist battered him alongside his jaw. Mulveen didn't even look at him again, but turned to the rest. Foley was where Mulveen expected him to be: slumped in the sawdust, unconscious.

"I owe some o' the rest of you fer that fool stunt." He looked them over balefully.

Suddenly he backhanded Clem Yoder in the mouth and, in almost the same motion, grabbed Simp Parsons and hugged him close.

"Christ," Simp gasped.

"Hear that?" Tobe asked him next to his ear. "That was a couple of ribs cracking. I oughta break 'em all. I could easy."

He pushed Simp away, and the man collapsed, fainting.

Clem Yoder was picking a couple of teeth out of his lip.

Mulveen eyed the crowd wickedly.

"Any man jack o' yuh ever double-cross me in a posse again, I'll do worse'n that. Now some of yuh pick them two up an' drag 'em over to the lockup fer me."

He stalked out, booting Clem Yoder ahead of him like a bear on the fight; two deputies herded the procession bearing Foley and Parsons.

After they'd put them in cells adjoining Dolf, one of the deputies warned Mulveen, "Look out fer them three from now on. All of 'em were in that hard bunch Pardeau brought in from Texas last year. Any one o' 'em might try ta backshoot yuh before he hits the trail back home."

Mulveen didn't reply—only grunted. "Go get Doc fer them cripples," was all he said.

As Dolf had observed, Tobe was the ideal sheriff for Pinebluff. Thanks to him, Dolf was still peacefully asleep when Mark Wheat and Judge Porter showed up at the jail. Doc Hennessey was with them. Mulveen had just returned from upstairs.

"Evenin', gentlemen," Tobe greeted them, not entirely surprised to see them. To Doc he said, "Got a coupla cases fer ya upstairs, but they'll wait."

It had been general knowledge that Wheat planned to give Dolf a job. The consensus to which Mulveen was a whole-hearted subscriber was that it would be a big mistake on Wheat's part.

Mulveen was hoping now that this train robbery had persuaded Wheat of the error he'd made.

"Evenin', Tobe," Wheat replied. "We're here about your new and famous prisoner, as I suppose you guessed."

Tobe nodded.

Judge Porter said, "If you don't have any objections, Tobe, we'll hold court in your office."

They all filed in.

The judge seated himself ponderously behind Mulveen's desk. Completely unself-consciously, he announced, "Hear ye, hear ye, this honorable court of the Fourth Judicial District is now in session. We're here to consider the case of Dolf Morgette for bail."

Sheriff Tobe Mulveen's face was a study in astonishment. Along with Hen Beeler and a lot of others, he'd mentally tried and convicted Dolf.

"Before we bring the prisoner before the bar, let's hear the witness for the defense," the judge said. He nodded to Doc to start.

Doc testified as to his and Dolf's whereabouts, and as to how Matt and Junior would be in to verify the same. Somehow he overlooked mentioning the Pinkerton episode. He was careful to emphasize that Dolf had willingly boarded the stage to Pinebluff, already having been informed by Beeler of what the result would be.

"Bring in the prisoner, Tobe. We'll adjourn for a few minutes while you go get him."

Porter took out a flask and had a pull, passing it around.

Tobe reluctantly but obediently went upstairs to the cell block, woke Dolf up, and brought him down to the hearing.

"A what hearing?" Dolf asked him again, on their way down, thinking he hadn't heard rightly.

"Bail. B.A.L.E.," Tobe informed him again. "The damn fools are plannin' to let ya out to cause some more trouble. I'll run ya outa town if you do."

Dolf grinned. "Then run me back in fer jumpin' bail, I suppose."

"Aw hell," Tobe said, exasperated.

He was in his second term, and nothing much had happened before now.

"Jist try to be good fer a little while, till they hang you, will ya?" Tobe pleaded.

"I ain't promisin'," Dolf told him. "And I didn't cause the trouble tonight. Your friends did. An' I didn't stick up that train, which I'll prove if your friends let me stay alive long enough. All I'm tryin' ta do is settle down an' let the past die."

"Well, I sure wish you'd a' tried it somewhere else," Tobe groaned.

Mark Wheat extended a cordial handshake to Dolf when he entered. "Happy to see you back, Dolf—not happy at the circumstances, but I'm sure we can clear this up."

He turned affably to Judge Porter.

"This, your honor, is Dolf Morgette. As you can see, he doesn't at all fit the picture of the monster we've been treated to in the papers."

He was warming up to a speech, as Judge Porter, who knew him well, recognized. Porter held up his hand.

"I can see that, Mark. Save the speech." Then he directed his attention to Dolf. "I'm sure you'll believe me when I say I've heard a lot about you, Mr. Morgette."

Dolf nodded and couldn't suppress a wry grin.

"You may not believe me when I say that some of it has actually been good." He paused for effect, no less pleased with histrionics than Mark Wheat. "In fact, Mark Wheat here thinks enough of you to personally put up the $25,000.00 bail I'm setting in this case."

Dolf couldn't believe his ears. Wheat had to want him free for a more pressing reason then the benevolent satisfaction of supervising his rehabilitation; that was certain. He harked back to Doc's analysis of the local powder-keg situation. Something in those circumstances must have Wheat scared bad. Twenty-five thousand dollars bad.

Doc cut his eyes across at Dolf, raised his eyebrows, and pursed his lips in a whistling position.

Amen, Dolf thought.

"For the record," Porter intoned in his best official voice, "so far as anyone here knows, there's not the slightest bit of anything but the flimsiest sort of circumstantial evidence to connect Morgette to the train robbery for which he's being held. In fact, this is a far-from-creditable example of the grossest sort of community prejudice against a man who's settled his debt with society. Also, for the record, I'd like you, Mr. Morgette, to recite your actions and whereabouts since you got on that train the day of your discharge from prison."

Dolf gave a brief account of his trip north, his meeting with Doc, and their subsequent ride to the line cabin. Unlike Doc, he didn't omit mention of their encounter with the two detectives.

"We weren't sure who they were but figured anyone on my back trail might be up to no good, so we had a little talk with 'em."

He put the best possible face on it.

He added, "I expected they'd have been around by now. They could be a couple of my best witnesses. An' of course Sheriff Lane can vouch I went as far as Redrock. The conductor ought to know I came all the way to the junction."

At mention of the Pinkerton and his pal, Porter gave Doc a severe frown. Doc found something on the ceiling that interested him about then.

When Dolf was through, the judge said, "Your story jives pretty well with Dr. Hennessey's, which would naturally have a bearing on my decision in this hearing. But somehow Doc neglected to mention those two detectives." He turned to Doc. "How does that come, Doc?" he asked.

"Slipped my mind, I guess. That Pink was so ornery I hate ta think about him."

"I see, and just what—if I may be so crass to suggest it— may I expect he will be accusing you of, assuming he shows up?"

Doc grinned. "Well, my medical opinion was that he looked overheated and that both of them appeared to have suicidal tendencies."

"So?"

"So I relieved the cheeky one o' his boots and overcoat to cool him down and both of 'em o' their six-shooters. A plumb humanitarian impulse, you might say," Doc stated benignly with an innocent face.

Even the sheriff couldn't suppress a grin over a whopper of that dimension.

Porter simply looked at Doc over the top rims of his glasses.

"Yes, one might say that," he allowed. "Then again *I* might not. We'll let their case rest till they show up, if they ever do. As to the case before me, I'm settin' bail at $25,000.00 cash in the circumstances. Mr. Wheat informs me he'll have it when the bank opens in the morning. Until then I remand the prisoner to the sheriff. Court is adjourned."

"And, off the record, Sheriff," he added, "you better keep a careful eye on him. It's my opinion a sizable part of this community wants him out of the way for some reason or reasons, not the least of which may be a general guilty conscience."

He extended a hand to Dolf.

"A pleasure meeting a celebrity." He smiled as he added, "Your horns aren't nearly as prominent as I'd been led to believe."

Mulveen was scowling as Wheat and the judge departed. He shook his head.

"Pays ta have friends, I guess," he said to no one in particular. To Dolf he said, "I ain't cancellin' my order for scaffold lumber yet." And to Doc, who had hung around after the others left, he said, "What the devil are you standin' around about? Them orphans upstairs need attention."

Doc smiled sweetly, not moving.

"I'm stickin' around fer my two dollars. You bet me Hen

would get outa driving that stage Dolf was supposed ta come in on the other night."

Mulveen reached into his pocket and pulled out two cartwheels, placing them carefully on his desk.

"I'll bet two more," the sheriff allowed, "that I'll have yer friend here back in the poke fer somethin' or other before a week's out."

"Bet," Doc agreed. "But I'll take these along in the meantime."

"C'mon," Mulveen motioned to Dolf. "It's back to the bridal suite till mornin' fer you."

"I'll be right back as soon as I get my bag," Doc said.

He went out between a pair of shotgun-wielding deputies who Mulveen had on the front door. Others similarly armed were posted elsewhere in the building at the various entrances. A couple patrolled outside, a precaution that Mulveen continued, even though the crowd was gone and the principal troublemakers were behind bars.

As Doc went through the door, Mulveen ordered, "Let 'im back in when he comes, but frisk 'im. He'll be upstairs awhile an' I don't want him slippin' Morgette a six-shooter."

Doc heard the words and sighed. He thought, *What a fool play that'd be with Dolf knowing he's gonna get out in the mornin' anyhow. He was sure right about Mulveen bein' thick atwixt the ears.*

After patching up the prisoners, Doc glanced in on Dolf under the suspicious eye of a deputy. Pinebluff's number-one celebrity was again peacefully asleep.

Doc grinned. *He needs all the rest he can get. If I'm any judge, this country'll keep him busy before too long. I hope not, but I've just got a hunch trouble's not far off.*

Doc's hunches paid off fairly often.

Doc had been gone perhaps five minutes when Mulveen received an unexpected caller to see Morgette. In most cases, at this time of night and with the uncertain state of affairs, the sheriff would have scoffed at the notion of someone wanting to see what he considered a highly sensitive prisoner. Somehow

Tobe Mulveen's mind was built so that he simply couldn't assimilate the fact that, for all practical purposes, Dolf was a free man unnecessarily detained. This visitor, to Mulveen's uncomplicated mind, was one of the big men of the community who, consequently, was entitled to special consideration. It was Ed Pardeau.

The sheriff was totally incapable of believing that, as Dolf had testified at his trial, Pardeau's mission when Dolf shot him had been to dispose of him, not arrest him; he was therefore equally incapable of conceiving that Pardeau's real purpose here at this time merited suspicion. Mulveen had been a deputy under Pardeau at the same time as Dolf and had been a good one. Also an honest one, which was why he hadn't been selected to go with the sheriff years before to arrest Dolf. If he had been, he might not have survived to become sheriff, a thought that had occurred to Tobe more than once.

"Came ta kill two birds with one stone, Tobe," Pardeau explained smoothly to him. "I hear a couple of my boys made a fool play tonight. I wanna give them a little Dutch uncle talk. An' while I'm here, I'd like ta see Dolf a minute."

He looked his most sincere—and Ed had a real knack for looking sincere as many people—mostly women—could attest, to their sorrow.

"Wanna tell Dolf I'm willin' ta let the past die if he is. We both gotta live here if he's made up his mind to settle. I got no grudge."

Mulveen looked admiringly at his old boss, and it showed in his expression.

"That's really big o' yuh, Ed," Tobe said, and he meant it. "About the boys—I sorta give 'em a little lesson they won't fergit real soon. I'd like to keep 'em overnight to cool 'em off."

Ed grinned. "Go ahead," he agreed. "Serves 'em right. Uh—by the way—would ya mind if I had a *private* word with Dolf?"

Mulveen wasn't surprised. He figured he understood—and said so.

Dolf was dimly aware when the other prisoners were

brought in. He stirred, hearing voices when Pardeau talked to his jailed riders. Then the familiar voice roused him to full consciousness.

"Pardeau," he said aloud to himself.

He was instantly alert, not at all certain what Ed's presence might mean here. He didn't think the man was capable of killing here, where he was sure to be caught. He wasn't even sure that Ed was the one who'd bear watching. Nonetheless, past associations triggered alarm bells in his consciousness.

Mulveen came to his cell first and rapped on the steel door.

"Hey, Dolf, you awake?" he said loudly.

"I'm awake," Dolf said.

"Got a visitor that you know."

Dolf was silent but prepared when Pardeau came to the barred window in the door. He hadn't changed much: still swarthily handsome with a dapper mustache unlike those worn by most men. His complexion under the hall lamp appeared a little more pallid than Dolf remembered. Knowing how vain Ed was, Dolf smiled inwardly to see that his hairline had receded greatly. However, the youthful face was still there, and the liquid brown eyes that the ladies loved, the eyes that could be so persuasive with sincerity. However, the face was a trifle puffy—liquor, Dolf guessed—and small crow tracks were visible at the corners of his eyes. Also, his forehead was developing parallel railroad tracks.

"Hello, Dolf," Ed said diffidently.

He looked at Mulveen, plainly wanting him out of earshot.

Getting the hint, Tobe said, "I'll leave ya to talk awhile if Dolf don't mind."

Dolf nodded assent. His curiosity was wonderfully piqued. He was absolutely sure Pardeau hadn't come to murder him here. Whatever other motive brought him there at that hour would have to be most compelling.

"I got your message from Doc," Pardeau started off, his voice uneven and a little hoarse. "Like I told Doc, that suits me right down to the ground. Let bygones be bygones. That's why I had ta see you."

He paused, as though uncertain how to proceed. Dolf's eyes never left his face. This man, he perceived, was laboring under some terrible fear or pressure.

Pardeau licked his lips, then plunged ahead. "I keep track of what goes on in the territory. I know ya probably won't believe me, but whoever took a shot at yuh with Bowden the other day—well, I didn't have anything ta do with that." His eyes pleaded. "You've got ta believe that, Dolf. Somebody swiped my hoss. Someone is tryin' ta git you ta kill me. That's the gawd's truth."

Dolf didn't speak for some time, looking poker-faced at the frightened, pleading eyes, the weak chin and sensual lips quivering with keyed-up tension.

"I believe you, Ed," Dolf said. "I figured that out from the trouble the fella went to so I'd be sure to see your hoss. I figured it from the poor shot—he was tryin' ta be seen, not beef me. Who d'ya think it was?"

Pardeau looked like a man on his deathbed who wasn't ready to go. Something was bothering him bad. He looked suspiciously around, as though spies might be hidden all over the place. He came as close to the bars as he could get.

"Come close," he said. "And promise not ta tell a soul I said anything."

Dolf put his ear next to the bars.

Pardeau again darted a furtive look around and whispered one word: "Wheat." Then he added in a husky voice, somewhat louder, "Don't ask me how or why. But I know it's him. At first I thought it might be Alby Gould—but it's him."

"Why?" Dolf asked.

"I can't say. But he's afraid you'll find out somethin' about him too. Jist remember that and watch out fer him. I guess I owe ya that much. An', Dolf, remember, if anyone makes another try fer yuh, it won't be me. All I want to do is live down the past an' live an' let live. I got trouble enough without havin' yuh on my trail. You gotta believe that."

Judging by the pathetically earnest, frightened look—really like a presentiment of some awful fate in store for him at any moment—Dolf was very much disposed to accept Pardeau's word.

"Take care, Dolf. An' good luck."

With that, Pardeau walked rapidly away. Dolf thought he could hear him talking to Mulveen for a moment downstairs.

Silence settled on the jail and town. A clock chimed downstairs. Midnight. It seemed like two days since he'd boarded the 5:30 stage at the junction. He blew out the lamp, stretched out on his back on the bunk, and, without undressing, pulled a couple of blankets over himself and lay staring up at the ceiling in the dark.

What do you know about that? he asked himself. *Old Ed Pardeau has changed his tune and his ways. Someone seems to be playing his own game with him.* Dolf couldn't say this development displeased him, if he could believe Pardeau.

Reservations tugged at his mind though, based on his bitter past experiences at the hands of this calculating man who had shattered his life.

He's tricky, Dolf thought. *And an actor too when he needs to be.*

Dolf had thought Pardeau was the last person he'd have expected to visit him, until the next one came, not five minutes after Ed left.

Dolf heard Mulveen's heavy tread coming down the corridor and hoped it wasn't to disturb him again. He was dog-tired and wanted some sleep. He heard keys jingling and then grating in his lock.

What now? he wondered.

It was Tobe again, carrying a lamp.

"You dressed?" he asked.

Dolf got up from under the covers so the sheriff could see he was. He wondered if he was being bailed out early.

"Probably a damn fool thing fer me ta do," Tobe said, "but I never could say no to a lady. You got another visitor says it's powerful important ta see yuh. I'm gonna fergit she was ever here. I'll be back in five minutes or so."

As he left, the mysterious visitor entered.

"Theodora." Dolf whispered the one word.

She tossed her head up in the old familiar way, looking at him with slightly averted features, her long black hair accentuating her dark beauty.

"Dolf." She came closer and touched his face with soft, warm fingers. He could smell her perfume.

"You're so much older," she said, somehow wistfully.

He said nothing, wondering what she had expected after five years in hell, wondering even more what she was here for now. He felt nothing, yet was still touched by her cameolike beauty, which had matured without aging her. She seemed more self-assured and yet childlike.

She looked directly into his eyes.

"Dolf, I made a terrible mistake."

He wondered, *Which one?* Still he was silent, not knowing what to say. He waited.

"I'm leaving Ed," she said. She stood silent, as though that needed no explanation. Actually, Dolf had come to believe she and Pardeau were remarkably well matched, in fact may have felt a twinge of pity for Ed now, if anything.

Curious, he asked, "Why?"

She looked away thoughtfully. "I don't know," she said impatiently. Then, "Lots of reasons. He's no man. Not a tenth the man you are, Dolf. I was such a fool. I loved you—I needed him. Can you understand that? I still love you. Always will."

He was suddenly angry, thinking: '*And I don't need him now,*' you think. *But when would the next Ed come along, and the next?* This was one hell of a thing to come tell him now. He knew she was perfectly capable of putting on an act like this. He eyed her closely. He didn't think she was acting. She was battling powerful conflicting emotions, and it was reflected in her eyes. She was not the kind to admit a mistake. Not if it killed her. Yet he'd just heard it. This wasn't the Theodora he'd ever known.

"Why are you telling me this now?" he finally asked.

"Don't you know?"

The strange part was he really didn't know. It never occurred to him that she might think he still loved her. His actual feeling about her had grown to almost the opposite. He might have been capable of hating her if he didn't pity her more.

"Don't you know?" she asked again.

He shook his head.

She looked disbelievingly into his eyes, saw nothing she could read there, and then stepped close to him, lips parted invitingly. He turned away and sat on the bunk to avoid the obvious invitation.

She changed tack. "Do you have any idea what Ed is doing to our children—especially Amy?"

That struck Dolf where he lived.

"I know," he said. "You should have seen the last letter I got from her before they let me out."

"And your son had to thrash him when he was drunk. Imagine what sort of man allows himself to be thrashed by a mere boy."

Dolf was beginning to get the drift correctly. She had been experiencing what was known as "finding someone out." *The mere boy who had thrashed Ed*, he thought, *is six feet tall, weighs about 180 pounds, and could probably whip his weight in wildcats.* He was beginning to be pleased at this turn of events.

Hearing Mulveen's purposely noisy tread returning slowly up the stairs, she said hastily, "We could start over, Dolf."

"Don't leave Ed on my account," he told her with unmistakable finality.

She looked disbelievingly into his eyes. What she saw there brought sudden panic, then anger to her face. Her black eyes snapped an ugly, hateful look at him.

"Do you expect me to believe you couldn't love me again if I wanted you?" she asked.

"Never. It's over," he said simply. "I pity you, but I could never love you again, Theo."

She flounced out. Noticing, Mulveen allowed her plenty of

time to get along her way before he locked the door and followed. He had noticed Dolf shaking his head in confusion as he took the lamp away. Women were a great mystery to Tobe. He respected those that deserved it, but he had never had the courage to try to court a respectable one for himself. He understood those down at Minnie Moore's place, those that couldn't afford to have tantrums.

Dolf was just comfortably back under the blankets when the explosion took place. It was at the other end of the hallway by the stairs. The whole place was instantly alight with licking flames. Dolf recalled that the stove was in an alcove down there, with a large stack of firewood piled up along the corridor.

Shouts of "Get us out o' here!" were already coming from the other prisoners closer to the flames.

The building, all log construction, was a firetrap. It would go up like tinder in minutes.

Dolf heard Mulveen's bull voice thunder, "Can't get up the stairs! Git some water! One o' ya ring the fire alarm!"

Smoke was already growing denser, filtering down the hall.

The cowboy in the cell closest to the fire, Simp Parsons, was screaming hysterically, "I'm suffocatin'!"

The cry tapered into a choking cough. Simp had already had trouble breathing, due to his cracked ribs.

The two others were also yelling wildly. "Hey, Mulveen, fer crissakes git us outa here quick!"

Dolf quickly lit his lamp, his eyes searching the cell for something to pry loose the window bars with. There was nothing.

The flames were now an ominous roar, fanned by someone opening the door downstairs.

"Shut that door down there!" he roared, hoping he could be heard.

Smoke was now taking on choking proportions. He heard the other prisoners gasping and gagging.

"Hey you guys down there," he yelled. "Soak a blanket in your water bucket and get yore head under it on the floor."

He was doing likewise as he yelled this instruction. The heat was becoming unpleasantly noticeable, even where he was. A minute or two remained at the most if they were going to be rescued. Before he ducked under the blanket, he took a last frantic look out the window. As he did, he saw someone's head just top a ladder on the first-story lean-to that adjoined the jail.

A whiff of smoke blotted the figure out and gripped Dolf in a paroxysm of coughing. His eyes were burning. Desperately, he held one eye open with his fingers to see if he could see the figure again.

It was Tobe Mulveen, dancing across the roof directly toward his window. The flames had burst through the jail roof above and now cast a pale flickering light on Tobe's figure. Fortunately, the hole burned in the roof acted as a chimney and seemed to suck the smoke upward out of the jail.

Dolf opened his window and caught a heaven-sent breath of fresh, cold air.

Mulveen yelled, "Here's the keys."

He jumped and tossed them in the window. They lit on the floor with a clatter. Dolf pounced on them.

"Go out the door at the other end of the hall ta get out," Tobe yelled in his bull voice. "I can't get in from that side."

Dolf was inserting key after key in his door. It was awkward work through the bars.

It'll be the last damn one, he thought, exasperated.

The smoke was now billowing back down the hall again. Flames were approaching the cell block. The heat was an oppressive wave.

He finally found the right key.

"I hope it's the same one for all the rest," he thought.

He snatched his soaked blanket and battled his way toward Simp's cell, thought he'd better get some help, and let Foley, in the next cell, out first.

"C'mon," he ordered. "I may need help."

A huge wave of flame licked at him. He fended it off with the blanket, advancing to Simp's cell.

Clem Yoder, still locked in, was crying insanely like a mortally wounded wild beast.

"Gimme them keys if ya ain't gonna unlock me yourself, ya son of a bitch! Gimme them gawdam keys!"

Ignoring him, Dolf opened Simp's cell. By now, the man was unconscious on the floor. Dolf grabbed his arm and dragged him into the hall.

"Take him," he yelled to Foley.

Foley wasn't there.

Dolf dropped Simp's arm to hand the keys to Yoder.

"Yer on yer own," he yelled, resuming his progress with Parsons, now dragging him by both arms.

Reaching the back door, Dolf found Foley insanely charging at it, trying to get it open.

"Nailed shut," he gasped, his eyes wild and insane.

He threw himself at it again and fell off it, wobbling.

Dolf looked for Yoder but couldn't see him. He ran back into the heat and smoke, shielding his face with his arms.

Yoder had got the key in the lock and had apparently passed out. Dolf turned the key, feeling the flesh on his fingers scorching. The lock gave slowly and finally ground open. He burned his hands badly on the bars, opening the door. His coat burst into flames as he grabbed Yoder. He snatched Yoder's wet blanket and draped it hastily over himself, doing a repeat of his transporting job on Parsons.

His senses were reeling when he reached the end of the hall. He was almost done. He staggered into the unlocked end cell and smashed the window with his hand. A reviving breath of air rushed in. His head was beginning to clear. Foley had followed him into the cell.

They both looked desperately around for some implement to attack the door with. It was then that Dolf remembered something from the past. He'd helped build this jail. The cell doors were simply lowered onto their hinges when open; closed, their frames locked them in place.

"Grab ahold," he yelled to Foley, hoisting the open eighty-pound door bodily off its hinges.

Foley got the idea immediately.

They took the huge impromptu battering ram upright between them and made a run at the door. At the first blow, it splintered. Their second run knocked it off its hinges.

A huge rush of cold fresh air greeted them. Right behind it came Mulveen and a half dozen volunteer firemen who had been about to take axes to the door.

Dolf wobbled out onto the fire escape landing and was just able to make it down the steps.

Gotta get away from the building before she goes up, he thought, dazedly.

He staggered out into the prison yard, where several scaffolds had graced the grounds over the years, and sat down, then lay down. That was the last he remembered till he came to, hearing Mulveen raging around.

"Where's Morgette? He slipped out while we was carryin' down them other two."

The damn fool, thought Dolf, and passed out again.

When he regained consciousness, he was in a clean strange bed in unfamiliar surroundings. He had the notion somehow that an angel was flitting around the room.

I wonder if I'm dead? he said to himself just before falling asleep.

CHAPTER 6

THEODORA Pardeau had known her husband was going to the jail and why. They had talked it over after Morgette had been brought in. They were staying in town for the night. She had seen Pardeau's mortal fear of Dolf's revenge in his eyes and lurking just below the surface of his manner. With difficulty she masked her contempt. This was doubly hard since she no longer cared whether it showed or not. After five years of marriage, she knew Ed Pardeau in and out in all his moods. The only one she cared for was his romantic mood. He could still be charming to her when he wanted to, but that had become less and less often. It was a failing that she had determined to make him pay for dearly.

They had not been married more than a year when she had discovered the horrifying magnitude of the mistake she had made. He had got drunk again and this time had tried to beat her. She nimbly dodged away, with him stumbling after her. He tripped and fell over the rag rug before the fireplace. When he got up he was looking squarely into the steady muzzle of a Winchester in her hands, held not three feet from his head. He was startled and shaken by the insanely furious eyes of his wife staring over the sights. It quickly sobered him.

"Easy on that trigger," he stammered, trying to grin and make it out a good-natured joke.

She didn't move, speak, or soften her glare. He took an uncertain step back.

"Go to bed," she ordered. "If you ever try that again, I'll pull the trigger."

He went to bed. He also never tried that again.

So Theodora knew her man like a well-read and reread book. That's why she thought he'd be at the saloon till well

72

after she got back from the jail—would probably never know she'd left the hotel room. If he did find out, she'd say she couldn't sleep and had taken a stroll. She was sure that Tobe Mulveen would keep her secret. She knew that, in his own doltish way, Tobe was in love with her. She doubted he recognized it himself. But she knew men.

When Ed returned she pretended to be asleep, although she'd just tumbled into bed. It had been a close thing: she had left the jail not ten minutes before.

He sat down in the single straight-backed chair and started to pull a boot off when the distant shouting penetrated the walls. He went to the window and raised the shade. The low, overcast sky was illuminated by the rapidly growing fire at the jail. He threw up the sash and stuck his head out.

"My gawd!" he exclaimed.

"What is it?" she asked, pretending to wake up just then.

"The courthouse!"

"What about the courthouse?" she asked, looking perfectly blank.

"Can't ya see the sky lit up? It's on fire!" he said.

Then a terrible thought occurred to him. "My God, I was just down there. Morgette'll think I did it ta try an' kill 'im! I gotta get down there an' help put it out." He rushed out the door, slamming it, not even taking his coat.

She sat up in bed, an inscrutable look on her white face. She lit the lamp and stared at herself in the bureau mirror.

"Morgette . . . Morgette," she said to herself. "Dolf Morgette. I hate him. Who cares if he's killed? I *hate all* men."

Then, contradictorily, her face took on a panicky look of concern. She ran to the window and looked up the street to where the flames were now leaping high into the air. She could hear the roar, smell the smoke, hear people shouting.

Suddenly she began to cry, flung herself on her face on the bed, and cried hysterically. Her fit was all over by the time Ed returned. She had dried her eyes and washed away the puffiness with cold water. She lay staring unwinkingly at the ceiling. The reddened sky was no more. She knew the fire was out. She tried not to close her eyes because whenever she did the same images returned. Dolf Morgette young, as she'd first seen him; Dolf Morgette gaunt and aged, as she had just seen him an hour before.

"Is he dead?" she whispered to herself.

Just then Ed Pardeau returned, and she asked him the same question. Ed had left before they found Dolf lying unconscious in the jail yard.

"He escaped!" Ed told her. "He's gone. He'll be comin' after me, sure as hell. He'll think I set that fire."

"Didn't you?" she asked unemotionally.

"No!" he almost shouted. Then, in a lower voice, "No. Why would I do a dumb thing like that, knowin' what'd happen?"

She looked dispassionately at him.

She said, "I thought you told me tonight you'd like to get rid of those three Texas troublemakers down in the jail because they knew too much. What did they know? That you sent them to egg that posse on to lynch Dolf?"

He fixed her with a mixed look of fear and outrage.

"That's a helluva thing to say to me. You wanna be a widow?"

She didn't answer.

"You bitch!" he hissed impatiently. "What a mistake I made!"

"You've made a lot of 'em lately," she said. "You may have just made your last one tonight."

Seeing his terror-stricken look, she laughed contemptuously.

"You think you made a mistake? You didn't make a tenth of the mistake I did."

That shook him. He looked at her in desperation. Quickly, he came to the bed, touched her shoulders, looked into her eyes.

"Darling, you're not thinking of leaving me, are you? I need you. That'd kill me quicker'n a bullet."

He leaned down, forced the lips she tried to turn away back to meet his and kissed her hotly, drew back, and then kissed her long and tenderly again. She closed her eyes, finally put her arms around his neck, and sighed deeply.

When he drew away she said dreamily, "I don't know what I think lately. Come to bed and forget it till morning."

Theo was not the woman to suspect herself of having been a miserably contradictory fool this night, or any other time.

The contrast between Theo and Victoria Wheat was almost a case of diametric opposites. Theo was dark with an ivory complexion; was tall, willowy, mercurial—quick to anger, quick to laugh.

Victoria was small and fair, composed yet unself-conscious. She'd been schooled in the East, read widely and understood what she read; and consequently she had thought a great deal about many things. Since she was totally aware of her intense womanliness, she made no small effort to be equally sure that she was capable of a man's achievements in a man's world—achievements that would probably be far more satisfying to her than motherhood.

She was thinking now, having let her book, Stendhal's *The Red and the Black*, sink to her lap. Doc Hennessey had appointed her to watch Dolf and to send for him at once if he woke up in pain. They still weren't sure but what his lungs weren't damaged by the intense heat.

"We won't know," Doc said, "till he comes to. He seems to be breathing okay, but only he can tell us how it feels."

He shook his head in anxious concern, then left.

Mark Wheat had insisted on having Dolf brought to his home. One fully in the know might have suspected he wanted him better protected than he had been in the jail. He had a plausible other reason, however.

"The so-called hospital in this town doesn't deserve the name," Wheat had said, then turning to Doc, "No reflection on you."

So they brought Dolf to the Wheat mansion and deposited him in bed in a second-floor bedroom.

Mark Wheat had told Mulveen with the positive assurance

of a man talking to one he knows is his political dog, "I want two damn good deputies guarding my house every minute of every twenty-four hours until Dolf is on his feet—and," he added, "they won't be there to see that he doesn't walk away, but to see that he stays alive. I'll pay their salaries myself."

But Victoria wasn't thinking now of those strange circumstances that had brought under her father's roof this tragic, violent man she had idolized as a girl. She was thinking of the man himself as he appeared then. She watched his face, which was sometimes serene, sometimes contorted in either pain or mental torture.

Once he'd said, "It's Pa," then after a long pause, dolefully, "he's dead. And Jim. . . ." He shook his head violently from side to side, as though trying to make it not so. Then, in a most mournful voice, "Poor old Jim."

He'd heaved a huge sigh.

She felt tears welling to her eyes. Here was one who had suffered.

He lost his father and brothers, she remembered.

She couldn't remember their names. Maybe one of them was Jim. Whoever it'd been, it was someone he'd loved.

She wiped her eyes and studied Dolf's once-more serene face. He needed a shave, but it didn't mar the still-handsome, lean features. She thought he had a very good nose. Also a wide, high forehead, and quizzical eyebrows now that he was in repose. His sweeping Imperial mustache was black, with just a trace of the same premature graying that had captured his temples. Beneath the mustache was a broad, heavy-lipped mouth built for mirth but compressed to severity from the habit of years of peril and adversity. In the chin was the strength that revealed how he had survived what he had. It was truly massive, though on him it certainly didn't appear overly large but instead reflected a granite determination. She recalled that his eyes were blue. When she had known him in a happier time and place, she remembered that they had usually been a mischievous shining blue.

"Poor man," she sighed aloud. "Poor, poor man. Maybe now they'll let you live in peace."

But that wasn't an expression of her true innermost feeling. Some deeper emotion than pity had gradually pervaded her consciousness as she sat watching and occasionally listening to his subconscious agony.

True, he had killed, but his people had been killed—killed ruthlessly from ambush, whereas he had killed fairly in broad daylight from the front and always with due warning. But for all of his dark background, one thing about him stood out. By any fair standard of judgment, despite the worst known about him, *this was a man*. And she was fascinated by him, despite her classical schooling in an effete, totally different world that would have condemned him with a totally uncomprehending sense of horrified revulsion.

She wondered what the two of them would find to say to each other when he regained consciousness.

She had looked away pensively into space, reflecting on this unsettling state of her mind. When she next looked at him, she was startled to see him regarding her solemnly with obvious puzzlement. He said nothing. She felt her pulse suddenly quicken.

"I'm Victoria Wheat," she said, finding words. "How do you feel?"

He still said nothing, regarding her with intense concentration. She rose, concerned that he might be delirious, or . . . with some panic, she thought he might be about to die. She was on the verge of summoning help.

He arrested her departure with a slow smile and said something totally unexpected by her. Normally awkward with words around women, he surprised himself as well.

"I remember you. You musta been twelve at the time. You came to a dance one night." He paused, remembering the details.

"I thought you were going to grow up to be a rare beauty—"

She felt herself starting to blush.

"—and you did," he concluded.

Still smiling, he turned onto his back and fell into a normal, exhausted sleep.

She stood for a long while thinking, a pensive little smile on her lips, the blush subsiding; then she remembered to sit down. Her breathing was fast for a moment, as though she'd just run upstairs.

"He's going to be just fine," she thought happily, watching the regular rise and fall of his breathing.

She slipped out of the room and sent a maid to give Doc the good news.

Tobe Mulveen was probably the only one in town who considered the fire totally unrelated to Dolf's presence in his jail.

"It was that drunken fool Billy Blackenridge," he raged, referring to the sometime jailer, janitor, and flunky, who also kept up the fires around the jail and courthouse. "I sent him up to start that fire when the prisoners come in an' the damn fool left the coal oil can sittin' on top o' the stove—I'd bet on it. Last time I caught him just in time. I'll wring his worthless neck when we find where he's sleepin' it off this time."

That was where the official investigation started and ended. When Billy showed up, Tobe took a pawful of his shirt by way of emphasis and, shaking him like a rat, started a short interrogation as a matter of form, but he was already convinced of what had happened. No threat could budge Billy from the adamant insistence he'd replaced the five-gallon can where it normally sat at the head of the stairs. There the matter rested.

"If I had a jail left, I'd put yuh in it sure as hell," Tobe blustered at Billy. "An' throw away the damn key."

CHAPTER 7

MARK Wheat kept an office at home. He'd had an outside entrance installed to maintain the privacy of his home. The office was just to the left of the main entrance. It opened onto the wide veranda that surrounded the mansion at the front and on both sides. Mark's desk was placed so his back was to the wall—also so he could see whoever approached.

Both fireplace and stove were available to heat the spacious room. This morning he had a fire going in the fireplace. He was sorting papers, occasionally consigning some to the fire. Built into the same brick wall as the fireplace was a double-door safe almost as tall as Wheat. Its doors were ajar. From time to time he deposited some of the papers he was sorting into a drawer of the safe.

A man in Wheat's business naturally accumulated a great many clients' confidential documents. A man with Wheat's past accumulated a great many more of his own. It was these he was sequestering or destroying.

He removed a shoe box from the safe. It was full of what appeared to be samples of coal, each one with a tag tied to it. This he placed on his desk; he sat for a moment, eying it. His thoughts were jumbled this morning, a very unusual condition for him to find himself in. He shook his head impatiently, casting his gaze out the bay window next to the door. Deep in thought, he absentmindedly pulled out a cigar, automatically trimmed the end with his pen knife, then lit it. He hoisted his feet onto the desk and stared unseeingly outside, still ruminating over whatever the box of coal had recalled to his mind.

"The cause of all the damned trouble," he muttered half-aloud. "The curse."

He was in this frame of mind when Doc clumped up onto

79

the porch and spotted him at his desk through the beveled glass door, turned, and entered.

"Mornin', Mark," he greeted him.

It was a typical gesture. Almost anytime, Wheat would have been glad to have Doc drop in. He found the man fascinating. Here was a former killer who was also a great humanitarian. Scores of people owed their lives to Doc's answering calls in any weather, day or night, no matter how inaccessible the victims were when disaster befell them. Doc was deeply loved and respected in the Pinebluff district. But Mark found his presence this morning irritating. He had to force himself to make the usual offer of a cigar.

He wished he'd seen Doc coming sooner so he could have shoved the coal specimens back in the safe. To his added annoyance, Doc's alert gaze spotted them immediately.

"I hope you ain't thinkin' o' switchin' ta coal with all the wood we got growin' in our backyard," Doc observed.

Mark forced a grin.

"Hardly. Once owned a piece of a mine back in Alabama. I knew it was gonna make the Wheats rich. Maybe it would have if the war hadn't come along."

Pretending to be casual, he picked up the box and shoved it under the desk on the floor.

"Sentiment I guess. I've dragged them around for years. Oughta put 'em in the fireplace."

Then, changing the subject, he said, "The patient is just fine this mornin'. Up and around. Joined us at breakfast. Why don't you go out to the kitchen and have a bite if you haven't yet? Libbie'll be glad to fix something. You can yell up for Dolf or go up."

Doc took the hint.

"Sounds good."

He left by the inside door into the entrance hall.

Wheat resumed his thoughtful pose, feet on his desk, puffing on his cigar.

The problem is, he thought, *Ed Pardeau. Ed has got to go.*

The fact was Ed knew too much. It had been unavoidable.

If he'd been willing to remain the junior partner, that would have been all right. In fact, if he'd just shape up now, it would still work out. But Ed was drinking again, and when he did, he got big ideas. He'd been in the legislature a couple of times and had a lot of friends. Furthermore, his name was well known, both from that and from the publicity when he'd tried to arrest Dolf Morgette and almost got killed in the attempt. Some of the boys up in the capital who didn't cotton to Wheat's independence had turned Ed's head. They wanted a tool they could manipulate as delegate to Congress and later as senator, in the event statehood ever became a reality.

"The bastards," Wheat swore under his breath. *They're moving fast too*, he thought.

He wondered how much Alby Gould's money might have to do with this surge of support for Pardeau. The two were getting mighty chummy, even going up to the capital together.

They think I don't know, he mused.

Wheat knew almost everything that went on in the territory. He'd carefully built a network of friends and people beholden to him for their livelihood, or at least for past favors they hoped might be repeated if the need ever arose again. In so many words, Mark Wheat was a master politician and no one, not even his enemies, denied that. So they tried to attack him through his weak, vain partner, Ed Pardeau.

I made a mistake, Wheat admitted to himself. *Should have backed Morgette for sheriff in the old days. I wouldn't have got a hold on the Morgette ranch, but what the hell good did it turn out to be? Especially with a treacherous partner.*

That brought up another point. Ed Pardeau's weakness for women. If he didn't watch out and Theodora caught on, he'd be out on his ear. Then even the tenuous hold they had on the best-watered ranch in the Quarter Lien would go down the drain.

Wheat sighed deeply.

What do I care? he thought. *I could have used the Morgette ranch if things had worked out. Let it go.*

But the rub was that a lot of people had died when that

scheme looked like the key to a fortune. In the process, Ed Pardeau had come to know too much—too much, that is, about Wheat.

Mark Wheat nodded, as though coming to a sudden decision. *I can still ride the Morgette horse,* he thought. *It's not too late, provided Pardeau has a 'melancholy accident,' as the papers put it. I've got to see that Dolf gets the right hints about what really happened to his pa and brothers.*

Dolf had slept almost around the clock. He was stiff, his chest felt a little tender when he tried a deep breath, but otherwise he couldn't see where he was any the worse for his narrow escape in the fire.

Doc had brought some of Dolf's clothes he'd been keeping for him and a toilet kit, since the other one had gone up with the courthouse and jail. Although Dolf didn't know it, Victoria had washed and ironed the shirts and underwear herself, also brushed and pressed the coat and pants.

He was gratified to find indoor plumbing that included a huge bathtub standing on ball-and-claw feet. He had almost never in his life had such luxury. He shaved, and then soaked the aches from his body in the tub.

By breakfast-time he felt almost as good as he had before his ordeal had started. Both his body and mind possessed wonderful resiliency and toughness.

Mark Wheat had graciously indicated to Victoria after breakfast that he had business he'd like to discuss with Dolf over coffee and cigars. She was used to such situations and shortly left them to themselves.

Wheat, with the acting ability that is necessary in any good politician, put on a studiously worried appearance, pretending to stare bemused into his coffee cup.

"I'm worried," he finally said.

Dolf watched him narrowly, reserving judgment, remembering everything he'd ever known about this shrewd man. He especially remembered Pardeau's one-word warning about who was behind all the local trouble: "Wheat!"

When the politician looked up at him with a carefully

calculated look of concern, Dolf showed outwardly only a poker-faced attentiveness.

"I'm mainly worried about you, Dolf. You're my horse. I've got $25,000 bet on you so far. Someone's trying to kill you. Have you any idea who?"

Dolf was deliberately silent for a long while. Finally he shook his head in the negative. He said, "I expected that Pardeau would have the motive, but I don't really believe he's behind it. He talked to me at the jail the other night. He's scared—really scared of something."

"Did you get a clue what he was scared of?"

Dolf decided to shatter Wheat's urbane aplomb and fetch this fancy footwork to a close with a solar plexus punch.

"You," he stated. "He warned me to watch out for you too."

For a brief moment Wheat's mask slipped; a bit of confusion or panic showed through. Then he almost instantly recovered. He continued to appear genuinely aggrieved, putting on an injured expression.

"Now that's just like Ed, lately. He owes me a great deal of his success. He was almost like a son to me once. But I've been finding out that he's an ingrate. He's not only biting the hand that fed him, but I've found out some other unsavory things about him. He's a sneak."

He paused to let that settle in.

He hadn't told Dolf anything he hadn't already learned from other sources, or from personal experience.

"I might give you the same warning about Ed that he gave you about me. Only I'll wager he couldn't give you more than innuendo; I can give you some concrete facts."

Dolf waited. There was obviously going to be more.

"For example," Wheat continued, "those three whose lives you saved up at the jail. Do you know what they are or why they were in jail?"

Dolf shook his head no.

"They're three of Pardeau's hardcases he brought in from Texas. They were in because they were the ringleaders who incited that posse into a lynch mob. That's Pardeau's speed. I'm breaking up our partnership as soon as I can come to some sensible sort of agreement with him. He wants to get the long end of the stick. And he's dangerous when he doesn't get his way. I wouldn't be surprised if he has someone try to kill me. And I'll level with you on that; I'm not going to beat around the bush. That's one reason I wanted you as a law partner. They'll think twice before they come around and start trouble with you around. Which reminds me. . . ."

He paused and went over to the buffet, pulled open a drawer, and produced Dolf's guns and belts.

"I figured you'd feel naked without these. Mulveen raised hell, but I told him you'd have the chance of a snowball in hell without your guns. Besides, half the kids in school carry six-shooters. It isn't as though carryin' one violates any deep community custom. We all carry one most of the time. Mulveen could see the sense of that—and that you'd get another pair somewhere else anyhow. But I wouldn't go anywhere without a six-shooter if I was you—not from now on until things settle down."

The rest of the conversation had to do with getting Dolf into the law business. Obviously, an influential sponsor was a good thing to have. It developed that Wheat was having the credentials committee up for some poker, at which time Dolf would pass his bar examination, apparently at the poker table if that's how he preferred it.

"All a formality," Wheat explained. Then he winked and added, "In this case, that is."

Dolf grinned. "I see. Well, I'm ready to go to work if you've got something for me to get started on."

"Rest up awhile," Wheat suggested. "Take a week or so to get back on your pins. But I'd appreciate it if you'd stay around pretty close in the meantime. Right now, if I was you, I'd go up and take a nap. Do you a world of good. But hang around the place if you know what I mean."

Dolf knew what he meant all right. Under the suave exterior, Wheat was as scared as Pardeau. Were they merely afraid of each other—or was something else going on?

On that note, Dolf had settled down for the nap Wheat suggested. He was surprised to discover how soon he'd got tired again, just from breakfast and a little conversation.

Doc woke him up. He hoped it was Victoria shaking him in the instant before he opened his eyes.

He saw Doc and grinned warmly. "Hi," he said, stretching and yawning.

"How d'ya feel?" Doc asked.

"Sleepy yet. Otherwise pretty good."

"How does your chest feel?"

"A little sore when I take a deep breath."

"Most likely the smoke. Let's hope yer lungs weren't scorched. If they were, you're apt to get pneumonia about the time you think you're well and croak overnight. Here, pull up yore shirt an' let me listen."

He pulled out a stethoscope and laid it around on Dolf's chest and back.

"Sounds okay to me," was the verdict. "We'd better do that about twice a day for awhile. And you stay inside."

"I've got things to do," Dolf protested.

"Like what?"

"I want ta see my daughter. She ain't apt to be comin' in here, so I was plannin' to go out there. I want to talk to Matt and Junior about some things too."

Doc avoided the subject of Amy.

"I reckon I mighta took care o' what ya wanted to see Matt an' Junior about." Doc said. "I sent Matt ta look up that conductor that oughta know ya got off that train. I sent Junior down ta see Sheriff Joe Lane. They're both supposed to bring back sworn statements. I had a notion you'd be needin' 'em. Is that what yuh wanted ta see 'em about?"

Dolf nodded. "Exactly, as a matter o' fact. That leaves Amy. If I ain't supposed ta go out, why don't you arrange fer her to come in?"

Doc looked uncomfortable. "The fact is," he admitted, "I talked to Theodora about that jist as she was heading back to the ranch the other mornin'. Amy doesn't want to see you—"

Then, seeing the expression on Dolf's face, he quickly protested—"Now wait a minute. She's only a kid. Give 'er some time. You know what the problem is as well as I do. He's skinned out, by the way. Left Theodora ta go out home alone. She laughed when she told me. He thinks yer gonna blame him fer settin' fire to the jail to try and kill yuh."

Dolf had naturally devoted some thought to that question. "How do we know he didn't? I wouldn't put it past 'im."

"Mulveen thinks that dunce Blackenridge set the kerosene can on the stove when he started the fire," Doc said.

Dolf shook his head.

"It sounded like the kerosene blew up all right. That'd account fer how fast it spread too. But it woulda blown long before then. The stove was already lit when I first went up there. It sounds just like Mulveen ta be that thick-headed. Ed coulda done it, but Tobe's almost as sweet on Ed as the gals are, so he'd never suspect him. He might check up on some o' them deputies he had too. Maybe some of 'em are my old friends that figure they owe me from the old days. Who knows?" Then, switching the subject, "So old Ed sloped? Fer good, I wonder?"

"No such luck. He'll wait'll things cool down. Prob'ly down at the capital. Everyone but Theodora knows he's got a gal down there. He'll come draggin' in one o' these days lookin' like he's been dragged through a knothole. Now, you git some more o' that shut-eye. Best medicine in the world fer yuh right now."

He slipped out and shut the door quietly.

Dolf stretched out on the big bed, his arms comfortably behind his head, fingers entwined, thinking about his prospects.

He'd be relieved when Junior and Matt brought back the proof of his innocence of the train holdup.

Then we can be out from under Mark Wheat's thumb, he thought. Lawyering didn't really appeal to him. Maybe he'd lay low till he was admitted to the bar and maybe not. Most likely not. It would be sneaky to let Wheat use his influence to secure his license and then tell him he had no notion of becoming his partner.

He still had a wad of cash. His plan was to put a few horses and as many head of stock as his roll would buy up on the range by the line cabin and to live there. It was sheltered in winter with lush marsh hay growing hip-deep. It was no problem for stock to rustle there winter or summer.

I can make a living at it, he thought, *and let the world go by. Maybe someday the right woman'll come along an' we kin grow old and fat up there together.*

That called to mind the picture of Victoria. He knew she was far above him, but all the same it was pleasant to dream about a woman like her. The fact was, in view of what had befallen him, he wasn't sure it would be fair to expose any woman to someone as mistrustful as he'd be. He knew that most prisoners released headed for the nearest available woman. He regarded any contact with the sex with a degree of panic. That had been his main reaction to seeing Theo the other night. No old embers remained to be fanned. Of course she *was* the authoress of his wary attitude, but some people might have experienced some lingering warmth from old shared passions. There had been none of this.

Must be the Injun in me, he reasoned. *I pity her—pity Ed almost as much. But it's definitely over. I owe her thanks fer givin' me sense enough to look over the next one a lot better—if there ever is a next one.*

With that thought still in mind, he dozed off with an image of Victoria behind his closed eyelids.

I sure hope she gets a good man someday, was his last thought before dropping off.

CHAPTER 8

MOST of the time these days, Hal Green was a farmer. One day a week he came to Pinebluff and was both editor and typesetter of the *Weekly Independent*. He helped write up the news his daughter Catherine collected. She was his only reporter, was a fair hand at writing, and could set type faster than Hal. Once, when Pinebluff was a boom town, the *Independent* had been a powerful voice in Territorial politics. In those days Pinebluff boasted five thousand people, with a thousand miners working shifts. Today the population was eight hundred, and perhaps thirty miners remained.

The Wheat-Pardeau interests had bought up the flooded-out mines, forming from them the Pinebluff Consolidated Mining and Milling Co. Some of the upper levels were still economically workable with pumping. They sold the pumped water for irrigation, which accounted for the fact that a considerable apple orchard business had sprung up when the mines shut down. This was Hal Green's main livelihood. The *Independent* was lucky to break even. In fact, in harvest season he shut it down completely so Catherine could help him and the boys pick and box the apples. She also helped haul them by wagon the thirty miles to the railroad, where they were then shipped to the coast for sale. Catherine had always been a tomboy. At nineteen she could drive a wagon as good as most men. She could also ride, rope, and shoot well enough to have a local reputation for competence at all three.

This was the reporter that came around to interview Dolf Morgette—a somewhat unconventional reporter for that day, but the best that Pinebluff could offer. Unlike Victoria Wheat, Catherine Green was no rare beauty. She was a sturdy, pretty, wholesome young woman, far older than her years. She'd had to become the mother of her younger brothers and sisters because her own mother died when she was eleven. There were four younger children: two boys and two girls. During the school months, Catherine lived in town with the girls on weekdays. The boys, Buck and Ben, at seventeen and fifteen, were out of school and helped run the farm.

Victoria called Dolf downstairs when Catherine arrived.

"An interview?" Dolf asked, surprised when Victoria told him who was there and what she wanted.

"Why not?" Victoria replied. "You're our only celebrity in Pinebluff. Besides, Catherine Green is a nice person. So is her father. Do her a favor."

"Did she grow up pretty?" Dolf asked slyly.

Victoria eyed him carefully, trying to look severe. The attempt failed. She smiled. "Pretty enough," she said.

She led him down to the parlor, entering first.

"He's ready to stampede, but I've got him haltered," Victoria broke the ice with a couple of localisms. She found them useful to offset predictable small-town reaction to her eastern education. "You two do know each other, as I recall."

"I reckon. She stole my horse when she was about ten," Dolf said.

Catherine appeared confused for some reason and blushed. Victoria noticed this and made a shrewd surmise about it. She looked quickly at Dolf to see if he noticed. He seemed unaware of anything unusual.

Victoria thought, *Do you suppose he's so modest he doesn't suspect how he affects women?*

Catherine found her voice finally. "I did *not* steal him. I rode him on a dare."

"And I paddled you when I ran you down," Dolf added. "Remember?"

Catherine fought off another blush, angry with herself over this loss of her usual poise, but pleased also.

She grinned, remembering. "You were my schoolgirl crush," she admitted, counterattacking. "It was better than not having you notice me at all. All the girls hated me for getting that much attention from you. We all had crushes on you."

Victoria frowned ever so slightly. She felt left out of this, then inwardly reminded herself she was being petty. "If you two will excuse me, I'll leave Catherine to her interviewing. Holler when you're through, and we can all have lunch together."

"My dad said he'd be over in a little while," Catherine said. "He wouldn't want to intrude."

"We'd love to have you both."

With that she glided out the door. But she would have preferred to stay. She wondered why, considered it briefly, then said to herself, *I don't mean a thing to him. So why should he mean anything to me?*

The subconscious knowledge of the answer to that question left her deeply troubled. She prided herself on controlling her life and making decisions logically. She wasn't being logical. And she wasn't controlling her feelings; quite the contrary. She found it most unsettling. But she was not angry.

Dolf and Catherine subjected one another to cautious appraising looks while they talked. He liked her type of girl: obviously competent yet not masculine—far from it. She had friendly brown eyes, a stubby nose that went with the wide attractive mouth, and a slight sprinkling of freckles. She wore her abundant brown hair in two long pigtails like a schoolgirl. Somehow it was most attractive worn that way with her plain gingham dress.

"Dad wants to run a front-page story on you, your plans . . ." She paused.

"My homecoming?" he suggested.

"That too," she admitted.

He grinned ruefully. "I'm not sure I should have come back. If I'd known how it was going to work out, I probably wouldn't have. I don't like the idea of going back to the pen a second time for something I didn't do."

"You know Dad and I never believed you were guilty the first time," she assured him, her brown eyes all concern.

"I knew your dad didn't." He smiled and added, "I hardly knew you except as our worst local horse thief of record."

"I'd have broke you out," she blurted, then blushed furiously.

She saw his sudden shrewd, appraising look when she said this, and it deepened her confusion.

He broke the tension by chuckling. "Then you were a hardened criminal type all around. I never suspected."

The arrival of Hal Green rescued Catherine from her temporary embarrassment. Victoria escorted him into the parlor and bowed out again. Hal crossed to Dolf and warmly pumped his hand.

"Good to see you back, Dolf," he said sincerely. "But I'm not sure you were wise to come; you can see what happened already. They're ready to hound you again. Guilty consciences."

Dolf nodded assent. "You're probably right. But I wanted to see my kids."

"I understand," Hal said. "But the community doesn't see it that way. They think you're here for revenge."

"What makes you think I'm not?" Dolf asked.

"I know you too well," Hal replied without hesitation.

Catherine had drawn in a sudden breath at Dolf's words. She, unlike her father, didn't know him that well. In fact, she felt that if she were a man, she herself might seek revenge in his circumstances. *Who could blame him?* she thought. But as she thought that, the answer also came to her at the same instant: *Everyone would blame him. Whether it's just or not.*

Dolf was deeply grateful to Hal for his expression of confidence. "Thanks, Hal."

"What're your plans now?" Hal asked, changing the subject, and then added, "I mean after we clear up this latest ridiculous charge against you." Hal snorted, "Talk about giving a dog a bad name."

The "*we* clear up" hadn't escaped Dolf. He felt another surge of gratitude for this old true friend.

"I don't know what my plans are," Dolf confessed. "I owe something to Mark Wheat. He put up my bail, gave me a job, and is going to see that I'm admitted to the bar, come hell 'r high water. So by rights I have to throw in with him like he expects. But to tell you the truth, I'd rather go back to ranching."

Recognizing that he was in Wheat's house and might be overheard, Green didn't say what he'd have liked to. Instead he said, "Good. I'd go for the ranching, and Dolf," he added, looking cautiously around, "come down to the *Independent* in awhile and we'll have a confidential confab. There's some things I want to tell you and someone I want you to meet."

The Greens made their excuses to Victoria on lunch.

"Press day," Hal explained, and they left.

Dolf had a snack with Victoria and then prepared to go down to meet Hal. He felt no responsibility to stick around since Mark Wheat had explained that he himself would be out somewhere all day.

Dolf was curious to know what the bee was in Hal's bonnet; also who he was apparently anxious for him to meet.

Dolf shoved a six-shooter in his belt under his coat. He put a dozen extra cartridges in his coat pocket. Thus prepared, he set out for the *Independent* building. He passed the charred ruins of the courthouse with its unpleasant memories. He was not surprised to see several people who had once professed to be his friends hastily cross to the opposite side of the street upon seeing him, then pretend to be busy looking the other way.

An outsized puppy with huge feet, obviously a hound and equally obviously a hungry stray, approached him cautiously, wagging its tail hopefully. Dolf got down on his haunches so the pup wouldn't be afraid of him and slowly extended the back of his hand for the pup to smell. It tentatively sniffed him, and finally allowed its ears to be scratched. Very soon he had its head between his hands, giving it a thorough rubbing, then he was rubbing its back and chest vigorously. When he rose, the pup filed in behind him and followed, sniffing at the back of his trousers.

Dolf stopped at the butcher shop and bought a package of meaty bones. He proceeded up the street to the bench in front of the Bonanza saloon, took a seat, and unwrapped his treasure for the pup, setting one bone on the boardwalk. The pup tied into it, grinding it to a pulp in a few big bites, then looking for more. Dolf doled out a second, then another and another to the same fate, watching in gratification as the pup's sunken flanks looked less and less raillike.

"Mop" Finn came out of the Bonanza just then. Dolf was surprised to see him still on duty as a swamper; he'd have expected him to be in an alcoholic's grave before then.

Mop's red-veined eyes focused on Dolf. The town's least citizen wasn't the type to avoid him, or anyone who'd been his friend.

"Dolf?" he said cautiously, coming closer. Then, happily, "Dolf Morgette. Heard yuh was in town." He came up, grasped and pumped Dolf's hand.

"Mop," Dolf greeted him, glad to see a friendly face. He put his hand on his shoulder and gave it a friendly squeeze. Automatically, he reached in his pocket for the price of a drink, just like in the old days.

Seeing this, Mop backed away and held up his hands to ward off the handout. "Nope," he said forcefully. "I ain't panhandlin'. I'm just plumb glad ta see yuh home. And," he leaned closer and added in a low tone, "I hope ya come on a skunk hunt. They's still plenty o' em around."

"Came ta see my family," Dolf told him. He never patronized the old soak.

Mop looked him over closely. "They'll try ta kill yuh, Dolf," he said soberly. "Human nature. They kicked yuh when yuh wuz down, now they gotta treat yuh like they wuz right—or hate themselves."

"Thanks, Mop," Dolf said. "You wouldn't know whose pup this is, would yuh?"

"Yup," Mop said. "Nobody's. Yours if'n yuh want 'im. Freighter left 'im here. Tied 'im to a tree an' drove off. Still be there if'n I hadn't cut 'im loose. I bin feedin' 'im what little I cud afford."

"You still got your shack out back?" Dolf asked.

"Shore have."

"Well, you take 'im out there an' keep 'im till I get back," Dolf said. "I'll take 'im."

He gave Mop the rest of the bones. "Give 'im the whole bunch," Dolf said.

Dolf found Hal alone when he reached the *Independent*. The paper was all that now occupied an imposing brick building that had once held the Mining Exchange, a hotel, a theater, and several offices. Dolf's tread echoed hollowly through the empty relic of an earlier prosperous era as he crossed the entry hallway to the *Independent* office.

It brought back memories. How many times he'd come here to discuss the affairs of the Law and Order Party that had backed him for sheriff. Those had been brave, optimistic times. Was he sorry they were gone? he wondered. It was an unanswered question. *Probably not*, he thought.

Basically, he was an optimist despite all the trouble that had come his way. He still held hope for the future. He was thinking, *We can't recall the past and live it different.*

In this mood he entered Hal's office. The editor was immersed in finishing an article. He passed Dolf a stogey.

"Set," he invited, "while I finish this before I forget what I was gonna write." And he added in explanation, "Old age."

Hal plowed on with his pencil. Dolf lit the stogey and stretched comfortably in a swivel chair that had once belonged to one of the two associate editors the *Independent* had boasted in the boom days.

Hal finished and tossed his pencil on his desk.

"I know you well enough, Dolf, to come right to the point. Mark Wheat is a lousy, no-good, scheming son of a bitch, and you shouldn't have a damn thing to do with him," Hal growled.

Dolf wasn't startled. This was what he'd expected to hear, or stronger. But the unavoidable fact was that Mark, like himself, might have been misjudged by the community. The man had put up a small fortune in bail for him without blinking. He had offered him a job, supposing he didn't have a nickel of his own. He had frankly admitted to Dolf his ulterior motive; he was afraid and relished the idea of having a combination partner and bodyguard. He had raised a daughter who was an angel in Dolf's view. Could someone all bad do that?

He thought all of this yet forebore to say a word in Mark's defense. He knew that where Hal was concerned, the effort would have been wasted. In the old days, Wheat and Green were the acknowledged leaders of opposing political factions. Their conflicts were sharp and bitter. Wheat looked tolerantly on the notion of a wide-open town; as district attorney, he had treated the murderous forays of the Rustler Gang as though its membership of thugs and blackguards were errant schoolboys. (So long as they handled his dirty work.) On the other side, Hal Green had thundered against them as a threat against civilization and progress, calling for martial law when enforcement under Pardeau became a farce. Moreover, Green had done this at constant risk to his own life.

These were the reasons that Dolf's loyalties were divided. Of course he knew that Wheat had been ruthless and tricky on his way to power. Many men were. But he seemed to have mellowed. On the other hand, Hal Green had always been straightforward, honest, and upright. He was the older friend. In a showdown, Dolf would have gone with Hal. It might come to that again. Dolf could feel something in the wind.

Hal was eyeing him now, trying to think where to begin.

Finally he said, "It's going to be just like back in '80 again. Wheat's land and cattle company is trying to freeze us little fellows out. He's already got everything but your old ranch, and he'd have that if his partner didn't as good as own it anyhow. Now he's raised the price of irrigation water again to squeeze us little fellows. We're all hocked to our eyeballs to his bank, or were till Alby Gould came along to bail us out."

"I keep hearing about Gould," Dolf said. "Just who is he?"

"You'll meet him in a little while. He's tough but honest in my opinion. He's an Easterner whose pa is filthy rich. He talked the old man into staking him to go into business out here. Came out on an elk-hunting trip and fell in love with the country. He's a college fellow but no sissy. Played football and baseball, was on the rowing and boxing teams. He can take care of himself. A couple of Pardeau's cowboys found that out, to their sorrow—jumped him over at the Bonanza, and he put a head on both of 'em. Knocked 'em both cold."

It was pretty obvious that Green was sold on Gould. Dolf wasn't so sure. From what he'd heard, it might be out of the frying pan into the fire.

Dolf said, "I heard he has some pretty hard boys workin' fer 'im."

"Has to," Hal said. "Wheat and Co. forced his hand."

"You say he's bankrolling you little fellows? What's ta keep him from playin' Wheat's racket on yuh?"

"You'll see for yourself. He's straight. Next thing he's gonna do is open a bank. He's got Wheat and Pardeau on the run. He'll be runnin' this country in another year—only straight, for a change."

"Why d'ya want me to meet him?" Dolf asked.

"He wanted to meet you. I think he's got a job offer that'll beat Wheat's all hollow."

"What kind of a job?" Dolf inquired warily.

Green shrugged.

"Wait'll you meet him. Oh, and that isn't all," Hal gloated. "He's courtin' Wheat's daughter, to add insult to injury, and old Mark is fit to be tied since the gal seems to like him."

This news prepared Dolf to take an exceptionally close look at this Alby Gould. Without analyzing his own feelings, he nonetheless felt that anyone who had intentions regarding Victoria had better measure up. Furthermore, the intentions had better be honorable.

Just then, a big man came in who he knew must be Gould. Something jarred about him at once in Dolf's mind. *The clothes*, Dolf thought. *He dresses like a dude. I wonder how long he's been out here.*

Gould was not as tall as Dolf but was heavier. He carried his bulk easily, apparently being in good shape. His face was somewhat blocky, but a relatively lean nose relieved it of plumpness. Amber eyes looked piercingly from beneath relatively heavy brows. With his florid complexion, the whole appearance reminded Dolf of a pink man.

Dolf could readily see how he might have been a boxer. His wide, blocky shoulders suggested strength, though he'd have been hampered as a boxer, Dolf thought, by relatively short arms. *Probably murder, though, as an in-fighter*, Dolf thought.

Green was introducing them now.

"I've heard a lot about you, Mr. Morgette," Gould said. "Some good, some bad."

He smiled abruptly, showing even, white teeth. His smile surprisingly turned his otherwise forbidding face quite pleasant. His eyes met Dolf's directly, without a trace of evasiveness showing in them at any time.

I can see how a woman would like him, Dolf thought.

Gould had a sort of magnetism about him reflected in all his movements. He seemed to be mentally shadowboxing as he talked.

Dolf made no reply.

Gould continued, "Hal here has praised you to high heaven. I've got a lot of faith in his judgment. Did he tell you I had a job in mind for you?"

Dolf's mind had been wandering. He was trying to place exactly where he'd seen Gould before.

"He mentioned it," Dolf said. He waited politely. If Gould expected some enthusiastic response, he was disappointed. And if so, it didn't show.

"I need a general manager for my operation here," Alby stated. "Someone that can't be pushed around or bamboozled. I understand you've studied law too. You seem like the ideal man for the job."

This was the last proposition he'd expected to have thrown his way. He'd expected that his guns were what Gould would want to hire. Dolf turned the proposition over in his mind. It sure would beat lawyering.

"Am I gonna be tied to a desk?" he asked.

"Only as much as you want to. You can get yourself an assistant to shuffle papers. I need someone who can make decisions. You'd be outside a lot on a horse, looking after things. I'm buying up timber rights; I've got one ranch and several farms down on the Quarter Lien, a general store here, the hotel at the junction, a freight operation that covers about half the territory, and will soon have a bank. I'll have a banker to run it, but you can handle as much of the legal end of it as you want. I think what I really need is a troubleshooter to keep the wheels turning smoothly when I'm out of the country, which may be quite often. In fact, I'm on my way to the railroad right now."

He looked over Dolf for a reaction. Hal Green was watching his friend, hoping he'd say yes.

"I suppose Hal told you, if you didn't already know, that I'm under a $25,000.00 bond as a suspect in that train robbery down below. As soon as I tell Wheat I'm not throwing in with him, he'll probably withdraw his bond."

Gould never changed expression. "I've placed $25,000.00 in Hal's safe to cover that contingency."

Dolf was beginning to see what Green saw in Gould. He was direct and tough. He did things in a big way and was obviously smart. He didn't know as much as he'd like to about Gould, but he knew more than he liked about Wheat.

On impulse Dolf said, "I'm your man. I'll tell Wheat."

Gould smiled briefly, extending his hand on it. "A deal."

"A deal," Dolf agreed, shaking Gould's hand. His grip was like a vise.

When he headed back to Wheat's, Dolf was walking on air. He hadn't realized how much he had hated the idea of being a lawyer—or being the partner of an old antagonist, as far as that went.

He'd already arranged for a new domicile. Hal offered him temporary use of the back room of the *Independent*. It had kitchen and bedroom facilities.

"Use it as long as you like," Hal offered. "But half the houses in town or more are empty and can be rented for a song."

"How about my pup?" Dolf asked.

Hal's eyebrows shot up.

"Pup? You don't waste time. Next you'll be engaged. Where'd you get a pup?"

Dolf told him.

"Bring him over," Hal invited. "Catherine and I both love dogs. What's his name?"

Dolf thought about that for a moment.

"Jim Too," he said.

"Ah," Hal observed. He understood. He'd known the other Jim and what he'd meant to Dolf.

Back at Wheat's mansion, Dolf got the surprise of his life. A huge six-horse covered wagon was parked at the front gate.

Doc was just coming out of the front door and spotted Dolf.

"Ah," he said. "I was just comin' ta git yuh. Your old granny is inside," he said, coming closer. And in a lower voice, "Wait'll yuh see the old gal. She's a four-dollar pistol. She and Victoria hit it right off like family."

"Her wagon?" Dolf asked.

"Yup."

"Who's drivin' it?"

"Her."

Dolf wasn't surprised. He remembered Granny, or "Mum," as everyone called her, very well indeed. She was, to say the least, a four-dollar pistol and more. She'd married at fifteen and followed her man to the frontier, which was then in Missouri; that had been in 1823. Shortly after that she loaded an Indian with buckshot when he tried to steal her colt while Granpa was down in the field plowing. The thieving Indians gave her place a wide berth after that.

Mum now met Dolf on the porch, Victoria not far behind, watching with gleaming eyes. Mum was tall and had taken on some healthy weight with the years. She grabbed Dolf in a bear hug, tears welling in her eyes. Then she held him at arm's length.

"Spittin' image o' yer pa when he went off ta the war," she said. "How old're ya now, Dolf?"

"Thirty-seven."

"Same age he was then, the dang fool. Went off and left yer ma an' you younguns ta look after the place. Then Jack an' Hen went too. The dern fool—jist like a Morgette. Shoulda let the young fellers fight."

All the same pride showed in her face at the memory. Then another thought entered her head. Her face saddened.

"Ya ain't caught the skunks thet killed yer paw an' brothers yet, I take it. I hope ya come back a huntin' 'em."

Dolf didn't reply right away. He hadn't expected this to be one of the first thoughts in Mum's mind. He wasn't thinking so much of revenge as peace. He wondered if she understood what he'd been through. *It probably wouldn't cut any ice if she did,* he thought. *She's from good old feudin' Tennessee mountain stock.*

Aloud he said, "We'll have ta talk about that. But first we've got to find you someplace to stay."

"Been stayin' in the wagon fer a thousand mile 'r more. No reason it won't do tonight."

Victoria broke in, "Please stay here, at least for the night. We've rooms all over. Father would enjoy some company too."

Mum looked at Victoria as though she just recalled something. She said to Dolf, "If'n ya got a lick o' sense, you'll court this gal."

Victoria, to her surprise and dismay, blushed deeply.

"Don't mind me," Mum said, recognizing Victoria's discomfort. Then she reverted to Victoria's invitation. "My boy Matt got me a house. Got the address here somewhere. I been travelin' a long ways. I wanna git under my own roof again afore dark. If'n we can't get my bedstead in, I'll sleep in m' wagon, but at least on m' own property again."

Argument didn't budge her.

Dolf shrugged his shoulders, looking blankly at Victoria.

"C'mon, Doc," Mum ordered. "Yuh kin show me where 'tis."

She pulled Doc along, taking it for granted Dolf was coming.

"I'll help her get settled a little," Dolf said to Victoria. "Then I'll be back. I gotta talk to yer pa."

Victoria sensed something in his tone and manner. "You sound serious."

What she really feared was exactly what was about to happen. Seeing the evasive look on his face, she said softly, "Dolf, we're awfully fond of you, even on short acquaintance. No matter what happens, remember I want to—" She stumbled, almost saying "know you better," which would have been considered unbecomingly forward. Instead she finished with, "be your friend."

He was shocked by her sudden seriousness, wishing against his better judgment that her attitude could mean more than he had any right to hope. He thought, *I'm a fool. She's only being nice.* Embarrassed, he couldn't find words.

"I'll be back," he said lamely, taking off hastily after Mum and Doc.

Mum was already in the high seat, reins in hand.

"Jump up," she said to Dolf. "This train is pullin' out."

Dolf was entirely in the dark on Matt's and Mum's plans. All he knew was that Matt had said she was coming. He hadn't said she was on the way.

The house they'd bought was a substantial two-story structure with a barn and corral behind. Tall spruces dotted the big yard. This would be a place for all of them to live. It was as appealing inside as it had been from the outside. As was often the case when a boom camp busted, the former owners had moved out, leaving almost all of their furniture in place. There was even a piano.

"I got some strong backs on their way over," Doc announced. "I'm more used to treatin' hernias than gittin' 'em."

In a short while Doc's hired men showed up. Mum put them to work unloading, supervising every move.

While that was in progress, Doc drew Dolf aside.

"I got some bad news," he confided.

He pulled a couple of telegrams from his inside pocket.

Dolf unfolded the first one; it was from Matt. It read: OUR PARTY GONE SOUTH. HAS RECORD OF PERIODICALLY SKIPPING OUT. HAVE SEEN HIS WIFE. CAN'T BLAME HIM. TOO BAD. HOME SOON.

The other one was from Junior, now over in the adjoining state. It read: SHERIFF JOE LANE KILLED CHASING HORSE THIEVES.

Dolf looked grim. He felt the old hopeless, sick sensation somewhere just under his ribs.

"That leaves our Pinkertons," he said.

"Fat chance," Doc grumbled.

"Maybe not," Dolf reasoned. "They want me out of the pen, not in. Have ya seen 'em around anywhere?"

"They were at the hotel," Doc said. "Playin' 'em close ta their chests. They jist rented a house down the street from Wheat's yesterday. Been watchin' fer you with field glasses to see if you make a move.

"How'd ya find that out?"

"Secret," Doc said mysteriously. Then, relenting, he explained, "Catherine Green interviews all newcomers to town. They were so suspicious-acting, she asked around if anyone knew 'em. Happened to ask me. The description fit, so I went down an' paid 'em a call. Were they ever surprised. The field glasses were still in plain sight."

Dolf grinned. "We'll keep 'em fer a hole card. I'm bettin' if I'm jugged again, they come up with my alibi. Let's hope so because I'm just about ta tell Mark Wheat I ain't his man. When I do, the bail goes out the window, I'm bettin'."

"Think that's smart right now?" Doc asked.

Dolf told him about the new offer he'd accepted from Gould.

Doc whistled. "That'll do it."

"Do what?" Dolf asked.

Doc looked at his friend as though he might be a slightly retarded child. "That'll blow this country sky-high. Surely you ain't so dense ya don't know Wheat hired ya in hopes you'd beef Pardeau fer him. On the other hand, Pardeau figured ya might find out somethin' an' kill old Mark."

"Find out what?" Dolf asked suspiciously, his voice suddenly harder.

"Maybe who was behind killin' your pa an' brothers," Doc guessed.

"D'ya know Wheat did that?" Dolf asked grimly.

"Just suspicions," Doc said.

"What motive would he have had?" Dolf demanded.

"I dunno," Doc sighed. "Maybe ta git his hands on the ranch."

Dolf shook his head. "It's a good spread, but no prize. At any rate, he didn't git it, though he may control it through Pardeau. What would a range hog like him need with another spread?"

"Best water in the country in a dry year," Doc suggested.

"If it was him," Dolf stated coldly, "or Pardeau, or anyone else, they'll answer to me. But I've gotta have more than suspicions."

"They'll tip their hands soon enough," Doc said. "If it was Wheat, and you're not under his thumb anymore, my bet is he'll be as anxious to see you dead as Pardeau. If you'd got Pardeau fer him, your number woulda come up next I'd bet. Just like right now."

CHAPTER 9

DOLF gave Wheat his decision that night. He read no surprise or shock on Wheat's bland face.

"Well, Dolf, I'd have been glad to have you as a partner. But a man has to follow his heart. You're an outdoor man, I guess."

He didn't mention the bail, and Dolf didn't bring it up. He did, however, tell Wheat that the alibis he'd counted on had eluded him.

Bright and early, even before breakfast, Tobe Mulveen showed up at Wheat's. He appeared slightly embarrassed for some reason, but not apprehensive.

"Well," he said to Dolf, who had spent one last night there, "I gotta take you in again. Got a requisition from Carbon ta take yuh down fer a grand jury hearing."

Dolf had been prepared for an announcement such as this, but it came at an unexpected time. He'd at least hoped to help Mum get settled. There was no thought in his mind of running for it. The evidence against him was purely circumstantial. Besides, it was certainly not the time to try running when he'd have to kill a dumb but honest sheriff, who, moreover, had recently saved his life twice.

"I'm puttin' yuh in the dinky little town clink till the stage leaves," he told Dolf.

Wheat was a witness to all this.

"Before you go, Tobe, I'd like a word with you in my office," he said.

"What about him?" Tobe asked, pointing a thumb at Dolf.

"You aren't going to run out on us, are you, Dolf?" Wheat asked.

"No," Dolf told him. "I'll be right here finishing my cigar."

Victoria had come in on the end of the conversation and guessed what was happening before Dolf told her.

"Oh, Dolf," she said, "I'm so sorry. But I'm sure it'll come out all right. You've had so much trouble."

Her eyes mirrored such sincere misery that Dolf felt sorrier for her than for himself.

Impulsively, she came up to him and kissed his cheek. He marveled at the soft tenderness of her lips. Her cologne tantalized him. A great hunger in him almost caused him to do something he knew he'd regret. She stood back and looked steadily at him. The look in her eyes caused him to stand up and take a short step toward her. He thought she would not resist. But just then, Wheat and the sheriff returned. Wheat's head rose sharply, as though he may have sensed the drama he'd just interrupted. If so, he chose to pass it off.

Wheat told Dolf, "Tobe can't go with you. Election coming up this year, so it's politicking time again. But I've got him to send his two best deputies. I'm paying them extra to see that nothing happens to you like the other night. I've got faith in you. I really wanted you to have the chance to settle down and live down the past."

Somehow he sounded wholly sincere, even a little wistful.

Tobe Mulveen's disgusted look clearly mirrored the fact that he thought Wheat was a soft-headed sucker.

"Good-bye, Dolf," Victoria said softly. Her eyes said much more, he thought, but he couldn't be sure. *Women are sentimental*, he told himself. *I'm imagining things—almost made a fool of myself. She's Gould's type—his woman.*

"If there's anything I can do . . ." she called after him.

It was then he remembered Jim Too. He held up Tobe long enough to get her to promise she'd look after the pup. That lifted a weight off his shoulders. He was already emotionally attached to the big doleful pup, Jim Too, who might have starved if he hadn't found Dolf.

Wheat wanted to talk to the two deputies that he had asked Mulveen to assign as Dolf's guards. What Wheat wanted from Mulveen he usually got. Dating from the death of Dolf's father, who had held the ranchers together as a voting block behind Hal Green, Wheat's star had been in the ascendant. Gradually his party assumed control. By the time Dolf was railroaded, Wheat was recognized as the czar of the Pinebluff district, which really was to say the northern half of the territory.

The two deputies involved were Wild Jim Ott and Quirt Hardin. Behind his back, the community called Ott, "Odd Jim Wild." He was wild enough in his own right and odd too; the "Wild" was probably hung on him because he wore long hair like Wild Bill Hickok had. Quirt Hardin was a Texan who claimed to be a first cousin of the infamous Texas killer John Wesley Hardin.

Both deputies were gunfighters with records. Both were actually in the employ of the Wheat-Pardeau interests, or they wouldn't have hung around after the boom camp days. They made peanuts as deputies, compared to the old days.

Shortly after Mulveen left with Dolf, the two deputies showed up at Wheat's home office. Mark shut both doors carefully and locked them.

Wild Jim watched this unemotionally, his narrow, greenish eyes almost unblinking. He had Indian features, was in fact believed to be a half breed. His long, straight black hair suggested it. So did his lean, flat frame; there wasn't an ounce of fat on all six feet of him. A knife scar on his cheek lent him a sinister look.

Hardin was a perfect contrast to Ott. He was short, chunky, and blond, with protruding light blue eyes, and actually appeared benign until aroused. Then the eyes could get mean and snappy, usually blinking rapidly at such times. The word around Pinebluff was: when Quirt Hardin bats an eye at you, run. Wheat considered him the more reliable of the two but didn't trust either of them. Besides, they both knew too much about his past.

Wheat eyed them in a friendly fashion now, since he had an axe to grind.

"I suppose Tobe told you boys you'll be escorting Morgette

to Redrock. I asked him special to put you two on it because I want to be sure Dolf gets there—in a pine box."

He let that sink in, his eyes narrowing to speculative slits. He knew what was going through their minds and thus added, "Naturally I'm willing to pay better than usual."

Hardin shifted in his chair and eyed Wheat with some surprise. He hadn't expected this.

"Yuh jist want we should shoot 'im?" he asked, to be sure he'd heard right.

Wheat grinned wickedly. "I don't care if you poison his tea. Just get him like you did his old man and brothers. He's in our way now. He just went to work for Gould. You know what that could mean. You've had it pretty sweet here; if Gould moves in, that could change." He paused, letting that sink in.

"Besides," he reflected, partly to himself because he realized as he spoke that it would go over their heads, "murder will out. If Dolf ever finds out what happened to his pa and brothers, he'll come after us."

"I can take Morgette," Wild Jim said evenly.

Hardin looked his partner over closely but was silent. Mark said it for them both.

"That's what a lot of them said. Maybe a dozen or more so far, maybe two dozen—who knows?"

He discouraged a retort and went right on. "Be damn careful. He's dangerous, even unarmed. Besides, he has friends. And make it look like he tried to escape; not that many would kick if it looked like that was how he was put out of the way."

"There's the little question of price we ain't discussed," Wild Jim said. "How much?"

"A thousand apiece."

Hardin whistled and said, "You really do want him iced bad, boss." He paused and added, "We'll get 'im fer yuh."

Wild Jim nodded his agreement. They shifted their feet, as though about to leave. Wheat held up a restraining hand.

"One other job," he said. "This one pays more. We'll have to dicker the price, I suspect."

The other two looked expectant. Wheat looked from one to the other, wanting to be able to measure any change in their expressions after what he had to say next.

"I want you to go down to the capital. Pardeau's down there. I want him to stay there—permanently."

He quickly shifted his gaze between them. They both looked surprised. In addition, he thought he could detect some uneasiness in Wild Jim's face.

"I'm not going to beat around the bush. Pardeau is broke flat. It's one reason I want him out. I'm willing to pay big."

He aimed the rest of his remarks directly at Wild Jim. "I'll double anything he offered either or both of you to put me out of the way." His eyes bored into Ott's. The gunman tried to meet his stare and couldn't, twisting uneasily in his chair. He didn't quite know how or whether to own up.

Finally he said, "Pardeau offered me two grand to beef yuh. I turned him down flat."

Wheat wasn't entirely satisfied with that. "Not enough money?" he needled.

Ott's face reddened. Not too ingeniously, he made an oblique answer that wasn't to his advantage.

"Everybody knows old Ed is broke, just like you said," he hedged. Too late, he realized what that implied but stood his ground, merely reddening some more.

Wheat turned to a new avenue.

"All right," he said. "I'm as good as my word. It's four thousand apiece to get Pardeau, and a bargain at that. I'm willing to put up the whole thing right now if you two will keep right on going after you do up Morgette and Pardeau."

The two gunmen exchanged looks. It was a fortune as far as they were concerned. In Wheat's eyes it was a real bargain, since he got rid of these two as well as the two they were to dispose of. Besides, his nimble mind had already developed a scheme that might get most of it back for him.

Hardin spoke up first. "I'll buy it. Besides, I don't like the cold winters up here. How about you, Jim?"

Wild Jim Ott nodded his head in assent.

Wheat didn't bother to shake on it. He preferred not to touch this sort of people. He'd have been amazed to know they were both grateful for a very similar reason.

He produced a carpetbag and showed them two bulky bundles of greenbacks inside. "Carry it like this so if anybody gets suspicious, you can tell them you're depositing it for me up at the capital. I even shoved in a faked deposit slip. There's a hundred fifties in each of those packages," he assured them.

"One final thing," Wheat instructed. "Don't beef Morgette before you get to Redrock. I want it done well out of this vicinity, just on general principles. And don't slip up."

Without amenities on either side, they rose hastily, and Wheat let them out the front door.

He sat down, carefully clipped a cigar, and lit it. He was deep in thought, feet on the desk, gazing out the window. He smiled in satisfaction. *The damn fools*, he thought.

Victoria Wheat had had Libbie lay out a bedroom for Mum the previous afternoon before she learned that Dolf's delightful grandmother couldn't be persuaded to stay overnight. It was one of the choice rooms, located directly above Mark's office, and had its own fireplace, served by the same chimney as the one in the office below. Rather than tell Libbie to replace the bedspread and put away the towels, Victoria considerately set about doing these minor tasks herself. She was still worrying about Dolf's plight as she did so.

With her little chore finished, she seated herself in a rocking chair near the fireplace. As a child, she'd often sat here alone, thinking, often cheered by hearing the familiar voice of her father downstairs transacting various pieces of legal business. Voices carried quite clearly up the chimney due to some acoustical accident in the construction of the two fireplaces, she supposed. She'd never let her father in on her little secret.

Victoria was deep in thought when she overheard the arrival of Wild Jim and Hardin in the office below.

She listened with some comfort as she heard Wheat's voice saying, "I asked him special to put you on it because I want to be sure Dolf gets there—"

Then he had paused. She knew what her father was referring to. Then she heard the next words, regarding how Dolf was expected to get there.

"—in a pine box."

She was thunderstruck. She felt faint and sick all at once. She hoped that she hadn't heard right. Now she strained to hear every single word. Although she didn't want to believe what she was hearing, she had no choice. It was the most wretched experience she'd ever undergone in her life.

When she heard her father casually saying, "If Dolf ever finds out what happened to his father and brothers, he'll come after us," she wished she could die.

Victoria left the room cautiously after listening carefully to the whole conversation and went to her own room at the back of the house. She had to think. She prided herself on not being the flighty, easily panicked type of woman, but just then her thoughts were totally jumbled. She fell into a chair, numbed. Her body felt heavy and useless. For a moment she thought of confronting her father directly, then rejected the idea as wholly out of the question. In the first place, part of her mental paralysis was due to the trauma of discovery that he wasn't her old dependable, indulgent father any longer. He never could be again—she knew that.

She had known that Dolf was in danger, afraid to admit to herself what the apprehension that caused her must signify. Then the danger had been real enough but still distant and nonspecific. Now the peril was imminent and from the most dreadful sources. And she knew what her fears for Dolf meant. She had never known a man like him. At any cost, she must see that he did not die now that she'd found him.

I've got to go to Sheriff Mulveen, she thought.

Then a sense of dismay promptly caused her to reject that idea. Not only could that send her father to jail as an accessory to murder, but she was also sure that the thick-headed Mulveen could simply not take it in. As soon as her father got to Mulveen to assure him smoothly that it must be something she'd eaten, Tobe would be ready to send her to a sanitarium if Wheat suggested it.

She couldn't believe this. Here she was dreading the machinations of the father she'd believed until a few moments before was the dearest person in the world to her. *How can this be happening to me?* she screamed inwardly in panic.

She felt physically ill. She sat as quietly as possible, trying to subdue her panic, hoping the nausea would pass. It did not help that she was obsessed with the dire need to do something and that it must be done swiftly.

Why can't I think? she asked herself in angry frustration, feeling her fingernails cut into her tightly clutched hands. Another thought paralyzed her with dread. *Suppose Father should come up to talk to me as he sometimes does? He'll see in a minute that something is wrong. If he does I'll hide in the closet*, she thought.

She almost swooned at the familiar sound of his footsteps on the stairs. She could feel her heart in her mouth. The footsteps only came halfway up and stopped. Her pulse pounded furiously in her ears. She only half-heard him call, "Victoria, I'm going out for awhile."

With a heroic effort, she was able to summon what she hoped was a normal voice.

"All right, Father. Will you be back for dinner?"

He stopped on the stairs again. She was praying he wouldn't return to kiss her as he sometimes did before going out. To her intense relief, he only paused to say, "I'll get a bite somewhere. Don't wait on me."

Then he hurriedly left. She rushed back to the front room to assure herself that he was actually leaving. She saw his familiar figure going down the street toward town.

After rejecting the sheriff as a source of help, her mind naturally turned to Alby Gould. Then she realized he was not in town. *Who else?* she asked herself.

Doc! the comforting thought occurred to her.

She knew enough about Doc to know he was capable of

killing Ott and Hardin to save Dolf's life if it came to that. She put on a bonnet and swiftly left for Doc's office. If she happened to run into her father and she had no bonnet, she knew he'd wonder what had caused her to leave the house so swiftly she forgot to wear one. This degree of forethought comforted her with the suspicion that her wits might be returning.

She congratulated herself on reaching Doc's little cottage, where he also had his office, without meeting her father.

She entered and called out, "Doc?"

There was no answer. She decided to sit down in a waiting-room chair to sort out her thoughts if she could. Her principal dilemma was already all too clear to her. If she told Doc everything she had heard, then he would tell Dolf. The man she thought she was falling in love with would then kill her father. What would that do to her life?

She moaned softly out loud. "And I didn't know what suffering was."

She shut her eyes tightly and pressed her hands to her temples like a confused child trying to make the memory of a nightmare go away.

I've got to swear Doc to secrecy, she thought in desperation. *But will he keep his word when he finds out how horrible the secret actually is?*

CHAPTER 10

AS he walked away from his house that morning, Mark Wheat was thinking, *A man can make one mistake and it will dog him all his life*.

Seven years before, the picture had been different. His power base had not yet been secure, but he was a free and happy man. It seemed to him then that the major force standing in the way of his ambitions had been the political power of the cattlemen. Dan Morgette, Dolf's father, who had been the first settler in the Quarter Lien, was their natural leader. Dan had only been there a dozen years himself, but that made him the most powerful old-timer. Assisted by four grown sons, he'd developed the biggest and best cattle ranch in the country. Wheat hadn't been interested in the Morgette ranch from the standpoint of cattle raising. His future plans looked toward the mines, the possible coming of a railroad, the development of timber. He had bigger visions.

Then he had discovered something about the Morgette ranch that had aroused his avarice and temporarily un-balanced his judgment. He had hired a geologist to survey the country who discovered that the portion of the Quarter Lien occupied principally by the Morgette holdings was almost completely underlain by a huge bed of coal. Wheat had gone to see for himself, taking Ed Pardeau and a posse of tough deputies along since there had been trouble with the Indians at that time. The two partners had left the deputies in their camp so their secret wouldn't spread.

Wheat was thinking now, *If Dan Morgette and his two boys hadn't stumbled on us, everything might have worked out all right. I could have made a deal with Morgette if he hadn't known what I was really after.*

113

There had been no open hostility between Dan Morgette —Dolf's father—and the Wheat-Pardeau crowd then, only rivalry. In fact, Dolf was still Pardeau's under-sheriff at that time. Therefore, when Dan Morgette and his two boys, out working the brakes for strays, had run across Wheat and Pardeau, there had been no hostile confrontation. Wheat confessed what he was doing and how he'd discovered coal there. There was a whole vein of it exposed on the spot.

"Thought I'd see for myself," he had admitted.

"You weren't plannin' on sort o' fergittin' ta tell me, were yuh, Mark?" Dan had joshed him.

Wheat was smooth. His mind had always worked like lightning in such situations. Boundaries were still vague in the Quarter Lien; his reply was based on that fact.

"Didn't know it was your land, Dan," he'd said blandly. "If it is, this'll make you rich. Could be the thing that decides the railroad to run a spur up here. Be good for us all."

There'd be some more good-natured conversation following, in which Wheat and Pardeau had accepted an invitation over to the Morgette chuck wagon to eat. Then they had left.

Once out of earshot, Pardeau had made the observation that set Wheat to thinking they might monopolize the secret for their own benefit.

Ed had said, "Be a pity if them three had an accident before the word got out."

"Mm–hmm," Wheat had responded idly, not yet seeing how that might be done right then.

What he was mainly thinking was that, with an election coming up in which he wanted to become county attorney, it would be nice to have Morgette neutralized. He had turned the whole thing over in his mind several times on the way back to their camp.

Pardeau knew people. He was quiet, letting Wheat's mind have time to figure up the odds. When he figured he'd had enough time, and before they reached their camp, Pardeau had stirred the pot again.

"Those deputies of mine back at camp'll do whatever I say. I could have 'em pull the shoes on their hosses 'n' it'd look like an Injun job if old Morgette 'n' his boys got beefed."

Wheat knew Pardeau's deputies. They were hired guns. Some were actually members of the Rustler Gang. Two of these had been Ott and Hardin. When Ed had brought up this idea, Wheat had pulled in his mount and looked over Pardeau speculatively.

All he had said was, "Ed, I guess I'll ride back to town. With old man Morgette out of the way, I reckon I'd be a shoo-in for county attorney. With me in office, we'd be sure no one did any time or stretched rope over a little killing, wouldn't we?"

He hadn't exactly told Pardeau to do it, and he hadn't exactly told him not to. But he'd thought he knew Pardeau. Yet even before he'd returned to Pinebluff, he was having serious second thoughts. He'd realized he didn't know if the coal was commercial grade.

And that had proved to be the rub. It had all been for nothing. After examining large samples, the railroad people had later concluded, "Too much slag—you can't get the heat out of that low-grade stuff—wood is better and there's lots of it here."

Thinking back now as he walked, Wheat sighed heavily. *All for nothing*, he thought rather hopelessly. *One damn mistake changes a man's whole life.*

One of the worst aspects of it was that this mistake had thrown him into Pardeau's power for too long. If his current plan worked, he might be able to get rid of at least part of the threat all at once. He didn't see any way that he stood to lose, no matter which way his plan came out. At worst he'd be out some money and get rid of both Dolf and Pardeau. He might do even better than that. He'd wired Ed Pardeau in their company code that it was extremely urgent to meet the two deputies on the train at Redrock. He'd neglected to mention that Dolf would be with them. He figured that Ed's curiosity over the cryptic wire would be enough to get him there. It was now a fair gamble that he might rid himself of all his problems at once. He had one additional thing to do to add more certainly to that gamble. He was on his way to do that now.

Pinebluff, a shadow of the former boom camp, had only a constable where it had once had a marshal and several deputies. Heavy law enforcement depended on Mulveen who, in view of policing the entire vast county, still had a half dozen deputies. Tobe, with no objection from the constable, had simply taken over the town's jail as temporary headquarters. It had a front office and a lockup with half a dozen cells.

Mulveen seemed mildly surprised to see Mark Wheat show up at the jail.

"I want to see Dolf privately for a few minutes," he explained. "He's still my client."

That seemed entirely reasonable to the sheriff. "Sure, Mark," he said.

He got the keys, took Wheat back, and left him in the cell with Dolf where they could talk privately.

Dolf was at least as surprised to see the lawyer as Mulveen had been. He was astounded to see Wheat pull two double-barreled derringers from his side pockets and urgently say, "These have clips on the sides. Shove them in your boot tops quick."

Without hesitation Dolf pulled up his trousers and concealed the two pistols as Mark suggested.

"They're loaded," Wheat said in a low voice, cautioning Dolf with his eyes and a finger to his lips. "They may be the best I can do for you now—I just found something out."

He went to the front of the cell and pretended to be seeing that no one was in earshot, then returned to Dolf, putting on a superb show of conspiratorial confidentiality. "I've learned that both of our lives may be in serious danger. We can't trust anyone."

He shifted his eyes warily, then continued. "Not even the sheriff. I learned that Ed Pardeau hired at least one of those deputies—Ott—to kill you and me. I can't have him taken off as your guard now, or he'd get suspicious. Besides, I'm not sure Mulveen isn't in with them."

He sighed heavily and shook his head.

"I'd have told you before you got in here, even if it cost me the bail money, but I just got the tip in the mail. I can't say who squealed, but it's someone I have to believe."

Dolf didn't know what to think since this had all happened so quickly. He simply had to go along with Wheat. When the lawyer was gone, several things occurred to him. The first was to see whether the derringers were loaded. He quickly checked each, careful to watch in case someone might be coming. They were loaded.

But, he thought, *the powder could have been taken out.*

At the time her father was at the jail Victoria Wheat had waited a half hour for Doc to return, becoming more impatient by the minute. The wait at least gave her a chance to think rationally. She concluded that it was possible to warn Dolf's friends, and perhaps even Dolf himself, without revealing the source of her information. She needed more time to consider before she was willing to forsake her father.

As the moments had passed, the need to talk to someone who might help obsessed her. The question was who? If only Alby Gould hadn't left town. Next she thought of Hal Green.

But he'll be back on the ranch, she thought. *It'd be too late if I told him.*

The thought of Hal brought to mind his daughter, Catherine. She lived in town. Without further hesitation, Victoria rose and crossed to Doc's desk. She borrowed a sheet of his paper and wrote him a note that read: "Must see you at once as soon as you're back. It is extremely urgent! I'll be at Catherine Green's or at home." She added the date and time, then signed her name. She prayed that Doc wasn't off on one of his rescue forays into the countryside somewhere.

Then she hurriedly headed for the Green's cottage, hoping Catherine was not out also.

She felt a great sense of relief when she heard quick footsteps coming to answer her knock. Catherine tried to mask her surprise at seeing her there. She'd never called before.

"I've got to talk to you," Victoria said urgently. "Are you alone?"

"Yes."

"The surprise clearly registered on Catherine's honest face. "Come in. What's the matter?"

"Dolf is in terrible danger," she blurted. "I just found out they're planning to kill him on the way to Carbon."

"Who?" Catherine asked.

"The two deputies that are going to take him there. Ott and Hardin."

"They're both killers!" Catherine gasped. "How did you find out?"

Victoria tried not to look evasive and said, "I can't say right now. But I know it's true. We've got to warn Dolf and his friends."

Victoria related all the details she knew of the plot. Catherine took them all in, a sense of cool purpose suddenly possessing her. She wasn't sure in her own mind how she felt about Dolf, but she knew she'd thought of him a great deal lately, and not in a merely casual manner. She had no intention of letting him be killed, whether he'd ever mean anything to her or not. She could clearly see what must be done as soon as Victoria finished talking. She outlined a plan of action.

"You'll have to go to the jail and tell Dolf. They probably wouldn't let me in. The sheriff is your father's man—he'll let you see him. There's no time to lose. The stage'll be leaving in less than an hour. I'll go get a hold of Dolf's brother Matt. I saw him come in this morning. He'll be up at their new house with Mum—"

She couldn't help but digress. "Isn't Mum something? I met her last night. She likes you."

Then she concluded by ordering, "You go to the jail right now. I'll take care of all the rest and get a hold of Doc as soon as I can. Hurry! And don't worry. We'll save him somehow. His brother and Doc will know what to do and how to do it."

Victoria felt a huge sense of relief as she hurried to the jail.

It was offset by dread at the possibility of running into her father somewhere, particularly at the jail. Not knowing that he had headed back home, her heart was in her mouth all the way.

At the jail, Mulveen looked even more surprised to see her then he had been to see her father.

"I'd like to see Mr. Morgette," she said, trying to sound natural and aware she wasn't too successful. She felt some explanation was expected and quickly devised one. "I've got a message from Father for him."

Fortunately for her, Mulveen assumed Wheat had merely forgotten something during his recent visit. She was relieved that he didn't appear unduly suspicious.

"Okay, Miss Victoria," Mulveen agreed.

He lumbered back to the cell block again.

"Visitor, Dolf," was all he said, and left.

Like Mulveen, Dolf was more surprised to see her than he had been to see her father.

When she was sure Mulveen was out of hearing, she blurted out, "You're in terrible danger, Dolf. The two deputies who are taking you to Carbon have been paid to kill you."

Dolf looked carefully at her, trying to read behind the look of panic on her face. His first thought was, *How would she know that?*

She read his thoughts. "Don't ask questions, please," she pleaded. "Just believe me. I know what I'm saying. They're supposed to stage a bogus escape somewhere between Redrock and Carbon, and kill you."

"Who told you?" Dolf demanded.

She tried to bring herself to lie to him. He read her look of confusion induced by violently conflicting desires. Finally she broke down, the need to absolutely convince him, so that he had a chance to save himself, overriding every other desire.

"Oh, Dolf," she said, "I don't know what to think. I overheard Father offer them a lot of money to kill both you and Pardeau. He knew they were in on killing your father and brothers too."

That was all she had time to say before they heard Mulveen returning.

"Be careful," she implored. Her eyes said the rest.

"Time's up, little lady," Mulveen said ponderously. "Hope ya got yer message said. Gotta get the prisoner ready for the road."

Ott and Hardin were in the office as she left. She tried to ignore them but felt a stab of cold fear when she met the insolent, baleful gaze of Wild Jim.

As she was going out the door, a cold chill ran up her spine at hearing Ott say, "I wonder what the hell she was doing here." Then she closed the door.

She didn't know where to go next but was sure she couldn't face her father and maintain a normal exterior without time to accumulate her wits. She headed back to Catherine Green's cottage.

CHAPTER 11

THE train's departure from Pinebluff Junction was delayed by the last-minute loading of three horses. These ranch-country trains usually had at least one freight car, one cattle car, and a number of passenger cars, plus an express car. The two bearded farmers who owned the horses sat at the rear of the car Dolf and his two guards were in.

Before they had entered the depot to get tickets, Ott had removed the handcuffs by which Dolf had been manacled to Quirt Hardin. The latter had looked the question at his partner, *Are you crazy?* But he said nothing. Wild Jim had always been the leader of the two. He'd answered the unspoken question.

"I hope old Dolf here does make a break fer it. I'll fix 'im like we did—" But he hadn't finished the remark. Dolf got the implication, thanks to Victoria's warning.

Then Ott had said directly to Dolf, "I owe you plenty fer gunnin' down Dan Reed and Hank Fry when they came with Pardeau ta arrest yuh back in '80. Just make yer run any old time. I'll git ya like a jackrabbit."

His eyes had glared wickedly when he said it. He'd been pulling steadily at a bottle on the way down on the stagecoach. Dolf wouldn't have been surprised if he'd made his play on the stage. He suspected what had stayed his hand hadn't been his orders from Wheat but the two other passengers.

The other two hadn't particularly surprised him when they showed up; in fact, he'd been more amused than surprised. They were Obadiah Peuke and Leverett Peeples. Neither had acknowledged they'd ever seen him before. Following their cue, he'd only grinned a trifle. He thought, *I'd bet a pretty penny they're on their way down to that grand jury hearing to*

121

see I don't go back behind bars. Too bad they didn't open up here and save me the trip.

He mentally shrugged off his annoyance. As much as had happened to him in the past seven years, this was a minor inconvenience. He thought he could see some light at the end of the tunnel. But only because he'd made a decision to burn his bridges behind him. He knew that in an hour or two at most, he would be forced to fight for his life. There was no fear in him. He didn't care whether he lived through the ordeal or not. He felt the old grim desperation taking its grip on him again. He planned to get Ott first if he didn't do anything else.

A man's never so free as with his back against the wall, like a trapped wolf watching the trapper coming for him, he thought. He grinned bleakly for just a moment, then saw Wild Jim Ott eyeing him narrowly from across the aisle. Ott grinned evilly behind his scarred face.

"Try it," he invited. "That's why I'm over here on this side o' the aisle. Yuh'll never git ta me afore I plug yuh. Go ahead."

"Hate ta spoil yer day, Ott," Dolf said, "but I happen ta know somethin' you don't."

He let that sink in and rattle around. He saw the look of bewildered suspicion capture Ott's phiz. Then it occurred to him he may have said too much and they might frisk him, suspecting he meant he had a hideout gun. So he explained his remark.

"I happen ta know the grand jury'll never indict me. I'm in the clear. Why should I run?"

Ott snorted. "Fat chance. What makes yuh so damn sure?"

"Just a hunch," he told him. "I feel lucky."

That brought a genuinely mirthful snort from Ott. Dolf knew what the other was thinking before Ott made a retort.

"Well, if'n yuh knowed what I do, yuh wouldn't feel so all-fired lucky," Ott said.

Ah, but I do know, Dolf thought.

He'd had time to think out his position. Two incredibly evil, scheming men, Wheat and Pardeau, were responsible for destroying his chances of living a happy, useful life. They had tried to use him against one another because each knew too much about the other. In addition, guilty consciences prompted the evil suspicion that each would somehow reveal only enough of what he knew to Dolf so that he'd take revenge on the other. So far, only Wheat had learned the folly of that hope and now planned to put Dolf out of the way, as well as Pardeau.

Dolf was equally sure that, in view of his past and what was hanging over him now, there was no way he could clear himself of killing his two guards, even though it would be self-defense. His future was clear to him. He would be a fugitive the rest of his life. The most anguishing part of it was that he'd probably never see little Amy again. Her worst suspicions about her father would be confirmed. Almost as bad would be the case with Victoria because he had determined that Wheat and Pardeau would pay for their past crimes. Since there was no way to bring that about within the law, it would have to be Old Testament justice. He knew he could never see Victoria again if he killed her father, even if she'd have had him otherwise. Another more pressing thought plagued him. *The big problem is that I can't be sure Wheat didn't set me up with a pair of empty derringers—may even have told these two he did it.*

But Victoria had said her father wanted the killing done beyond Redrock. If the two deputies were keyed to move only on his play, which could happen anytime, that wouldn't be the case. Dolf thought he divined Wheat's real motive. *He doesn't care if I get them or they get me—probably hopes we'll get each other since he has something to fear from each of us.*

In that case the derringers would probably be loaded.

"*If they ain't,* he thought, *those two ain't any more sure o' that than I am. So I'll make my play first an' git their shootin' irons. I know theirs'll be loaded.*

The question was where should he make his move? He knew the country like a familiar face. The best place would be where the tracks crossed the Mustang River. He could take to the river in the dark with a driftwood raft and float down into the badlands for fifty miles or more. That way no one would pick up his trail for days, if ever. By then he could make it into the high peaks and find shelter from his own hunted breed. In a few weeks he could make it over the Canadian line. The Mounties didn't ask questions of people who behaved themselves. At least few of them probably had pasts that didn't bear close examination. Men that tough couldn't be recruited from English prep schools. Later he'd make a *pasear* back again and do what had to be done. After that, maybe he'd go to Alaska. What he'd heard of that strange, wild land appealed to him.

Like here when we first came twenty years ago, he thought. Thinking of the chance to start over with a clean slate was pleasant indeed.

While he was thus lost in thought, he only half-noticed the two clumsy-looking bearded farmers moving down the car, probably to get closer to the stove. One of them limped heavily and carried a cane he'd noticed before. His first warning that something was afoot came when the cane-user swiftly swung it from behind Ott and beaned him with it. The deputy slumped over, out cold. On Dolf's left, Hardin made a quick move for his six-shooter and was an instant late. The crash of the .45 in the hands of the second farmer announced that fact. Hardin had an angry red hole right between his eyes.

Thinking he might be next, Dolf grabbed for the derringer in his right boot.

"Easy, Dolf," the man who had shot Hardin said quickly. "It's me."

Dolf was thunderstruck to recognize Matt's voice. He could barely see the resemblance behind the bushy whiskers.

Matt said to his partner, "Pull the emergency cord, and keep anyone from comin' in that end o' the car."

They were in the front car and so had only one entrance to cover.

"We got hosses on board," Matt said. "We'll get you ta hell out o' here."

The few other passengers were frozen in terror. Matt swept

his six-shooter back and forth over them. "It's all right. Don't try anything funny an' nobody else'll get hurt."

Dolf was amazed at how cool he sounded right after killing a man. He recalled how sick his brother had looked over the simple encounter with the two detectives a few days before. He was puzzled over the contradiction but dismissed the question from his mind just then.

The engineer didn't seem to be responding to the emergency signal.

"Probably heard the shot," Matt said. "Maybe thinks it's a stickup." To his partner he said, "I'll climb over the tender. You stay here. I'll get 'im stopped."

Matt went out the door.

Thinking to arm himself more adequately, Dolf stooped to retrieve Hardin's pistol and belt. He had forgotten Ott. Something warned him to look behind his back. He turned just as Ott was tortuously trying to clear his head enough to get a steady bead on him. The demonic look of concentration on the evil scarred face was almost incredible.

Fast as Dolf was at flipping Hardin's pistol into his hand and trying to dodge out of the way, Ott's shot went off, the flash and powder blast almost blinding him. He knew he was hit bad but threw off the shock by a mighty effort of will long enough to shoot back. His last conscious recollection was of seeing Ott clutch at his heart, then slump onto the seat, dying.

Maybe me too, was Dolf's last fleeting thought before he fell. He felt no fear or concern.

The train came to a grating halt. Matt came back, herding the engineer and fireman to make sure they didn't try to start up again.

"C'mon," he yelled, sticking his head in the car. Then, seeing Dolf on the floor, he swore. "What the hell happened?"

The other bearded one pointed at the dead Ott.

"He's hit bad. We'll have ta carry him. I'll git the hosses."

Just then, the two detectives burst in from the next car. Peuke had his six-shooter in his hand.

"Drop it," Matt ordered in a voice that suggested no foolishness. "I oughta shoot you two. If you'd have come clean, my brother wouldn't be layin' there maybe dyin'."

The two detectives took in the scene at a glance.

"The damn fool shouldn'ta tried to make a break for it. We were comin' ta testify an' get him off," Peuke complained.

"Fine damn time ta say so," Matt grated. "He wasn't makin' a break. We was makin' it for him. Them two had orders to kill him."

"How do you know?" Peuke asked.

"Shut up!" Matt ordered. "You two carry Dolf outside an' be quick about it. Take it easy too, or you'll be with 'im."

As they picked Dolf up, a huge spurt of frothy blood squirted from the hole in his left breast.

"Christ," Matt said. "He may be dead already. Git movin'," he ordered the two detectives savagely.

Outside, the other bearded one was bringing the horses.

"I'll carry 'im in front of me," Matt said. "Git 'im up here so I can get a hold of 'im."

It was a struggle in the dark. They finally all managed it.

"Lead the other horse," Matt ordered his partner. "We may need to switch off, with two of us on one horse."

To the two detectives and train crew he left a parting warning.

"You tell anyone that wants to follow ta come a foggin'! They've done enough to Dolf. I'm shootin' ta kill from now on. An' I'll be back to settle the score with the snake that sicked them two in there on Dolf. Tell that to the world. If you sons of bitches had played square, he wouldn't be maybe dyin' now. If he does, you'll answer ta me."

With that he kicked his horse in motion. It was one of Mum's six-horse team; all they could get on short notice and still beat the stage to the junction.

Out of earshot of the train, Matt said, "It's a damn good thing Doc and Junior are meetin' us. Maybe it ain't too late for Dolf."

They pressed along urgently in the darkness, Matt cursing

the overhead branches that slapped at them. His ears strained for the sound of the river ahead where he expected to meet Doc. A tight sense of urgency gripped Matt's chest.

He mumbled aloud, "Lord, I'll take every one o' those beatings he gave me over again if yuh just let 'im live."

He's still warm, Matt thought. *So he ain't gone yet. Hang in there, Dolf. We'll git yuh to Doc soon.*

A huge sense of relief engulfed him when he spotted the flickering fire through the trees ahead. They had figured no pursuit would get organized so quickly they couldn't use a signal fire to rendezvous by. Matt thanked their lucky stars they'd taken the chance.

"Ho the camp!" Matt yelled, riding in.

Doc and Junior stepped out of the concealing trees, Doc with his scatter-gun, Junior with a rifle.

"Dolf's hit bad," Matt said.

"I'm not blind," Doc muttered. He was already grabbing him. "C'mere, Junior, an' give me a hand—quick."

They lowered Dolf's limp form as gently as possible to the ground.

"Build up the fire," Doc ordered, "so I kin see what the hell I'm doin'." He checked Dolf's pulse, then got his stethoscope and listened.

"Missed his heart," he said with a professional calm he was far from feeling. "If it hadn't, he wouldn't have any pulse by now. Sounds like it nicked his lung. Not much we can do out here but plug him up and hope. Pull those blankets off the hosses—we gotta keep 'im warm. Put 'em right beside the fire an' we'll wrap 'im up."

They got him as close to the fire as they dared.

"We got till at least mornin', I think," Doc said. "Junior, build a long fire an' warm up a stretch o' ground like the Injuns. Then we'll put 'im on that. I'll be right back."

Doc was gone down the riverbank for several minutes. He returned with his handkerchief full of the moldy fungus that grew on the trees there.

"Injun remedy," he explained. "Couldn't do any better with

that hole in the best hospital in the world." After cutting the clothing from around the wound, he began to carefully work a long piece of the handkerchief with the mold wrapped in it down into the wound, using a plain pencil to push it. When he felt he'd hit the bottom, he stopped.

"Not scientific," he allowed. "But I've seen it work. Now I do the prayin' while ya tell me what went wrong up there."

They told him the whole thing from start to finish. When they were through, Doc was silent for a long while.

Finally he said, "So that son of a bitch Odd Bill Wild finally got his. I shudda done it to him years ago. . . . Well, we can't risk takin' Dolf back to town now. They'll jist have another mark against 'im. Good thing Junior and me had a stroke o' genius an' swiped a big scow to come over here in. Our hosses are back on the other side."

Turning to Matt, he said, "You an' Mum git these nags on the other side an' lead any posse that comes out here on a merry chase. Me an' Junior'll float Dolf down into the badlands. We'll git word to ya in a few days."

By then Mum and Matt had pulled off the stage whiskers they'd used as a disguise.

At first light they tenderly packed Dolf into the big scow wrapped to his chin in saddle blankets.

"He's breathin' better," Doc said. "Good sign. Looks like his color is okay too."

A hundred yards down the flood of melting mountain snow, Doc stood up and waved his hat. Junior was plying the oars to steer.

"Good thing yuh took actin' in that dude school back east and had them phony whiskers," Mum observed.

"Lucky, provided Dolf pulls through," Matt agreed. "If he doesn't, there's a lot o' skunks'll pay for it," he added grimly.

With that he forced his horse into the Mustang River, Mum following.

"We'll pick up the other nags an' head fer the high country," Matt allowed. "At least I will. You can go back ta town if you'd like, Mum."

She gave him a withering look. "Not on yer tintype, sonny," she snorted. "I ain't never been up a real mountain afore. Only looked at 'em."

CHAPTER 12

THE smooth sheet of water at the launching spot continued placid but swift for the first couple of miles. As the morning light increased, it was possible to get a better idea of their swift progress.

"Doc," Junior said nervously, "I don't remember ever seein' the Mustang move this fast."

"Been a big spring melt in the mountains this year," Doc guessed.

"You ever been down here in a boat before, Doc?"

"Cain't say as I have."

They swept along at an accelerating pace without conversation for some distance. They were entering an area where the banks sometimes rose steeply on both sides, forming miniature canyons in spots. Then the river narrowed, their speed increasing sharply with the water rising in long, greasy-looking swells. Junior was having trouble keeping the scow right end to, not being used to rowing.

"Keep this thing straight," Doc cautioned. "We can't afford to dump your pa in the drink. By the way, can you swim?"

"Tol'able."

Doc was silent for awhile.

"I can't swim a stroke," he said. "If we do go over, try ta get your pa ashore."

"What makes ya think we might go over?" Junior asked apprehensively.

"Hear that noise like a train comin' closer?"

Junior cocked his head and listened. What he heard didn't reassure him.

"My idea is that's a rapids," Doc said. "My guess is this scow was built special fer this stretch o' water. I sure as hell hope so."

They were racing along now between another set of rocky banks, gaining momentum again.

"Gimme an oar," Doc ordered. "This thing's got a place back there ta use one fer a rudder. I'll steer. You see your pa doesn't get thrown out the best way yuh can. My idea is we're in fer the ride o' our lives."

They swept around a sharp bend and could see the river dropping steeply before them into a narrow canyon with white water aplenty.

"Stow that other oar under the seats in case I lose this'n or it breaks," Doc yelled over the growing din. He knew that white water meant rocks. At their speed, a head-on collision with one would stove in the boat. It might survive a glancing blow, but not a direct hit.

"If yuh know any prayers, start in on 'em," Doc yelled to Junior.

After that he got too busy to talk. The steering oar twisted like a live thing in his hands, trying to wrench itself out of his grip. He tightened his hold, bracing his feet on the thwarts. At all costs, they must avoid the roiling spots of white water. He felt them being sucked down into a trough as though some huge beast had them in its grip and was preparing to devour them. They hit bottom and shot up a huge swell, almost flying out of the water, then dipped abruptly into a still-steeper trough completely out of sight of what might await them further down.

The roar was deafening now. They were hoisted again like a chip, hurling over another crest that almost catapulted Doc out of the boat. He wedged his feet beneath the seat in front of him, straining like a maniac. Fleetingly, he saw Junior spread-eagled face-down across Dolf, his feet under the forward seat and his arms under the one Doc had wedged his feet into from the other side.

"I'll try to hold yer feet," Junior yelled, but his words were lost in the roar.

Doc felt Junior's strong hands grab his boots, anchoring his shins tightly to the seat.

Good man, Doc thought.

A huge swell spun them broadside to the current just then. They lost their forward momentum that had given the steering oar its bite. Doc glanced over his shoulder, desperately, flailing the oar to turn them. They were racing down broadside into a patch of white water dead ahead. With a superhuman exertion, Doc plied the oar like an eggbeater.

Gotta straighten us out! he told himself.

He could feel his gut muscles straining themselves into knots, but the boat was coming around. They scraped ominously over something beneath them, then ricocheted off the very top of a rock that normally would have stuck up ten feet above the river's usual surface.

Doc was panting, painfully striving for life-giving air that he simply couldn't gulp in fast enough. Sky and horizon had become a blur to his reeling senses. Bright spots swam in his vision. Sweat poured off of him.

Lord, he prayed, *if yuh ever loved me, I need yuh now*.

They popped into a stretch of swift calm water just then. *Enough ta make a churchgoer o' me*, Doc thought.

Junior popped his head up and looked around. Seeing where they were, he got up on the seat in front of Doc.

"Shall we beach her?" he yelled.

Doc shook his head, trying to get breath to answer. Finally he was able to gasp, "Too close to civilization. Better ta drown than get caught—some smartacre might get the idea ta come sniffin' down the bank this far."

"Want me ta spell you on the oar?"

Doc could feel some strength coming back, was beginning to get his breath again, and wasn't sure how well Junior would do at steering. He shook his head in the negative.

"Maybe that was the worst of it."

Very shortly, the crescendo of sound issuing from the canyon ahead spoiled that notion.

Junior hovered down again over Dolf, straining to keep any weight off him, and at the same time to hold him in.

Doc braced himself for the renewed battle. As yet, he could see no huge swells such as they'd encountered before, only a series of riffles. They curved crazily around another bend in this choppy sort of water. Ahead the canyon narrowed again abruptly. A fog of water spray clung densely above the gorge.

Lordy help us, Doc thought. *We'll never make that one.*

The scow was almost wholly out of control from the moment they crested the first huge torrent. They swapped ends completely, Doc waving his oar futilely, facing upstream. Then they swapped ends again just in time for a swift maneuver by Doc to skin them by a jagged finger of rock.

The walls here rose almost sheer, several hundred feet out of the water, flashing by as fast as a train, it seemed to Doc. The huge volume of water in this narrow place carried them above most of the rocks. However, another problem presented an almost equal hazard. They were taking water over the sides. There was nothing to bail with. Neither could have spared a hand to bail if there had been.

Dolf was now laying helplessly in a rising pool of sloshing icy water. Doc thought, *Before it drowns him, we'll sink—some consolation. We gotta get outa here or it'll give him pneumonia sure as hell.*

Then he had to get ultra-busy with his rudder oar again. He maneuvered them cautiously into the center of the torrent, where a huge glassy crest of water arose due to the friction at both sides where water battered rock. Riding this slick ominous rope of water, they rushed headlong around a sharp bend. The centrifugal force from their huge momentum slid them off the crest. It was like sliding off a high-centered road on ice. They were headed inexorably downhill to a fatal collision with the jagged canyon wall.

Doc pulled his rudder oar out of its socket and rushed over Dolf and Junior to fend the boat off the wall. The tremendous force of their motion snapped the oar from his grasp, thrusting him backward at the same time. He tripped over the gunwhale into the icy water, trying too late for a handhold on the boat. His head went under, and he began to choke as water rushed into his nose. He flailed the water like a typical non-swimmer. His leg seemed to be held by something. Then he felt himself being hoisted by the front of his coat. When his head came up he saw that Junior was hoisting him back toward the boat. His effort was tipping the scow dangerously, but perhaps was what caused it to narrowly miss a collision with the canyon walls.

Junior partially rose and shifted his grip. As he did so, Doc spotted a tree behind the boat. He thought he might be a little out of his head, but then another tree came into his view.

They had drifted into a broad, smooth stretch of the river, and were actually in a backwater at the mouth of a branching canyon. Junior was able to get up and help Doc back into the scow. The older man was still coughing and sputtering. Junior pounded him a couple of times on the back. When he thought he was all right, Junior took the remaining oar and paddled and poled them to shore.

They had landed where a stretch of meadowland sloped upward to rimrock. Cottonwoods grew densely along the banks, the flood waters lapping partway up on those closest to the river.

"Gotta get your pa dry," Doc wheezed after they secured the scow. "Gimme a hand an' we'll carry him up the bank."

"My matches are probably soaked," Junior said in dismay as they were hustling their inert burden up onto the grassy meadow.

They deposited Dolf as carefully as they could onto the grass.

"I got a watertight match container," Doc said. "I'll get started on a fire. You wring out them blankets, then bring me the driest one. Hang the others on the bushes to start dryin' while I git the fire goin'."

After the fire was started and going good, Doc rigged a blanket lean-to over Dolf.

"That'll reflect some heat on 'im," Doc explained. "Now bring them other blankets over here an' we'll dry 'em out. Then help me collect a big pile of wood."

While they were collecting the wood, a curious deer stepped out of the trees, watching them without fear.

"Dinner," Doc said in a low voice. "Move slow an' git your rifle. I'll keep 'im interested."

Doc started to slowly move his hand up and down in a rhythmic motion. The deer first ran a few steps, then whirled and stopped to look again. Doc continued the steady rhythm. From the corner of his eye, he saw Junior disappear below the bank. He didn't see him again until he heard his rifle shot from somewhat further downstream. The young buck dropped in his tracks.

Thank gawd all the Morgettes kin shoot, Doc thought.

He was famished from his struggle with the rapids. They were soon spitting strips of venison on sharpened sticks over the fire.

Dolf's first conscious recollection after he was shot was one of a seemingly endless ride. Sometimes he thought he was trying to turn a stampeding bunch of cattle. At others he thought he was running away from some people chasing him. Through the whole thing, he remembered that his horse had run him against a sharp branch, which was still jabbing him agonizingly in the chest. Once or twice he'd tried to lift his hands to pull it out, but they were heavy as lead. He suspected that was because he was really having a bad dream. He tried hard to make himself wake up, but he couldn't. Occasionally he'd fall back into a deep sleep again, but then the dream would recur. Later he dreamed he was swimming. For a brief moment he'd get his eyes open, but everything was spinning around. That nauseated him, so he quickly closed them again. He felt cold. Icy cold. It drove away the nausea.

When he first came fully to his senses, the stars were out. He recognized them first. Then he saw the fire and turned his head to look at it. The motion cost him a terrific pain in his chest. He groaned and closed his eyes again. When he re-opened them, Doc's face was swimming above him. He tried to get it in focus.

"What'sa matter me?" he muttered.

"Yuh been shot," Doc said. "Gotta be quiet an' lay still. You're gonna be okay, I think—provided yuh do what I say. I'm gonna prop your head up an' try ta git somethin' down yuh fer the pain in just a minute. It'll hurt when I move your head, but you'll get some good rest afterward."

Doc prepared some laudanum from his kit. *Damn good thing that didn't go overboard*, he thought.

Gradually Dolf got the dose down. Doc was right. As he had already discovered once, it hurt like fury to move. Then after a bit, he began to relax and drift away. The pain was letting up. He was glad Doc said he was going to live. He had a lot of things to do—only he couldn't remember just then what a single one of them was. He slipped into a gentle sleep.

Doc looked at Junior. He suspected the young fellow had been close to tears ever since they'd brought Dolf in.

"Barrin' pneumonia," Doc reassured him, "he's gonna make it. And if we keep that fire goin' he ain't apt to git pneumonia. While we're adoin' that, we better figure out how ta git a better camp fixed up afore a late snow blows in. I think our best bet is fer ya to walk out an' bring some supplies back in here."

As he said this, his expression suddenly changed, and he made a grab for his shotgun leaning against the tree next to him.

"Whup, podner, we're plumb peaceful," a voice called out of the darkness.

Junior turned to where Doc had been looking and actually jumped at the sight of two silent blanket Indians standing at the edge of the firelight. Then a third figure joined them, a pure-quill buckskin-clad, greasy Squawman if he'd ever seen one.

"Seen yer fire," the Squawman said. "Don't git many pilgrims up here."

He squinted closely at them, giving a particularly hard stare at Junior.

"You be a Morgette, I guess," he said. "Wouldn't be one o' old Dan's boys, wouldja?"

Junior shook his head. He pointed to the blanket lean-to.

"My dad is, though."

The Squawman came closer and peeked in at the wounded man.

"Dolf Morgette!" he exclaimed. "By the saints!"

Then he took a closer look at Doc. "Goin' blind," he explained. "Dint recognize yuh, Doc."

"I recognize you, yuh old buzzard," Doc said. "And am I ever glad to see you! Dolf's been shot up bad. We need somewhere he kin rest up where he'll be warm and dry—an' no nosy varmints apt to stumble onto 'im."

Doc took the Squawman's paw in a friendly shake.

"Junior," Doc said, "I want yuh ta meet a pure-quill legend—Bitterroot Tom."

The Squawman took Junior's hand in his own huge dirty paw and gave him a bone-crushing shake.

"So you're Dolf's boy?" He sized him up slowly.

Junior stood open-mouthed. He'd heard stories of Bitterroot Tom since he was in diapers. Without him, the Morgettes' first winter in that country might have been their last. Until now, this old-timer had seemed more legend than reality.

"C'mon in an' bring yer friends," Doc invited. "We got a whole buck ta work on."

As Doc knew, nothing made a friend of an Indian quicker than filling his bottomless stomach.

A little later Bitterroot was explaining, "I'm stayin' with Chief Henry's bunch. He jist come back from Injun Territory where they sent 'im when he busted off the reservation seven yar ago. Like ta kilt off half the tribe. He's some bitter but damn glad to be back on his home range. Him 'n' old Dan Morgette was close. Dan allus had an extra beef whenever Henry's outfit was hungry—which, as yuh know, was most o' the time. He'll hide Dolf, I reckon—an' lift the ha'r o'anybody as comes snoopin' a'ter 'im, I'd guess. Anytime yer ready ta move 'im, you'll be plumb welcome."

That pretty much settled the question of hiding Dolf. No one would expect him to be with the Indians.

"We'll need a hoss fer the kid here," Doc said. "I want him ta bring me out some stuff. Got a nurse in mind too—one that'll do 'im more good than medicine. You reckon Chief Henry'll mind a white gal in his camp, Bitterroot?"

The old Squawman cackled, "Hell no. Probably try ta swap ya a bunch o' ponies fer 'er."

Doc gave Junior some careful instructions regarding what he wanted him to do.

"Mornin'll be plenty soon," he said. "We won't move yer pa till then. Too apt to stumble over somethin' in the dark."

The next day they moved Dolf to Chief Henry's camp on a travois. He and Doc were provided a tepee next to the chief's.

The old chief was an original: a staunch friend and a terrible enemy. He said what he thought in his best English.

"Sumbitch cum for son of Dan Morgette, Injun knife tickleum heart!"

Doc conjured up a delightful picture of Peuke and Peeples stumbling onto their trail with their dumb luck. *I hope they do* he thought.

Doc's last caution to Junior was, "Don't go into Hal Green's place until after dark. Someone might be watchin'. An' scout it out good afore yuh go in. If they're watchin', ketch one o' the boys out on the range an' give 'im the word."

CHAPTER 13

VICTORIA Wheat often left on short notice to visit friends overnight, or even for a week or two. Her father was used to the fact that she was her own person with a mind of her own. Perhaps because she had been left without a mother very early, he had been extremely understanding of her desires. At any rate, he was used to her coming and going with no more ceremony than leaving him a note. Therefore he was not surprised to find a scribbled message from her stating that she would be visiting. He *was* surprised to learn where—at the Green ranch. He hadn't realized that she was particularly close to Catherine Green, as indeed she hadn't been. Nor did he suspect the reason for this sudden unexpected absence. Nonetheless he was grateful. He also realized that his daughter had become quite fond of Dolf. That, perversely, pleased him more than not. The thought of Alby Gould as a son-in-law turned his stomach.

Wheat had also become fond of Dolf in spite of himself. The situation left him deeply troubled. He was trapped; the whole year-long affair had gone entirely contrary to the fundamental conditioning of his own conscience. He was a man sick at heart. In this mood, it was a relief not to have to face his daughter.

Victoria always marveled at the gothic rusticity about the Green ranch. It was more like a farm, surrounded by level, tree-bordered fields greening with the coming of spring. Orchards clung to the gently rolling hills above. Sheep and goats grazed serenely among cattle and horses. Chickens, ducks, geese, and turkeys wandered contentedly around the many sprawling log buildings. The main house was a model of snug domestic tranquillity, at least one hundred feet long with deep, full-length porches on both sides. Chimneys sprouted from the roof, denoting stoves or fireplaces in every room. The delightful aroma of burning pine pervaded the premises.

Catherine settled Victoria in a room of her own and soon arranged to have a fire lit for her.

"Why don't you just lie down and rest awhile, my dear," Catherine suggested. "A nap would do you good if you can manage one."

Victoria would have thought a nap would be the furthest thing from her desire in the turbulent state of emotions in which she found herself, yet Catherine's suggestion reminded her that she was deeply weary.

"I believe I'll try," she agreed.

Alone, she took stock of her situation. It was anything but enviable. No one recognized her tragedy better than she did. She was trapped in a body as ancient as Eve's with a mind as modern as tomorrow. Perhaps a man like Dolf, an anachronistic sort of Lancelot, could make her happy. But would it last when she outgrew the passion of youth? What if they should one day look at each other from wiser eyes and realize that something precious was dying? And—more tragic perhaps —what if the experiment was never to be? How could she expect the love of a man whose life had been ravaged by the same blood that flowed in her veins?

These numbing conundrums coursed through her mind and, perhaps from their sheer tragic weight, drove her to sleep for release. Her last consciousness was an image of Dolf as he had looked at her when he first awoke in her home after his ordeal with the fire at the jail.

She heard again his calm voice saying, "I thought you'd grow up to be a rare beauty—and you did."

The remembrance curved her lips into a faint smile as she dozed off.

A later generation would learn that when Dolf Morgette rode the territory, the earth trembled when he passed. That night Tobe Mulveen learned from the whispering wires that his two deputies had died and that the nemesis was now abroad again. He swore and raged—and also organized a posse. All had been turmoil since the day that Pinebluff had learned Dolf was coming home. Tobe Mulveen saw it as one of his highest responsibilities to those who had elected him to see that turmoil was not a part of the community's life. He moved ponderously but surely into action.

"I'm going after Morgette personally," he stated to his under-sheriff, Morgan Casey. "While I'm gone, I want you to find out where Doc was when this happened—also Dolf's brother and young Dolf. He had to have outside help."

Before twenty-four hours had passed, the sheriff had a tolerable picture of what had happened. By then he had visited the scene of the escape, dispatched his posse on the trail in the charge of Morgan Casey's brother Ed, and gone on down the line to Redrock to interview the witnesses who had been held off the train by Mulveen's local deputy.

From Peuke and Peeples, who were actually the only useful witnesses, he learned something that pleased him and something that did not.

Peeples, tired of Peuke's cat-and-mouse game and its consequences, alibied Dolf for the robbery of which he'd been suspected in the first place.

Mulveen exploded. "This is a helluva time ta be tellin' me this," he growled. "If you'da spoke up sooner, none o' this woulda happened." He was happier to learn from the two detectives that one of the bearded parties had referred to Dolf as his brother.

"Matt Morgette," he gloated. "I'll land him behind bars too."

"Don't forget," Peeples reminded him, "that Matt Morgette or whoever it was said those two deputies were planning to kill his brother."

"How the hell would he know that?" Mulveen interjected.

"I dunno, but he sounded all-fired convincing. If I was you, I'd ask him when you catch him."

Mulveen gave him a disgusted look. "Thanks fer the

suggestion," he muttered. Then, fixing Peuke with a poisonous look, he said, "I'm juggin' both o' yuh fer obstructin' justice."

"You can't do that!" Peuke protested.

"The hell I cain't," Mulveen told him. "I'm also holdin' yuh both as material witnesses."

Peeples gave his *ad interim* boss an angelic smile. It would be a pleasure to go behind bars in view of the circumstances, he thought. Listening to Peuke sputter soothed him a great deal for past indignities.

"At least let me wire Chicago," Peuke requested.

"I'll think about it," Mulveen told him.

With that, he had his Redrock deputy throw the two detectives into a cell.

"I want a lawyer," Peuke yelled as he was going into the lockup.

Mulveen smiled benignly. "Nearest one's in Pinebluff or Carbon. I'll put an ad in the paper fer yuh. Maybe one'll come bustin' down on the next train." With that, he left them.

Peeples rolled into a bunk and calmly corked off to sleep. He hadn't felt so good since before he'd signed on with Peuke.

Within forty-eight hours of Dolf's escape, Mulveen was back in Pinebluff with a fairly accurate picture of what had happened with respect to Dolf's escape. He was not too dense to recognize the tragedy of the situation.

The sheriff was thinking. *He done his time and was in the clear. Maybe we all misjudged him. If them two detectives hadn't been playin' games, my two deputies would never o' been killed. Now we're after ol' Dolf fer murder, all fer nuthin'. An' he won't surrender this time, I'll bet—if he's still alive.* Mulveen's brow creased in a frown. He thought, *There'll be more dead ones before we see the end of Dolf, if I'm any judge. An' now his brother Matt is on the owl hoot trail with 'im.*

He shook his head solemnly. *I wonder if Doc is with 'em, or jist out on one o' his rounds. If he is with 'em it'll be the Morgette Gang all over again. We'll soon know.*

He'd left a note for Doc to come see him as soon as he hit town. While he was at Doc's, he read Victoria's note to Doc still on his desk. He wondered what that was all about. *Probably the vapors,* he thought.

Women weren't Mulveen's favorite subject. He preferred not to think about them if he could avoid it. Fortunately for Victoria, this prevented him from speculating further about her urgent message to Doc. A few blind spots such as this didn't render Mulveen a complete fool, however.

If Dolf is alive and holed up in this country, he reasoned, *he'll need supplies. Now where'd he be apt to get 'em?*

This thought prompted him to set a watch on Mum's place and Hal Green's ranch. That was how he discovered that no one was home at Mum's except Mop, whom she'd hired as her caretaker. *What d'yuh know about that?* he asked himself about her absence. *Now what in thunder does that mean?*

A cross-examination of Mop revealed that he knew absolutely nothing worth knowing.

"She told me ta feed 'n' water the hosses an' I ain't seen 'er since," was all he got out of the former saloon swamper. Mop loyally neglected to mention that three of the horses now in the corral had been gone for twenty-four hours, then mysteriously reappeared. *None o' his business,* Mop thought. *Besides, what he don't know ain't apt ta hurt anyone.*

Matt had led Mum cross-country to Pinebluff.

"If we're gonna outrun anyone trailin' us, it'll have ta be on faster hosses'n these," he told her, referring to her draft nags. He figured they would be at least twenty-four hours ahead of any pursuit that would develop.

"We'll drop these big plugs off 'n' get some grub and blankets, then head for the tall tules on Doc's and Junior's horses. If I'm any judge, none of Mulveen's men'll follow where I'm goin'. We'll lay down a trail that'll throw 'em completely off the track of Dolf."

"I wonder how Dolf is," Mum said. She had almost insisted on going along to nurse him. By now she was wishing she had.

"Doc said he thought he'd live, didn't he?" Matt reassured her. "He's the best in the West on gunshot wounds—had enough practice on 'em."

Mum snorted, "Never seen a sawbones yet with a lick o' sense. If'n he's got any, he'll be the first one."

The two waited until dark before coming into Pinebluff, hastily reprovisioned, and pulled out as quietly as they'd come, heading for the high peaks and owl-hoot country. As Matt had guessed, Deputy Sheriff Ed Casey and his posse were almost a day behind them. When the trail led back into town, Casey reported to Sheriff Mulveen.

"We lost the trail right here on Main Street," he complained. "Ain't no way ta track amongst a thousand hoofprints."

"Great Lucifer," Mulveen roared. "Do I have to do everything myself? Hasn't anyone around here got any brains?"

Ed Casey looked crestfallen. "Wadya want I should do now?" he asked Mulveen, looking over at his under-sheriff brother Morgan for moral support that wasn't forthcoming.

Mulveen eyed him in disgust. "Who d'ya suppose was on them three hosses?" he asked.

"There was five hosses all told," Ed stated guilelessly.

"What?" the sheriff bellowed again.

This was entirely too much for the slow mind of Mulveen. "Explain how there got ta be five hosses," he demanded, speaking slowly and carefully.

"Well, we swum the river an' circled ta picked up sign. Injun Jack found the trail o' them three big nags right off. Pretty soon they went down ta where two more hosses had been tied, then they all headed up this way in a bunch. We lost the trail right out here, practically."

Mulveen stroked his chin thoughtfully. "Now who in tarnation d'ya suppose was ridin' them five nags?" he wondered out loud.

"Wasn't anybody ridin' three uv 'em," Casey stated.

"How the hell d'ya know that?" the sheriff inquired.

"Injun Jack said so. The two we found across the river an' one o' the big uns after it got across."

Mulveen collapsed back in his chair, clapping a huge hand to his forehead. "My gawd," he sighed.

He sat for a moment in stunned silence, then turned a stern eye on his deputy. "Ya know what ya let happen, don't ya?" he asked disgustedly. "Ya follered a phony trail, like a damn fool. Dolf was hit bad, accordin' ta them two fool detectives. He's holed up back there somewhere right around the river. My bet is whoever helped had a boat—that's why Injun Jack didn't find their tracks."

He lapsed again into a thoughtful stance, leaving Ed Casey uncomfortably awaiting his next outburst of wrath.

"We dunno who that other bearded jasper was," Mulveen mused out loud. "It's certain t'other one was Matt Morgette, from what he said. We dunno who rode them two hosses this side o' the river either. My guess would be it wuz Doc an' somebody—or maybe it wasn't Doc since they was lookin' fer Doc, since Dolf is hit bad. Hmmm."

For a not-entirely-bright specimen, Mulveen's mind worked surprisingly well at this sort of reasoning. His blind spot was in judging people. As a mouse, he'd have trusted cats and been suspicious of sparrows.

"Wadya mean one o' them bearded fellers was Matt Morgette?" Casey inquired.

Mulveen explained how he knew that.

"Whoever we're dealin' with," the sheriff concluded, "we gotta get back down there ta the river fast. I'm guessin' we'll find our party camped not three miles below where they crossed the Mustang. Any farther down they'd o'gone inta the canyons an' we won't hev to worry about seein' 'em again—with the head o' water they'll have down there this year, that'd be sure death."

Turning to his under-sheriff, Ed Casey's brother Morgan, who'd been taking in his older brother's discomfiture with relish, Mulveen said, "I'm takin' that posse back to the river. I want you and Ed here ta scout around town fer anybody suspicious—if any o' the Morgettes or Doc show up, hold 'em till I git back."

"Even their grandmother?" Morgan Casey asked.

Mulveen looked a little nonplussed. He hadn't remembered her. If he'd known her better, his orders might have been vastly different.

"Of course not, yuh idjit!" he snapped. "Howsomever, if she shows up, I'd like ta know where she's bin."

He paused, trying to think of anything he might have overlooked. "Oh, yah, one other thing. If ya don't find anything in town, circle fer sign. Have Ed here show ya them tracks an' see if any uv 'em heads on through. Them two might circle around an' lead us right ta Dolf. If'n they do, don't make any fool plays. Come after me. An' don't slip up."

He hurried out the door, then ducked back in and addressed his under-sheriff, "Ya might as well pull in the boys we got watchin' the Green ranch. But keep someone on the Morgette house. I wouldn't put it past 'em ta try and smuggle Dolf in right under our noses soon as he's in any shape to move."

This decision by the sheriff foreclosed the one chance he had of being led directly to Dolf's refuge. The watcher at the Green ranch might have detected Junior Morgette's visit.

Doc had sent Junior to the ranch to enlist Catherine as a nurse. He knew she'd be found there on the weekend.

Doc explained to Junior, "These Injuns're all heart, but I don't want some medicine man dumping my 'evil potions' in the crick while he uses a drum and rattle on Dolf. Besides, a gal nurse is good medicine all by herself. I gotta make an appearance in town pretty damn soon or end up in the poke myself if'n I know Tobe Mulveen. So as soon as Dolf's outa the woods, I'm goin' on in."

"What about me bein' nurse?" Junior protested.

"Uh uh," Doc shook his head. "You ain't a gal. Besides, you're gonna need an alibi too. We're goin' in together. We'll cook up a story about me bein' back o' beyond treatin' somebody yuh stumbled onto hurt while yuh was huntin'. Mulveen won't believe us, but unless he can prove somethin' else, he'll be stuck with our story. 'Sides, if he tosses me in the poke, some expectant mama'll bean him with a fancy umbrella an' he knows it."

"What's ta keep 'im from juggin' me?" Junior asked.

Doc smiled. "Nothin'," he said.

By the time Junior reached the Green ranch, news of the shooting on the train had already spread all over the Pinebluff district.

Junior timed his arrival well after dark and reconnoitered as best he could, to be sure the sheriff had no one watching. He came in on foot, the dogs barking him up as soon as he got close. Hal himself answered the door. It took Junior only a couple of sentences to explain what he'd come for.

"I'll get Catherine out of bed," he said. "It's up to her."

Victoria, lying awake in her room, heard the disturbance of Junior's arrival, the voices, then Hal's footsteps going to arouse Catherine.

Her mind had been in torment ever since she'd heard of Dolf's being seriously, perhaps fatally, wounded. She had tried to mask her feelings around the Greens, especially Catherine. But, in the way that women are able to divine one another's hearts, they both sensed the other's anguish.

False modesty was crushed by fear in Victoria's case. In her most secret heart, she wailed, *Oh my darling, I've just found you. How could I bear to lose you now?*

She suspected that the affliction might not be as acute in Catherine's case because she hadn't seen as much of Dolf since his return. But Victoria knew that Dolf's appeal to women had laid siege to Catherine as well, and that all was confusion in that innermost "keep" of her castle that is every woman's heart.

She could not help but crack her door and eavesdrop on the conversation in the nearby Green parlor. She heard Junior's words, "Doc says he's gonna live if he doesn't git pneumonia." She almost swooned from relief. *Please God*, she prayed, *don't let him get pneumonia*.

When she learned that Catherine would be alone nursing

Dolf, a new fear assailed her. She wanted to rush out without shame and shout, "Let me go too!" But then she realized how impossible that was. How impossible it all was. Dolf knew her father's part in engineering his tragic life. How could she ever expect him to do other than despise all the Wheats?

She lay awake a long time after she heard Junior and Catherine depart into the night. Tears ran softly down her cheeks—tears of relief, tears of frustration.

"There is no hope," she whispered to herself softly. And more tears followed.

CHAPTER 14

DOC lay back on his Indian-style couch of buffalo robes and watched the fire slowly flicker down to glowing embers. Dolf slept quietly on another snug pile of robes across the tepee, covered to his chin. Bitterroot Tom had stayed to gab with Doc until a few minutes before. Dolf had even been awake a little while and had felt well enough to get down some broth, and also to put away a lot of water—both good signs.

Doc was puffing away on the short pipe Tom had provided him. He'd lost his cigars in the river.

A *dinky dudeen*, Doc thought, looking over the stubby pipe. *Likely came off a dead cavalryman.* He knew no cavalryman went on a campaign without his indispensable dinky for comfort.

Tom had even produced some real tobacco, observing, "Kinnick-kinnick is great fer Injun ceremonies an' sich, but even them heathen buggers 'druther hev 'baccy."

Doc was now possessed by a great sense of contentment. He believed Dolf would pull through. It'd been touch and go for the past forty-eight hours, but the signs were all good. Doc had determined that if his old friend died, he was going on the warpath to even the score. A fury had possessed him over the unfair manner in which everyone had jumped on Dolf without giving him a chance. He'd savagely thought, *I've got two special bullets with Wheat and Pardeau engraved on 'em. Next come them two detectives. I might even get that blockhead Mulveen.*

As Dolf's chances looked up a little, Doc's revenge list shortened. Doc was relieved without exactly knowing why. Finally it came to him. *I guess I'm too old for the owl-hoot trail,* he thought with an inward sigh. *If I beefed them skunks,*

I'd have ta go on the dodge. Actually, he was a year younger than Dolf, though he looked older. *Old or not,* he promised himself, *if Dolf doesn't do it himself, I'm gonna rub out them two skunks Wheat an' Pardeau.*

He'd even forgotten that vow for the moment, contented with the peace of his surroundings and the satisfaction derived from Dolf's marked progress. Dozing a little, he was aroused by a noise at the entrance of the tent. Someone was coming in, packing a roll of robes behind them; they're fastened the flap against the raw spring breeze outside.

"Who're you?" Doc asked, realizing at the same time that it was an Indian that probably understood little or no English.

He was in for two surprises.

"I'm Margaret Henry," a woman's voice replied in very good English. "Chief Henry is my father. He sent me to keep the fire up so you can get some sleep."

Well I'll be a . . . , Doc thought. *Don't that beat a hog flyin'?* Aloud, he said, "Well, I dunno as we need any help." He could sense that she was looking unhappy in the dark.

"Father won't take no for an answer. It's Indian hospitality. If you send me back, he won't understand."

"Well, Margaret," Doc said, "if that's the case, hop to it. I could use some shut-eye."

He put out his pipe, pulled a robe over him from the pile he was sprawled on, and settled down comfortably. In a short while, she heard his gentle snoring. She smiled slightly, quietly placing more wood on the fire. Then she arranged her robes so she could sit up facing Dolf, to be sure to know if he showed signs of discomfort. As the fire burned higher, it brought out the highlights on his now-gaunt, strong face. She thought the high, broad cheekbones flanking the strong nose resembled an Indian's. She crept close to him and cocked an ear to listen to his breathing. It was steady and regular. She smiled again in the darkness. She wondered if she dared feel his forehead to see if he was feverish. At risk of waking him, she did it anyhow. He stirred slightly. She was happy to discover he had no fever.

"I'm all right, Ma," he mumbled. "Go to bed."

The words had a strangely appealing effect on her. Her heart went out to this helpless man who thought he was a little boy again. She'd learned in the white man's school at Carlisle that some of the *Wasichus* were as good as Indians. Her father had sent her to their school to save her from the fever that killed half his people their first year of banishment in Oklahoma. That had been seven years before. When he had been allowed to return home with the tribe just the year before, she had joined her people—"gone back to the blanket," as the *Wasichus* said.

Indianlike, she sensed in her whole being that Dolf had a good heart. She was made happy by the notion of helping him get well. She thought of this and many other things in the peaceful stillness of this night. At intervals she placed more firewood on the fire to keep the tepee warm for the sick one. She gave no thought to herself. Warm or cold were all the same. Inside she was always serene and contented. She knew that she was different from the other Indian girls—always had been from the earliest time she could remember. She ran laughing to play with them, but she never indulged in their silly giggling. She also had long solemn times when she wanted to be alone to think.

She was thinking now, *Is this why the young men of my own people are shy around me, because I was always different, or is it because I've gone to the white man's school and they think I'm spoiled for them?* She didn't know. At least, they didn't make the signs that young men did when they wanted to come courting. Chief Henry noticed, but he didn't care. She was now twenty and unmarried, but he was happy to have her still in his tepee.

"I have dreamed that someday a great warrior will come for you," he told her. "You will know him when he comes. You will have a child by him who will also be a mighty warrior."

She wondered about Indian visions such as her father's. They told her at Carlisle that these were foolish superstitions and that she must forsake them for the path of Jesus Christ, but she wasn't sure. Her schooling there, she suspected, had unfitted her for either the white man's or the Indian's way. But inside she was still content. What had happened to her was the will of the Great Spirit. What would happen to her yet was His will. Confidently, she waited for what was to be and was happy.

If a great warrior comes, I will know him, she told herself.

She regarded Dolf with speculative eyes. The urge to touch him possessed her again. She approached and placed her hand on his forehead. He opened his eyes and turned his head toward her, studying her carefully. Her cool hand was still on his forehead.

"Who are you?" he asked.

"I am Margaret Henry, Chief Henry's daughter. He sent me to nurse you," she told him.

After thinking that over, he smiled slowly.

"I dreamed you were Ma and I was a little boy again," he confessed.

"I know," she said. "You said, 'I'm all right, Ma, go to bed'; you have a good heart to think of others when you are so sick yourself."

He studied her in the flickering firelight. He liked what little he could make out. "Could you get me some water?" he asked.

She had to hold up his head so he could drink. His great weakness was terribly apparent to her. She powerfully willed some of her own sturdy strength into his injured body and soul. He was asleep again almost as soon as she let his head down.

"I will be his strength," she vowed.

Keeping her vigil the rest of the night, she prayed to *Wakan Tanka* and Jesus Christ, and also the spirits she felt in the wind tugging at the outside of the tepee. She believed that those who prayed from the heart were heard, no matter whose name they invoked in crying out for help. This she felt sure of, for all the confusion her unhappy past had induced in her young mind.

She knew part of the story of Dolf's tragedy. She, as a girl out gathering berries, had seen the wicked men shoot down Dolf's father and brothers without warning. With the wisdom of a young animal, she had stayed hidden, knowing that if the killers discovered her, they would silence her for their own safety. When they had gone, she had run to tell her father. He and some of the warriors had come with her to see the bodies. Her father had vowed his revenge there on those who had killed his friend Dan Morgette. But he himself was hunted. Earlier, the young warriors had killed some other bad white men. Then the soldiers had come, and all the Indians had run away. That very day, the scouts had warned her father that the soldiers were near again, just as he was about to take the revenge trail after Dan Morgette's murderers.

Chief Henry had then led his people on a long march to escape the soldiers. In the end, it had all been for nothing. She remembered that summer of constant terror when they were always running and fighting. Many she had known as uncles and grandmothers, or just as good friends, had been brutally killed and sadly had to be forsaken by the long trail in their haste to escape. When it had all ended far to the north, in the moon of the falling leaves in the early snow and bitter winds of oncoming winter, the White Father had sent them to the strange, barren South. There malignant fevers had killed many.

Her own long aloneness had begun then. It had put iron in her soul. She had never cried again after the first lonely nights at Carlisle. She never would, she knew.

When Doc arose in the morning, she told him, "Your friend was quiet. I gave him water once."

"Good," Doc said, going to look at Dolf.

When he turned again, she had silently gone. But she had left her robes behind. In awhile she returned with something for them to eat. Doc was thinking, *If I'da known Margaret was handy, I might not o' sent fer Catherine. I wonder how the gals'll get on together?* He grinned over the possibilities.

Catherine arrived with Junior that afternoon. Doc introduced the two women. He couldn't quite put a word to their mutual reaction to each other. Surprise was the closest he could come. He was happy to detect no resentment. That would have disrupted his plans. Since discovering Margaret, he was aware that an around-the-clock nursing schedule was possible. That, in his opinion, was all Dolf needed now. Someone to feed him, give him water, and see that he didn't get uncovered, especially at night, and catch pneumonia.

Doc stayed one more night. By then Dolf was able to talk a little with him.

"I figure I'd better get back," Doc explained. He told Dolf of his plan to alibi himself and Junior. He knew Dolf didn't want to condemn his son to a life like his had turned out.

"If by some chance that bonehead Mulveen does figger out where yuh are," Doc told Dolf, "Chief Henry's gonna run yuh back in the hills somewhere on a travois. I think you're in good enough shape ta move if need be. I left instructions fer Bitterroot to come git me if yuh need me."

The next morning Doc and Junior pulled out.

Catherine watched their departure with mixed feelings. She was a self-sufficient young woman, but she knew absolutely nothing about Indians except that this very tribe had scared the whole district out of their wits, herself included, just seven years before. She was certainly glad to find Margaret Henry the apparently civilized person she was.

Bitterroot Tom also reassured her quietly.

"Case yuh got any fears o' these heathen, young lady, you're safer in Chief Henry's camp than town any day. He'd cut out the heart o' anyone botherin' yuh."

She was spared from the Indian method of eating out of a community pot with her hands by having brought some eating utensils of her own on Junior's advice. She had found him a thoughtful young man, wise for his years, a younger copy of his father.

She was alarmed to see how gaunt and pale Dolf was. "Do you really think he's all right?" she asked Doc in alarm.

"Yup," Doc assured her. "Fer a gent shot as bad as him, an'

less'n a week gone by, he's lookin' better'n average by a jugful. Yuh jist ain't used to seein' gunshot patients. All we can give him now is nursin'. That's up ta you. The rest is up ta him. He's got a strong constitution. He'll make it."

Nonetheless, when she was alone before the flickering fire with Dolf laying across the tepee under his robes, the wind eddying mournfully around the smoke hole above them, doubts tugged at her mind. She was somewhat reassured by the presence of Margaret Henry, now napping nearby. A strange girl, but a great help both with hands and heart. Catherine couldn't help but like her, though earlier she had felt a pang suspiciously like jealousy upon seeing Margaret skilfully lift Dolf's head to give him a drink, or to spoon broth to his lips.

She is a pretty thing too, Catherine had to admit.

Soon enough she had her own turn and was rewarded by Dolf's recognition of who she was and the obvious gratitude in his eyes.

"Thanks, hoss thief," he acknowledged her services the first time she awkwardly fed him.

"When yuh say thet, smile," she said, imitating cowboy talk.

Happily, she thought this return of his spirits confirmed what Doc had told her. *He's on the mend*, she thought. *Why am I so happy?* She thought she knew, but wouldn't admit it even to herself yet. She was so glad she had this opportunity to be close to him when he needed her most, whereas she might never have contrived to see him otherwise. *How selfish of me*, she chided herself, but she was buoyantly happy nonetheless.

Her happiness hadn't long to last. Margaret had told her she'd taken some nurse's training at Carlisle. Catherine noticed the Indian girl feeling Dolf's brow several times, then looking worried. At the time, she was lying in her own robes trying to drop off to sleep. Somehow she'd been restless.

She'd noticed Dolf stirring several times under his own robe. For the first time, he seemed not to want to sleep on his back. Once or twice she heard him mumbling in his sleep. When

Margaret went again to feel his forehead, it was more than Catherine could stand. She felt instantly apprehensive.

"What's the trouble?" she asked Margaret.

The Indian girl turned to look at her. "He has a fever," she said. "It'll probably break before morning. Night is always the worst time for fevers."

The Indian girl remembered that most of her people had died at night in the miasmal Indian Territory. People seemed to have their lowest resistance at night, even to depressed spirits.

"Try to get some sleep," Margaret told Catherine. "You've got to be strong for him. If I need help, I'll wake you."

"Do you think we should send for Doc?" Catherine asked.

"Not yet. I think we can expect these little feverish spells. If he gets real bad, we'll send for Doc."

Catherine was not comforted by the fact that it would be a twenty-four-hour round trip to get Doc back here. Furthermore, the sheriff would probably be watching him for just such a call. Worrying about these things, Catherine was only able to drop into a restless doze.

A blood-curdling yell raised her out of her sleep, and she sat bolt upright. She looked toward Dolf. Margaret was trying to hold him down and was having trouble.

"Help me!" she cried. "We can't let him break the wound open again!"

Catherine rushed to her side. Both of them tried to hold his shoulders. She felt the delirious strength of his struggle, weakened though he'd been. His eyes were open, a crazed stare in them.

"Don't!" he said urgently. "They're coming! Let go of me. I've got to. . . ."

He never finished the sentence. The insane stare left his face. He laid back down quietly and seemed to fall asleep again. The two girls exchanged relieved looks.

"Maybe it's over," Margaret said, not too convincingly. "I'm going to check his bandage."

She uncovered the wound and inspected it in the dim light.

"He's bleeding again, a little," she said. "There's also some pus in it. That could be good," she added doubtfully. "That could be the cause of the fever."

Catherine was sickened by the overpowering fetid odor. She thought, *I can't help him if I get sick.* She tried to fight it off and succeeded for the moment.

"I'm going to change the bandage," Margaret said. She threw the blood-encrusted rag into the fire, then put more wood on to get some light.

Dolf's yell had set the dogs barking. This, in turn, brought Chief Henry himself. He spoke to Margaret in their language. She seemed to be arguing with him over something, at the same time placing a new bandage over the horrible, bruised bullethole, which had already partially closed.

Chief Henry left.

"He wants to bring the medicine man," Margaret explained. "He's gone to get him."

With a sinking heart, Catherine remembered Junior's laughing repetition of what Doc feared from the medicine man. Unlike Margaret, the white woman had absolutely no faith in medicine men.

"He mustn't," Catherine protested.

Margaret fixed her with an intense, unreadable look from her dark eyes.

"Sometimes," Margaret said, "his medicine is stronger than the white man's. I have seen wonderful things that are in no books."

Seeing Catherine's doubtful look, she laughed. "For right now," she said, "he can at least help us hold him. They don't call him Strong Bull for nothing."

Strong Bull was all that Catherine had feared. He wore a headdress of buffalo horns shaved paper-thin and carried his medicine bag.

Unable to think of anything else to do to stave off his heathen ministrations, Catherine moved beside Dolf herself and felt his forehead. He was burning up with fever. *He's going to die,* the sudden fearful thought possessed her. *He's going to die, and there's not a single thing I can do in time to save him.* She thought of running to find Bitterroot Tom. She didn't even know what tepee was his.

The iron arms of Strong Bull picked her up and moved her away.

"For God's sake!" Catherine screamed at Margaret. "Send for Doc!"

The Indian girl's face was an impassive mask. "No," she said with finality. "It would be too late if this is the crisis. We must pray and have faith in Strong Bull."

Dolf again let out a hoarse cry, half-human, half something else undefinable, then tried to get up. The brawny arm of the medicine man held him down easily, where the combined strength of the two women had failed. Some power transmitted from this strong touch seemed to quiet Dolf.

Strong Bull withdrew his sacred pipe from his bag. He also took out an eagle-bone whistle, saying something to Margaret. She took it and moved to the east side of the tepee, facing west, her eyes closed, head back.

Watching her in fascination, Catherine noticed that Chief Henry had soundlessly slipped back inside and was seated impassively in the shadows behind his daughter. Margaret began to sound various low, piercing notes on the whistle in a sort of rhythm. As she did, Strong Bull was methodically filling his pipe with Kinnick-kinnick. When he had tamped it to his satisfaction, he extracted a live coal from the fire with his bare fingers and dropped it into the pipe. Catherine was awed to see no expression of pain or flinching on his part when he had very deliberately handled the red-hot coal. Something about this whole unreal experience caught her up in its rhythm; she felt an eerie power entering her feet and flowing upward through her whole body. Her former resolve to stop all this totally left her, without leaving a memory. She became part of some arcane, ritualistic stage play, powerless not to act her part.

Strong Bull puffed once or twice to get the pipe going strongly, then rose and commenced a sort of singsong talking, prefacing each stanza with "Hey-hey-hey." Singing, he solemnly offered the pipe to the south, then the west, north, and east in turn. Each time he paused for a minute or more, imploring the aid of the grandfather of that direction. Then he offered it to the sky and earth. Finally he seated himself and smoked, at last putting the pipe out and returning it to the bag.

Catherine, who had expected every moment to see Dolf go into another delirious outburst, was amazed to see him lying perfectly in repose. She watched Strong Bull pick up the drum he had brought with him. He placed it in the hollow of his crossed legs and, by a rapid motion of his hands, coaxed a rolling sound like thunder from it. Catherine felt the hair raise with a creepy tremor on the back of her neck, followed by a chill tremor through her whole body.

Margaret had ceased her blowing on the whistle when the pipe ceremony had started. She was now seated, staring fixedly to the west, as was her father. They appeared to be hypnotized. Catherine knew that, like her, they had become a necessary part of Strong Bull's ritual and must play their roles like altar boys. By now Strong Bull had commenced a steady, low rhythm on the drum, chanting in his weird singsong. As he did, the feeling of some supernatural presence flowed again through Catherine, imbuing her with a strong feeling of anticipation as well as a sense of hope. She tried to pray in the conventional manner, but no sensible words formed themselves in her mind. She was thinking in pure ideas that she was never afterward able to verbalize.

Dolf felt hotter than he ever had in his life, dreaming deliriously. *It's the drought this summer*, he thought. *I'll open the windows so Theodora can sleep.* He knew he was getting up, and she was not in bed. Somehow he had a feeling that this was all a dream he'd lived before.

He started to open the window that faced down the porch and saw three shadowy figures outlined by the starry sky. Someone was letting them in the front door. He felt alarm signals going off in his brain. He groped for the six-shooter he always kept at the head of the bed. It was not there. He raced to the closet where he knew another would be hanging and reached it just as the three men stealthily entered the room, one carrying a lamp. The lamp carrier set it on the bureau just as a voice said:

"He ain't in bed. Look out."

Then they turned and saw him. They raised their pistols. He knew then that they were there to kill him; he fired at them so fast the sound of the shots blended together.

"Theo!" he cried. "Theo! Are you all right?"

Theo rushed into the room and took in the scene. Eyes wide and frightened, she rushed to Ed Pardeau, lying on the floor.

"You've killed him," she moaned, trying to cradle his head in her lap.

She fixed Dolf with wide dark accusing eyes. "You've killed him," she said again in a low, anguished voice.

Then he knew, and his world had never been the same after.

Catherine, seated in the tepee, had heard Dolf's last anguished cry from his dream and thought she knew what he was reliving.

Then this nightmare faded from his mind, and Dolf heard a welcome sound of thunder. He had been thrashing around the bed back at the old ranch trying to sleep, too hot even without covers. He smiled now, half-awake, realizing that a cooling storm was coming and the drought would break.

"Leave the windows open," he said. "Let it rain in. Who cares?"

Then the scenes shifted again in his fevered brain. He saw the muzzle flame, felt the bullet strike him with the force of a hammer blow as Wild Jim Ott fired at him. This time he didn't fall. The sound of the shot seemed to echo and re-echo again and again. He was flying through the air at terrific speed, headed straight for a bright star. He could still hear the echo of the shot, even though everything else was absolutely still.

He came to rest on a cloud. All around him were white

ranges of hills and mountains like banked clouds. He was lying on a cloud couch. From a blacker cloud directly overhead, he saw two men coming at him, their bodies pointed like spears.

He heard a whispering sound, then a rolling like thunder. Suddenly it was cold; he shivered. The two men had turned to rain. It had only been a thunderstorm after all. He turned his head to see if the water was forming puddles. This was when his old hound Jim came up beside him and licked his face. He was so glad the old dog wasn't dead after all. As he tried to pat his head, the dog receded some distance, and Dolf could see that now he was actually his old horse, Big Fool.

Then the sky was full of horses and dogs running. He heard the terrific thunder of the thousands of hooves, the neighing and barking as a sky full of Big Fools and Jims gamboled together.

Then it came to him what was happening.

So this is what dying is like, he thought.

Suddenly there was a flash of lightning and another roll of thunder. All of the duplicates disappeared, and only one Jim and one Big Fool were left. He was not surprised to see both of them turn into his father's face.

"You won't die yet," his father said. "Your time isn't here yet."

Then the face was growing older and older, as old as the earth and stars. Receding rapidly, it said, "Drink this and live. We have won."

Then Dolf saw a hand offering him a cup of water. Eagerly, he raised his head toward it. He felt helping hands lift his head to receive it. He drank it all, despite a slightly bitter taste. It was cold and wet and good.

Only then did Strong Bull focus into his vision.

"Who are you?" Dolf asked. He heard Margaret Henry's voice answer him from behind where she was still supporting his head.

"He is Strong Bull," she told him. "If you do as he says, you will live."

Then the last words of his father in his dream recurred to him: "Drink this and live."

"He says if you have faith, you can stand and walk. If you walk around the tepee from left to right, you will return, lay down, and get well."

Dolf heard this, the strange chant of Strong Bull, the roll of the drum; he felt the same weird strength enter his body that Catherine had felt. He found himself standing somehow, without having experienced pain.

Margaret led him to the south side of the tepee. "Start here," she said.

In a sort of half dream, Dolf walked around the tepee to the west, north, east, and back to his starting point. He felt remarkably strong. Then Margaret led him back to his bed. As he stooped, he felt something rupture painlessly inside his wound, and a great gout of fetid, bloody pus flowed out and continued to drain.

Margaret cleaned it away. "Lay down now," she ordered. "I'll put a new bandage on it."

Catherine had sat as one totally hypnotized through this whole affair. When it was finally over, she wasn't sure she hadn't been dreaming. When she finally came to her senses, Strong Bull and Chief Henry were gone. She felt drained of all strength.

Margaret had got Dolf back in his robes. He was breathing regularly and deeply.

"Come feel." Margaret invited her to feel his brow.

Limply, she complied. It was cool and slightly damp. The two women exchanged a long look.

"Did all that really happen?" Catherine asked.

"Yes," Margaret said. "And his fever's broken. He'll live. Now you'd better get some rest. I'll watch him."

A *miracle*, Catherine thought dimly as her fatigue was dragging her into a heavy sleep. Then her white man's logical skepticism recaptured her mind. *Or the hard way to lance an abscess?* she asked herself.

She wondered what Doc would say when she told him.

CHAPTER 15

AS soon as the news reached Mark Wheat of the outcome of the shooting he'd instigated, he knew he must go away. There were too many threatening aspects to the situation that he wanted time to think out. One of them was the apparent presence of Matt's brother and the bearded stranger just in the nick of time to release Dolf. Did this indicate that Dolf or someone close to him knew he'd been set up before Wheat had told him that at the jail and given him the two derringers? More likely it was a coincidence. It was natural enough for Dolf's brother to engineer his release since it looked like a fair bet he was headed back to the pen. As for the other possibility, it was too remote. Dolf wouldn't suspect him.

However, the thing that really bothered him was what his partner's reaction would be. Pardeau was shrewd enough to figure out what Wheat's intent had been in wiring him to meet the two deputies at Redrock without having mentioned that Dolf was with them. That clearly had enough of the earmarks of a possible setup to get rid of Pardeau and Dolf at the same time to make him highly suspicious, since he knew Wheat would like him out of the way.

Ed was also capable of doing his own killing in a pinch. Wheat wasn't quite ready to die just yet, or to forsake his political ambitions either if he could salvage them from this mess. Of course, if he had known that Victoria was onto him, his view would have been entirely different. He probably valued the love and respect of his beautiful daughter above everything in life.

He would have liked to see her again before he went away, but there was no time. It was hard to tell how soon Pardeau would come back to Pinebluff, but come Wheat was certain he

163

would. There was no time to lose, even though he was sure that Ed Pardeau was not the type to come directly off the stage gunning for him. Ed would rather potshot him through a window at night. So there was a little time.

He packed enough clothes into two suitcases for a protracted absence. Then he sat down and wrote Victoria a note, advising her that business would take him east for perhaps a month and that he would write from there. He hired a messenger to carry that to her at the Green ranch, then left town by buckboard. He didn't intend to run the risk of accidentally bumping into Ed Pardeau due to a possibly mutual stage connection at the junction. He would have the train flagged further south.

Another less immediate danger was troubling him as much as the thought of Ed Pardeau. This led him to hope that Dolf Morgette had crawled away somewhere in a hole to die. He understood he'd been hit hard.

He's a good man, Wheat thought. *I'd hate to see him go. But if he lives there's always the chance he may find out someday, especially if he goes after Ed and makes him talk before he kills him. Can't be sure one of those deputies didn't blab either, thinking he wouldn't live to tell the tale. It would have been Ott, with his sadistic temperament and hatred for Dolf, if one of them did. In either case he'd come for me sure as hell.*

Getting her father's note solved Victoria's tremendous dilemma: how she could face her father again, or explain satisfactorily to him why she had stayed away so long. She made up her mind to return home now, even though she loved the tranquillity of the Green ranch. She and Hal Green had discovered in each other kindred spirits with a love for discussing classic literature and philosophy. He was a pleasant contrast to her father, with whom she'd always wished she could talk of great ideas; Mark Wheat was a worldly man who grew impatient over talk about anything that didn't relate to money or power.

She had grown to believe in just a few days that she could

trust Hal Green. One had to believe one could trust someone after such a great disillusionment.

One night, after Catherine had been gone for a couple of days, Victoria came close to opening her heart up to this gentle, understanding man who was Catherine's father. Only one thought restrained her. He would insist that justice for Dolf demanded that she go at once to the authorities. If they believed her, by no means a certainty, she would destroy her own father. And, devastating as the thought was to her, maybe Dolf was dead by now. What necessity would there be in that case to move with haste? She wanted more time to think this through. Only one thing was certain: she must, in any case, move out from under his roof and become her own woman.

She could hardly bring herself to consider the possibility of Dolf's dying, as though such a weak thought might itself diminish his chances of survival.

Why do I love this man of violence? she asked herself.

She knew that that fact alone could well destroy a woman of her temperament in the end. Look what it had done to her already. The only satisfactory answer that came to her—and it was a question itself—was, "Why did Guinevere love Lancelot?"

The lines from *Don Juan* came to mind, where Julia sits in unhappy exile in a convent and writes Don Juan after their forbidden love has been discovered:

'I loved, I love you, for this love have lost
State, station, heaven, mankind's, my own esteem,
. . .
Man's love is of man's life a thing apart,
'Tis woman's whole existence;
. . .
Men have all these resources, we but one,
To love again, and be again undone.'

Yet, she thought, *must love be woman's whole existence? Or undo her either?* She wondered. And as she wondered, she considered the puzzling fact that she was in love, yet scarcely had touched the man whose fate wrenched her heart so harshly. She, who hadn't known a few days since, knew what suffering was now.

When Doc and Junior returned to Pinebluff, they found Sheriff Mulveen remarkably receptive to their story regarding their mutual protracted absence.

"Well," Doc had explained to the sheriff when he visited him in response to his note, "I was on my way to go testify at Dolf's grand jury hearing when Junior busted in with news about this pilgrim that accidentally shot himself up in the hills. My duty was perfectly clear. I wired the D.A. down at Carbon an' pulled out with Junior. Yuh kin find the telegram on file. We stayed a few days nursin' that pilgrim. Then his pals packed 'im out the way they came in, over on the east side o' the range."

Doc congratulated himself on his foresight in having sent that wire as an advance alibi. The trouble was Mulveen knew Doc was just shrewd enough to have done it for that reason. Doc was certain the sheriff would check it out anyhow, in case there'd been no such wire sent at all.

I hope he fergits to check out that shot pilgrim, Doc thought, but he knew better. He shrugged, inwardly thinking of his next alibi. He could see himself telling Mulveen, "How in the hell do I know what hole they come out at—maybe the pilgrim took down ag'in an' they're holed up at some ranch."

Mulveen eyed Doc blandly.

"I'm buyin' that thin story fer the time bein'. Meanwhile don't be leavin' ta tend another pilgrim without yuh check with me first. Yuh kin pass that word along ta Junior too."

As Doc was leaving Mulveen's temporary office, he thought, *Yah, Tobe, an' I know why yuh bought that thin story so easy. Yuh'd play hell havin' one o' us mebbe lead yuh ta Dolf like damn fools if we were in your poke.*

Mulveen settled down to a waiting game. His posses had

drawn a complete blank. But Tobe was a patient man. He smiled contentedly, thinking, *If Dolf's still alive, somebody'll lead me to 'im sooner or later, or else he'll pop up somewhere all by himself. Shot up bad as he was, I give him about six weeks ta be up an' around ag'in.*

The one person that it didn't occur to Tobe he should watch was the only one he should have: Catherine Green. Three days after Dolf's crisis had passed, she returned to the Green ranch alone.

"Dolf is definitely mending," she told her father. "I think I'd better be seen in town for a few days. Besides, the girls might say something at school that would set the wrong parties to thinking. If Dolf had to run for it now, it might give him a setback or even kill him."

She also carried this word to Doc, who had been doing more than his share of worrying about his friend. His reaction to her description of Strong Bull's healing rites was not what she had expected.

Doc was pensively silent for a long moment. Finally he said, "Yuh never know, Catherine. If it works, don't knock it. Did yuh find out what was in that cup o' water Strong Bull gave Dolf?"

"Ugh, yes!" She looked revulsed. "Ground red ants."

Doc let out a little yelp of appreciation. "I'll hev ta git me some," he said, then changed the subject and added, "In a few days I want yuh ta go back out there to check on Dolf. All the rest of us are bein' watched. When yuh go, take him out that pup Jim Too. He can be powerful medicine about now."

Victoria soon learned that Catherine was back. She couldn't stay away, for need to hear how Dolf was. Embarrassment over knowing that Catherine felt exactly as she did about Dolf couldn't deter her.

As soon as Catherine had admitted her to the Green cottage, Victoria spilled out the words, "How is he?" Realizing how she had shamelessly bared her feelings, she felt the blood rushing to her face. Catherine kindly helped her cover her confusion by pretending to be busy getting tea ready.

"He's just fine," Catherine assured her. "Chief Henry's daughter, Margaret, is nursing him."

"A squaw?" Victoria blurted.

"Not exactly; she studied nursing back at the Indian school in Pennsylvania. She speaks English as well as we do."

Victoria almost asked, "Is she pretty?" Then she rephrased it in a less revealing form.

"What is she like?"

Catherine sensed what the question implied. "I'm afraid she's as pretty as sin."

Then they both laughed.

"I don't think Dolf is ready to take up the blanket yet," Catherine assured Victoria.

They both laughed again. On Catherine's part, it was whistling in the dark. She'd seen Dolf's eyes on Margaret as she'd fed him.

"Will you be going back?" Victoria asked. Seeing Catherine's hesitation, she hastily explained, "I've got something he'll want."

She picked up the portmanteau she'd brought with her and opened it on the table, pointing inside. "His guns," she said simply.

Catherine nodded her understanding. "Leave them here. I'll be going out. The sheriff is watching everyone else, Doc thinks."

Mum and Matt returned to town the way they'd left: in the wee hours of the morning.

"They'll be looking out fer me," Matt said. "I shoulda kept my big mouth shut at the train and they'd be lookin' fer some bearded jasper they'd suspect Dolf hired."

"Two of 'em," Mum chimed in. "They're lookin' fer me now, remember?"

They had decided the safest place for Matt to hide was the most obvious: Mum's house.

"Sheriff'll never think o' lookin' there," Mum stated positively.

"If'n he does, I got a thousand rounds or so fer m' old Remington Rollin' Block. You 'n' me 'n' Junior can stand that sheriff off till Election Day, when they might git a new one with some brains."

It wasn't long after Mum's return that Doc showed up at her house. He'd asked Junior to let him know as soon as Mum was back.

"Where's Matt hidin' out?" he asked Junior first of all.

"At the house."

Doc thought that over, then smiled broadly. "Good place. Mulveen's too dense to think o' lookin' there."

At Mum's the four of them had a conference. Since none of them knew the key information that Victoria could have provided, the main question was how to keep Dolf and Matt out of the toils of the law till they figured out some way to clear them. Victoria's name did come up, however. Catherine Green had naturally told them that Wheat's daughter was the source of her tip-off regarding the aim of the two deputies to kill Dolf.

Doc's guess went right to the heart of the issue.

"I'd bet Victoria overheard her sneaky pa schemin' ta hev it done. The sheriff's office is right under Mark Wheat's thumb. If it wasn't Wheat put them two up ta it, 'twas Pardeau did, an' Wheat knew about it somehow. But in any case, yuh kin bet Wheat didn't tell her direct. She had ta overhear some o' his schemin' or got inta his papers. She's protectin' her pa. She's a straight, honest girl, an' it must be jist about killin' her to find out the kind o' skunk she's got fer an old man. My bet is she'll come clean pretty soon, pa or no pa, and let the chips fall wherever—"

Mum asked, "D'ya think I oughta go see 'er? She could prob'ly use a shoulder ta cry on. Maybe she'll tell me."

Doc didn't think so. "Let her come ta you if she makes up her mind. If we rush her, she might git balky. Sooner she spills it, though, the better fer us."

"Suppose she doesn't?" Matt wondered. "What then?"

"Then," Doc allowed, "we gotta git Dolf outa this country

complete unless we wanta risk his havin' ta kill or be killed again. Same with you, Matt. We're the only ones that know killin' them two deputies was self-defense. Till we kin prove that—if we ever can—you an' Dolf are gonna disappear as soon as he's well enough to travel. I got a little money. That'll keep yuh both awhile."

Matt exchanged laden glances with Mum, a question plainly in his eyes. She nodded assent.

Matt cleared his throat. "We won't need any money, Doc. We got plenty."

Doc looked interested, raising his eyebrows and awaiting clarification.

Matt looked embarrassed, not knowing how to start.

"I got a little confession to make," he said. "I'da had to tell Dolf soon 'r later anyhow. I got the best part of a hundred thousand dollars, or at least Mum has—she's been keepin' it fer me. I was the lone bandit that stuck up that train Pardeau used as an excuse to come after Dolf an' try ta kill 'im."

He waited for the effect of that. Doc was silent, waiting for the rest.

"Wouldn't've done any good ta own up. They never even tried Dolf fer that. He was sent up fer shootin' Pardeau and his two deputies. The only reason he was suspected of the train job at all was family resemblance. My damn handkerchief got pulled off my face."

Doc wasn't easily surprised. He thought up till then he'd heard almost everything under the sun. He had to admit he'd been wrong.

"I'll be damned," he whistled. "O' course, robbin' railroads an' banks ain't rightly illegal in my book. Kinda takin' 'em at their own game, only more honest. Yuh ain't figgerin' to come clean now, are yuh?"

"No way. Those Pinkertons would love that. It ain't exactly the principle o' the thing; it's the money. We need it worse 'n the Express Co. right now."

"How'd ya come ta pull it off?" Doc asked admiringly.

"Well, I was sittin' in the railroad station down at the capital, thinkin' about how I'd tied one on an' missed my train, an' how I should be ashamed the way Dolf had to scrape to get the money ta send me off ta school in the first place. I bought a ticket on the next train an' was waitin'. About then I saw this messenger sneak off a train with the Express sack about 2 A.M., playin' it sneaky. I was still feelin' that giggle water, and no one else was around, so I put a handkerchief over my face, kinda as a joke, an' stuck my six-shooter in his ribs. The whole trouble was he put up a fuss an' grabbed my mask before I hit him over the head. I hid out fer almost two hours, figgerin' they'd know it musta been me. I reckon, though, no one ever thought of Dolf's kid brother. He was the big news then with pictures in all the papers. The worst part of it was it gave Pardeau a halfway excuse ta get a warrant out for Dolf."

Doc said, "If it hadn't been that, it'd been somethin' else, or else a shot in the back."

Matt nodded solemnly. "Anyway, I stole a horse an' lit out into the country a ways. You coulda knocked me over with a feather when I lit a match an' found all them greenbacks in the sack."

"How'd yuh git away?" Junior asked.

"I just turned the horse loose and walked back into town after hidin' the loot, an' caught my train. No one noticed a thing. It was the dumbest thing I ever saw. I even had on the same clothes. I guess no one expected the highwayman right back at the R.R. station. The next summer I came back and got the sack and hid it again in a better place."

"Where'd ya hide it first?" Junior asked.

"Climbed up a tree an' tied it up there with a latigo string," he said. "Wonder some sharp-eyed kid didn't spot it since it wasn't over half a mile from town."

"Are yuh gonna tell my pa?" Junior asked.

"I reckon," Matt said. "Anyhow, we ain't gonna need your money, Doc, thanks anyhow."

"Don't mention it," Doc said, still flabbergasted. "Old Jesse James himself," he muttered. "Wadya know about that?"

Pardeau returned to Pinebluff a couple of days after the shooting. He had a great deal to think about. Foremost of his worries was why Wheat had apparently tried to get him tangled up with the two dead deputies and Dolf. He suspected he knew but couldn't be sure as he would have been if he knew that his tricky partner had supplied Dolf with the two derringers. He thought he'd have a little showdown with Wheat anyhow but discovered he'd left town. That confirmed his suspicions.

His second problem was Theodora and her waning interest in him. He was a vain man, yet a realist. He admitted inwardly that he fell far short of being a real man. He was more of a Georgie-Porgie and was honest enough with himself to realize it. In his whole life, the biggest boost to his ego had been stealing Dolf's woman. He'd envied Dolf first, then hated him. It was probably the main reason he'd married Theodora—to prove to himself and the world that he really had stolen her. The ranch was secondary. This same psychological quirk prompted him to cut Dolf down even in the eyes of his daughter Amy. He recognized the mental rottenness that this implied even as he knew he had to go through with it, regardless.

His third problem was the least tractable. It was Mum. She'd showed up at the ranch during his absence.

Junior introduced Mum to his mother. Theodora was taken aback. She'd been dimly aware that Dolf had a grandmother, and that was all.

"Make yourself at home," Theodora invited. "I'll get coffee and something to eat if you've time."

"Got all the time in the world," Mum told her. "I wanta see my great granddaughter."

"She won't be home from school for hours yet," Theodora told her.

"I'll hang around and look the place over. Matt and I are planning to build on the ranch."

"You can't do that," Theodora protested.

"Why not?" Mum asked ominously. "It's half Matt's."

"You'll need my permission," Theodora protested weakly.

Mum speared her with a definitely hostile eye. "When did you ever ask Matt's permission to do anything?" She answered her own question. "Never, ain't that right? Well, yuh might as well git ready fer a change."

Theodora, needless to say, was not enchanted with Mum right off. To her intense disgust, Amy, like almost everyone else, was definitely enchanted with her great grandmother. Theodora watched in wonder as Mum and Amy sociably munched cookies together, the young girl wide-eyed as Mum told her about killing the Indian who'd tried to steal her horse so long ago.

"I fetched him dead-center with a load o' blue whistlers," Mum was saying. "Yuh kin bet it left him fatal sick. I fed him ta the hogs."

Instead of being horrified, Amy giggled. "I'll bet you're just sayin' that, Mum," the young girl guessed.

Mum chucked her in the ribs and winked. "I'm tellin' this story, Amy. Makes a better story thataway, don't it?"

Amy nodded.

Mum grinned.

"Got some other good uns ta tell ya too."

Theodora was even more disgusted to see the look on Amy's face that clearly showed she could hardly wait. Theo's attitude only changed when she saw how Mum handled Ed Pardeau. Maybe a few years earlier she would have sided with her husband. Now she drew an almost poisonous satisfaction from anything that discomfited him. She'd found him out good, and Mum *did* discomfit him.

Theo provided him no warning. Amy saw no reason to. Hence Ed anticipated a visit from a nice old doting great grandmother soft on Amy. Theo waited for Mum to personally read him in on her plans to build on the ranch.

"Yuh can't do that without our permission," Ed stated.

"The hell I cain't," Mum replied, fire in her eye.

Ed appeared as shocked as he actually was.

"I'm startin' tomorrow. If'n you're tired o' livin', jist git in m' way. I'd as soon let yuh hev a load o' buckshot as look at your slick face."

"She already killed an Injun," Amy burst in.

Pardeau gave his stepdaughter a withering look. He was losing face and thinking fast. He looked a little sick.

"I didn't say yuh couldn't build," he crawfished.

"An' don't!" Mum cut the discussion short.

Theodora smiled wickedly, but Ed, stalking from the room in a huff, missed seeing her satisfaction. It was lucky for her he didn't. Dangerous pressures were building up in him that she was too smugly contemptuous to recognize. She was also preoccupied with wondering whether Dolf was still alive or not. She got no satisfaction from Mum or Junior on that point.

Junior only shrugged, which answered for both of them.

"Does Doc know anything?" she asked her son.

"If he did, he wouldn't say. Be afraid he might git Pa killed if he ain't already dead. Doc's mighty close-mouthed anyhow."

The same question was bothering Pardeau more than he'd like to let on. He asked Theo if she'd learned anything from Junior and Mum, and she frankly told him, partly because she knew it would add to his already obvious apprehension.

"Someday he'll be comin'," Pardeau said. "If he's alive."

Theo's eyes sparkled devilishly. "And what'll you do then?"

Pardeau shrugged. He still had some hired gunslingers among the cowboys. *If I know he's comin'*, Ed thought, *it won't work out like last time.*

Already he was turning over in his mind the first rude thoughts about how he could get Dolf to come at the time and to the place of his own choosing. If he was alive.

CHAPTER 16

DOLF was getting stronger every day. Almost a month had passed since he had been shot. This day he mounted for the first time the splendid black horse Chief Henry bestowed on him as a gift. Margaret translated the chief's little presentation speech.

"My father says: 'For the son of my old friend Dan Morgette to repay a little the many generous things he did for me and my people. And—' " here she hesitated; it was obvious she didn't want to tell him the next words, but she did—" 'I give this horse also for the great warrior son of my friend that he may use it when he takes the war trail to avenge the death of his father and brothers.' "

Margaret had already told Dolf how those deaths had actually occurred. She didn't know the men but knew they were lawmen by the badges they'd worn. She described their leader: Ed Pardeau. The Morgettes had surrendered to a sham arrest and given up their weapons. Then the posse had shot them down in cold blood. Dolf felt a hardening of his resolve to settle more than one score with Pardeau.

"The horse's name," Margaret told him, "is Wowakan. In our tongue it means 'supernatural.' "

He rode Wowakan now, farther each day, Jim Too following wherever they went. Dolf noted with satisfaction that his own strength was returning as well as the developing strength of the pup's muscles. He knew that young dogs were apt to give out on the trail without strenuous hardening. Jim Too was an exceptionally strong dog, already almost tireless.

Dolf was now seated on a log, with Wowakan and Jim Too nearby. He came to this secluded spot daily to regain his dexterity with pistols. The soreness that had slowed his move-

175

ments was almost gone from his left side. It only gave him an occasional twinge. He stroked Jim Too's ears, the dog looking up at him adoringly with his large, intelligent eyes.

"We've got a long trail ahead of us, pardner," Dolf told him.

Wowakan nickered softly behind them, as though to say he too understood. Dolf reached back and stroked his soft muzzle.

"Yeh, you too," Dolf acknowledged. "I've got a feeling our soft days are about over—just a feelin' in my bones."

This premonition, like that which had warned him of impending danger when the riflemen had shot at him in Bowden's buckboard, almost never erred. It made him restless. But because of it, he would not be mentally unprepared when the dangerous time came.

The catalyst of the trouble was Theodora again. She had always, in late years, been his Jonah.

Theodora wanted Dolf back. It was a wholly unreasonable desire. She didn't even know whether he was alive. But she was satisfied that he was from the contented attitude of their son. Junior was not mourning, and she knew he worshipped his father. She was sure Junior would have heard from someone if Dolf was dead.

Most of all, Theodora wanted Dolf because he had told her he didn't want her. She knew why he shouldn't want her, if he was in his right mind, but she also had a simplistic view of men. They were all very much alike in her mind. And she was still a beautiful woman. She had the added advantage of being the mother of the two children Dolf adored. Coupled with her desperate desire to get rid of Pardeau, these facts moved her powerfully to want to change her life pattern. She knew her mind. Now she needed an instrument to carry out her desire.

Before she could devise a plan, other forces were in motion that may have accounted for the sixth-sense warning Dolf was receiving.

Alby Gould's return to Pinebluff was what impelled Victoria Wheat to tell all she knew. It started when Hal Green brought Alby up to date on local events. When Alby learned of Victoria's warning that saved Dolf from being murdered, he drew about the same shrewd conclusion Doc had. Moreover, he thought he was close enough to Victoria to get her to reveal the source of the information. Alby thought her father was an evil influence in the territory that should be crushed. He was not too scrupulous to use the woman he aspired to marry to destroy the power of her own father. He considered it simply a matter of "all's fair in love and war."

Accordingly, accompanied by Hal Green, he confronted Victoria at her home. She tearfully confessed to them the whole sordid story. Her high regard for Hal Green helped her dissolve her misgivings.

Alby, a careful man, even checked out the acoustics of the fireplace before he sent for Mulveen. The sheriff was not under Gould's thumb, as he was Wheat's, but Gould was the kind of man who overawed the sheriff. Gould represented money and power and had the self-assurance they engendered.

Confronted with Victoria's story, Mulveen was at first stupefied. He had her tell it again. Then he checked the fireplaces himself to hear how clearly they transmitted voices.

Finally, in a last desperate effort to circumvent reality, he asked, "How can you be sure it was your pa's voice?"

Gould exploded. "You dunce! You listened to our voices. Did you have any trouble identifying them? Now get busy and do your job, or I'll wire the governor and have you suspended from office before the sun goes down. We'll get a special prosecutor and the U.S. marshal on the way up here. It's obvious as the nose on your face that you've been dim-wittedly persecuting an innocent man. It's equally obvious that there's been a conspiracy of some sort going on here under your nose for years. It's about time it gets a thorough investigation."

"Jist the same," Mulveen still mulishly insisted, "I'm gonna take a posse out and arrest Morgette. Till we git this straight, I ain't lettin' him pull his freight."

Alby registered his disgust.

"What do you need a posse for?" he exploded again. "To

start some more trouble? If Morgette sees a posse coming, it may lead to more shooting before he gets the right idea. Could even lead to trouble with the Indians. Suppose Mr. Green and I be your posse. We can take Catherine Green to show us where Chief Henry's camp is. With a woman along, we'll be pretty sure no promiscuous shooting will start."

Very reluctantly, Mulveen acceded to that arrangement.

"Another thing," Alby reminded him. "You'd better send one of those posses you're so fond of out to arrest Ed Pardeau for first-degree murder. Also wire wherever Wheat is and have him held."

"I'm the sheriff here!" Mulveen blustered.

"You won't be," Gould coldly reminded him, "if I send off just one wire. Now which'll it be?"

Victoria felt drained when her mortal ordeal was all over at last. She didn't know what to think. One thing was clear in her mind; they were doing the right thing. She was sick at heart, knowing her father must pay for his crimes like anyone else. At his age, it would destroy him to go to jail even for the minimum sentence.

How can I testify against him? she asked herself. Her despondency over her father was lightened by the knowledge that Dolf was going to be a free man.

She was suddenly bone-weary.

I don't know what I think if the facts were known, she told herself dully after she was alone. *How will I ever face Father?* was the thought that kept recurring to her.

She knew it would be dreadfully unfair to think of Dolf as the cause of her having finally learned about suffering. She thought, *He also taught me what being in love is.* Her spirits picked up over this reflection.

Dolf, who was rapidly recovering, would just as soon have let the law tend to Pardeau. He also knew that he could not really go after Wheat because of his feelings for Victoria. But there appeared no chance the law would mete out justice to either of them. He hated that idea. In addition, he himself was again a fugitive, with little hope of ever being able to clear himself of any of the charges hanging over him.

He had no idea that the means of his salvation in the persons of his friends soon might be at hand. Equally, he had no means of realizing that other forces were still at work that could thwart them.

Theodora's tragic influence was about to come into his life again. Whether Dolf was still alive or not, she wanted to get rid of Pardeau. Ed had sensed this in his wife for some time. It drove him to desperation. He would lose the one coup he felt made him a better man than Dolf in the eyes of the world. The more he turned over this proposition, the more he came to believe perversely that Dolf, not the fickle Theodora, was somehow the root of the problem.

The explosive situation reached a crisis suddenly. Ed had finally demanded a showdown. She had been taking long rides alone that he thought demanded an explanation. The fact was that she needed to get away to think. Suspicious, Pardeau had tried to follow her. Simp Parsons, one of their cowboys whom she'd always treated well, and one who was particularly fond of Amy, had warned Theodora that Ed was following her on her rides. Out of spite, she took to masking her trail by deliberately riding on rocky terrain where only an Indian could have trailed her.

"You're hidin' Dolf yourself!" Pardeau exploded at her. "I shoulda known! That's where you've been ridin'!"

She almost blurted out, "You must be insane." Then she recognized how this was a ready-made opportunity to twist the knife in him again.

"What if I am?" she demanded. "I'm going to get him back too. You and I are through."

He cursed wildly, drawing back a hand to hit her. The look of pure murder that swiftly came into her eyes forestalled him. He remembered the ancient scene with the rifle in her hands. He stumbled blindly from the room, cursing.

His plan had been already almost worked out. Her vicious decision to torment him put it into effect.

The next morning Ed was gone. Theodora found a note from him under the lid of the coffeepot, where she'd be sure to see it first thing. It read: "Tell your precious lover if he wants to see his 'precious' daughter alive again, he can come try to take her away from me at his old line cabin on Spruce Creek. We'll have it out man to man. If he brings anyone with him, I'll shoot his brat. I guess this'll bring him out of his hole, sweetheart."

Theodora was suddenly brought to her senses by this. She truly loved her daughter, selfish though she was. In a panic, she searched the house to be sure it wasn't all a perverted drunken joke. Amy was gone. There was no doubt about that.

What have I done? she asked herself. *What shall I do? I don't really know where Dolf is; why did I tell that insane man I did? Dear God, what shall I do now?*

At that key juncture, Junior and Mum dropped in. After they had struck a truce over the building issue, Theodora had actually enjoyed having them for breakfast occasionally, on their way to the site of their construction project.

Wordlessly, she showed Junior the note. Her eyes pleaded with him. "If you know where your father is, you'd better show him this."

Junior read the note to Mum, who claimed she had trouble seeing without glasses; actually she had as much trouble reading with or without them.

"Git your pa," Mum told him. "I may head up ta this Spruce Crick with m' scatter-gun an' shoot some sense in Pardeau myself," she added.

"Don't do that!" Theodora pleaded. "He's insane. I know. He'll do what he says."

Junior rode to Dolf with this note early on the same day Alby Gould finally pried the truth from Victoria.

Consequently, when Sheriff Mulveen and his party reached Chief Henry's camp, Dolf had left. Bitterroot Tom, who acted as interpreter, assured them that no one knew where. He neglected to tell Mulveen that they wouldn't have told him if they had.

Margaret drew Catherine aside and told her, "Junior came for him last night. They left in a hurry. We really don't know where. My people could trail him, but they will not do it for the sheriff."

Mulveen actually considered trailing him, then thought better of it. "I think he'll show up somewhere pretty soon. We can wait."

This didn't satisfy Catherine, but she kept her own counsel.

"Please have someone follow and tell him we have the testimony that will clear him. He's free to come home," Catherine privately and urgently begged of Margaret before they all departed.

Out of Mulveen's hearing, she told her father and Alby—who had misgivings similar to her own—what she had arranged.

"Good girl," Alby said.

CHAPTER 17

THE starlight was bright enough to travel by, and a moon rose later. Dolf and his son rode at a fast trot, Jim Too padding along beside. Dolf had tried to send Junior back to town but met with stubborn refusal.

"She's my sister," Junior argued. "Besides, Pardeau is sneaky. He won't meet you in a fair fight. If he gets you, I'll at least get him."

Dolf also knew Pardeau would never meet him fair and square; hadn't expected he would. He simply decided he'd have to take that chance; there was the almost certain probability that Pardeau would have some of his hired guns to back him. Dolf was gambling on his knowledge of Ed's personality and on his guess about the motive in making this insane move. He was sure that Ed would want to take time to bluster and gloat. That would give him his opportunity to grab him. He had an ace in the hole. Years before, Bitterroot Tom had made him a master at knife throwing and fighting. He'd borrowed what he needed from Tom before leaving the Indian Camp. He had a heavy throwing knife hanging down between his shoulder blades in a quick-draw sling.

He was betting Ed wouldn't let him in the cabin with his six-shooters—probably had his men posted to intercept him and take his guns. He prayed they'd miss finding the knife. With it held in Ed's ribs, he and Amy might escape—if she was still alive. He refused to even think she wasn't.

"You can't be seen with me anywhere near the place 'r they may kill your sister," Dolf warned. "It'll be gettin' light by the time we git up there."

"I'll drop back an' Injun up from the other way," Junior

said. "Know the country back that way like m' own face. They won't know I'm comin'."

Dolf had confidence in his son. He knew that he himself could have done the same at Junior's age. The boy was another ace in the hole. He felt a tremendous sense of pride in his son, which lifted his spirits.

They parted as the eastern sky first began to pale. The moon was still overhead.

Dolf gravely shook hands with Junior, knowing this could be a final parting. They sat their horses side by side for a moment, gripping each other in solemn silence.

"Good luck, Pa" were the only words that passed between them, then Junior reined his horse away and spurred into the forest.

Jim Too was puzzled for a moment, not knowing whether he should go that way. Dolf called him back.

"This is our trail, boy—maybe our last one."

He was thinking solemnly of what had happened to old Jim with his pa and brothers.

Let's hope this one works out different, Dolf thought.

He lifted Wowakan to a gallop now. It was certainly the right name for the horse. He seemed to glide over the ground as effortlessly as if he really were a spirit of some kind. Dolf's regard for the horse's intelligence, as well as his speed and bottom, had increased every day he rode him.

The trail rose steeply now on the final ridge before reaching Spruce Creek. Dolf had slowed Wowakan down to a walk. Here it was still almost as gloomy as night, due to the heavy overhanging growth of evergreens. This gloom transmitted its mood to Dolf. He wondered if he'd ever be free of battling uneven odds in a fight to regain normal existence. He was on edge, expecting a challenge, or perhaps even an ambush at any moment. Wowakan suddenly threw up his head, scenting something ahead. At the same instant, Jim's hackles raised and he growled threateningly.

"Whoa up right there," a loud voice ordered.

Dolf pulled in Wowakan. Jim Too uttered a growling half-bark.

"Call off the mutt before he catches a slug," the same voice sang out.

Dolf reassured Jim Too, who came to him and sat down nervously, whining his protest.

"That's better. Now put yore hands on the saddlehorn an' keep 'em there."

A figure approached, covering him with a rifle. Dolf recognized Pardeau's broncbuster, Stud Foley, whom he'd rescued in the jail fire. *Some gratitude*, he thought but remained silent.

"There's another rifle on yuh back there, so don't try nothin' funny," Foley warned.

He came around to the left side of the horse, still keeping the rifle on Dolf, taking no chances.

"Okay, Clem," he yelled. "Yuh kin come on up now."

Clem Yoder approached cautiously, also packing a rifle that he kept trained on Dolf. He stopped almost at point-blank range.

"Now," Stud ordered, "git down real easy and keep yer paws on the saddlehorn while I git yer shootin' arns."

Dolf did as he was told, feeling the weapons lifted from each holster.

"Now tie up thet hoss an' the pup. Boss wants ta see yuh down below," Stud Foley told him.

When he had done that, Foley asked sociably, "Yuh wouldn't have a hideout 'r two on yuh, would yuh, Dolf?"

Dismay captured Dolf's mind at the thought they might find his knife, his one hope to bring a whole skin out of this, with Amy alive.

"Pull up yore pants-legs," Stud ordered. "I read in the paper yuh had a dinky in yer boot on that train."

Dolf obeyed, grateful he had nothing for them to find. Maybe that would disarm their suspicions. It was a vain hope.

"Turn around," Stud said.

He felt him all up and down for a hideout. He was just

finishing, and Dolf was about to congratulate himself on his luck, when Stud's cheek accidently came in contact with the knife as he stooped to pat Dolf down on his trouser-legs from behind.

"What's this?" Stud crowed, feeling for the knife. He reached down and pulled it out, throwing it in the underbrush.

"I never cared fer knife-wielders," Stud observed nastily.

Dolf's hopes sunk into his boots. Now only a miracle could pull them out of this predicament. He wondered where Junior had got to by now.

"Let's go," Stud said, shoving him ahead. "And no funny moves, or the show's over right here."

"Is my daughter alive?" Dolf asked.

"So far," Stud said.

Foley whistled to signal those at the house as they approached. Simp Parsons opened the door and looked up the trail toward them. Dolf could see he had a double-barreled shotgun.

They sure ain't takin' any chances, he thought. *Helluva thanks fer pullin' their worthless carcasses out o' that fire.*

Parsons had reentered the cabin. He carefully covered Dolf with the shotgun as Stud poked him through the door with his rifle.

"You stay out there," Stud told Yoder. "He mighta been dumb an' brought somebody with him."

Pardeau was sitting insolently in one of the rope chairs, with a leg idly slung over the arm. He directed a hate-laden look at Dolf.

"Well, well, well," he sneered. "The great Dolf Morgette, terror of Pinebluff. Oh yes," he added nastily, "and great lady-killer."

Dolf had no way of knowing what the last remark meant, not knowing that Theodora's lying shrewishness had toppled Ed off the deep end under the misconception that she was returning to Dolf.

"Where's Amy?" Dolf asked, ignoring the jibes.

Ed indicated a bunk with his thumb. "Drag 'er out, Stud," he directed.

The cowboy rolled and heaved the girl from the bunk. She had a gag over her mouth, and her hands were tied with a handkerchief.

Dolf felt his anger rising over this needless cruelty.

"What's the idea of the gag?" he asked.

"She's as mouthy as her mother," Ed said. To Stud he said, "Take the gag out."

Dolf looked kindly at his daughter. It was the first time he'd seen her in five years. Naturally, she'd grown a lot. At twelve she was almost as tall as her mother and beginning to show signs of the same beauty. Her eyes were snapping furiously with anger, not fear, Dolf was pleased to note. She shook her head fiercely to help get the gag out.

As soon as it was, she gasped, "He says he's gonna kill us both, Pa."

There were tears of frustrated anger in her eyes. "He told me all those bad things about you, and I believed him." She turned her remarks on Pardeau: "You're the bad one. If you don't kill me, I'll shoot you the first chance I get."

Pardeau was reminded of the look he'd seen in Theodora's eyes over the sights of that rifle. He believed she might shoot him. He laughed nastily. "Shut up," he said, "or I'll have that gag put back in."

Then ignoring her, he turned to Dolf. "I'm gonna settle some old accounts today. You owe me plenty."

Dolf silently watched him, contempt in his eyes. The man was sick. He had the "who-owed-whom" entirely backward, like his kind always did. Dolf thought of that knife lying useless out in the brush and wondered again where Junior was. He didn't have long to wonder.

Yoder herded him through the door with his rifle.

"Look what I caught snoopin'," he chortled. "I was out where we left Dolf's hoss, an' the pooch let me know he was acomin' just like a good fellow. He stumbled right inta my arms."

Junior looked crestfallen.

"I'm sorry, Pa," he apologized.

Pardeau crowed, "We'll make it a family affair. I want these two brats to see me beat their pa fa'r 'n' squar' with six-shooters! Tie him up an' gag 'im," Pardeau ordered.

Yoder and Stud did as they were told, Amy and Dolf watching helplessly.

"Put 'im in a chair where he can see the show," Pardeau told them.

"Now," he said, turning his attention to Dolf, "I got a surprise fer yuh. I'm plannin' ta shoot it out like I said, fa'r 'n' squar'. Only everybody knows yer a lot faster'n I am—so ta do it fa'r 'n' squar', here's how it's gonna work."

He took out his six-shooter and removed all but one shell. Then he carefully adjusted the location of the cylinder.

"This shell comes up last, Dolf. Now I'm puttin' the six-shooter right here on the table. Yuh kin make a grab fer it 'n' start shootin' anytime after I count three. If yuh git me, I told the boys ta let yuh go."

He started to count. Dolf realized he had no choice—was glad he'd practiced as he had up at the Indian village.

"Three!" Pardeau shouted.

Dolf sprang forward and snatched the gun, clicking it as fast as a machine gun three times, then suddenly stopped. Pardeau hadn't moved. He stood grinning slyly.

"Go ahead. Click the rest uv 'em," he goaded.

"Yuh pulled the powder on that shell," Dolf said. "Why should I?"

He was now prepared to die. Had run out his string. His greatest regret was that his children would die too. "Go ahead 'n' shoot."

"Not yet," Ed said. "I got a couple more things ta tell yuh. Theodora told me she hired that hairpin ta take a shot at yuh with the warden. Wanted yuh ta think I did it. She also set thet kerosene can on the stove at the jail. Did it 'cause she was mad yuh didn't wanna take her back, she said. Pity yuh changed yer mind."

Suddenly a great deal became clear. Dolf could see the fine scheming hand of Theodora in this whole mess. Obviously she'd thrown Ed over and told him she was going back to him. Ed had reacted like the jealous fool he was. What a mess. He hoped she'd live a long while to think about the harvest of her selfishness.

Pardeau very deliberately reached for his pistol.

"Wait a damn minute," Simp Parsons protested, lifting the shotgun to cover Pardeau. "This ain't the way yuh said it was gonna be."

He swung the scatter-gun to cover his fellow cowboys as well. "Don't nobody make any rash moves. This man saved our lives. What kinda skunks'd we be ta let him git killed with no show atall? Now, are ya with me 'r again' me?"

Yoder and Foley exchanged sheepish looks. Stud shrugged. "I guess we're with yuh. This ain't the way it was supposed ta work out."

Before anyone could change their minds, Dolf stepped over and took Pardeau's six-shooter. No one made a move to restrain him.

Waving the six-shooter to emphasize his order, Dolf said, "Untie the two kids."

Ed Pardeau's face had turned ashen. He was already imagining what was in store next. As usual, he wanted to talk.

"I wasn't really gonna do it, Dolf," he quaked. "I just wanted ta throw a scare inta Theo."

"I'll bet," Dolf grated.

To Parsons he said, "Bring him outside an' give 'im the scatter-gun. We'll git this over with like he wanted. Fa'r 'n' squar'."

"No!" Ed protested. "No. I swear I wasn't gonna kill the girl. I wasn't gonna kill anyone. Tell 'em, Amy."

Dolf looked at his daughter for confirmation.

"He's a liar," she said. "He told me all them things about you, Pa. I don't believe him. But please don't kill him. I don't want you to kill anyone anymore."

Dolf grinned. This little square-shooting lady was his

daughter—somehow she was growing up with a big heart, and he'd bet it was no thanks to her mother or stepfather. *Probably Junior's influence*, he thought.

"I wasn't really gonna kill 'im," Dolf told Amy. "Jist throw the fear o' God in 'im.'"

Turning to Ed, he said. "If yuh got a hoss around here, fork 'im 'n' slope. If I ever lay eyes on yuh in the country ag'in, I'll kill yuh sure. Now git.'"

"Whud ya do that fer, Pa?" Junior asked after Pardeau had spurred away.

"Fer yer ma, I guess." He shook his head. "I don't know. Maybe I'm tired o' killin'. Jail wouldn't do his kind any good. Makes 'em worse. Besides, the kind o' law we got here, he'd get off anyhow."

To Parsons he said, "I'm mighty beholden to yuh fer bein' square when it counted. Put 'er there. Same goes fer you two," he told Stud and Yoder. "I reckon yuh still got jobs back at the ranch after Amy puts in a good word fer yuh, if yuh want 'em."

"What're yuh gonna do now, Pa?" Junior asked.

"Hug your sister," he said, grabbing Amy up in his arms.

"Oh, Pa," she sobbed. "I do still love you."

"I love you too, honey," he said, his eyes stinging with grateful tears. "I love you too."

The three cowboys stood by grinning.

"I'll git the little lady's hoss," Parsons said. "Reckon yuh'll all be headin' back to the ranch."

"You too, Pa?" Junior asked.

"I guess so. There'll never be a better time ta try an' clear my name. If I don't, I'll be runnin' the rest o' my life, an' your sister'll never have a pa."

CHAPTER 18

DOLF rode on around the old home ranch, headed for town, leaving Junior to drop off Amy and tell their mother what had happened. Dolf had a couple of calls to make. The first would be to thank Catherine Green for nursing him. Then he knew he must face Victoria.

Can I ask her to make a choice between me an' her pa? he speculated.

He'd seen the adoration in her eyes when she had been with Mark Wheat. It was also clearly a choice, as he saw it, between right and wrong. Her decision might tell him something about her he was afraid to learn. He'd have been a lot happier if he had been aware that she had already made that decision. As it was, he was debating not putting her in that position and, instead, going on the dodge himself. After all, she had tried her best to save his life; what more could he ask? He was thinking now how lovely she was and how soft her lips had felt on his cheek; also about that look of invitation in her eyes. But the whole thing was impossible.

I'll cut out for the tall tules, he told himself. *Mum can look after Amy—an' Junior; he's already done a pretty fair job o' bein' a pa to her.*

He definitely decided he wouldn't see Victoria after all. In this frame of mind, he hitched Wowakan out of sight in the corral behind the Green cottage. Jim Too followed him to the back door. He knocked softly. One of the two younger Green girls, who had been washing dishes together, answered the door. She looked at him in wide-eyed surprise, as though a knight in armor had suddenly come calling.

"You're Dolf Morgette," she said, sounding and appearing awed.

190

"I'm afraid so," he admitted. "Can I come in?"

"Sure," she said. "I'll get Catherine." Running by her smaller sister at the sink, she hissed, "It's Dolf Morgette!"

Her little sister almost dropped a plate, turning to look.

Dolf came in with Jim Too and closed the door. The young girl continued to look at him with slightly open mouth, eyes wide. Jim Too went over to her, tail wagging.

"You're real," the little girl said.

Dolf grinned. "You bet." Pointing to the dog, he said, "That's Jim Too. He's real too. He wants yuh ta pet him."

Catherine entered the room swiftly.

"Dolf," she murmured. "I'm so glad you're here alive. Where did you go?" Without thought, she hugged him and gave him a not-quite-sisterly peck on the cheek.

Then she stepped back, blushing. The two little girls were taking it all in with interest.

"Wadya mean, where'd I go?" Dolf asked, not understanding how she'd known he'd gone anywhere.

She explained, then gave him the good news.

"You're practically in the clear now. Everyone knows those two deputies were hired guns. They'll never hold you after Victoria Wheat testifies."

He felt like a huge weight had been lifted from his spirit.

"Can I fix you something to eat? We've finished, but we have a big ham. I can fix fried spuds to go with it in a jiffy."

He remembered he hadn't eaten for twenty-four hours.

"You've got a customer," he agreed.

She seated him at the kitchen table, which was covered simply with a checked oilcloth.

"I'll put on the coffeepot while I'm getting the other things ready. I've got some scraps for the pup too."

She questioned him about his whereabouts for the past day while she was fixing supper. Several times, she made little exclamations of surprise.

When he finished telling his story, she said, "I can't believe you let Ed Pardeau go, after all he did to you and your family!"

"I guess I'm tired of killing," he explained wearily. "Besides, I figured there wasn't much chance o' doin' anything to him with Mulveen in charge. You know no court would accept the testimony from Chief Henry's tribe either."

"You'll be lucky if Mulveen doesn't charge you with something for turning Pardeau loose." She laughed. "He's got typical sheriff's brains; got to charge somebody with something."

Dolf shrugged indifferently. Suddenly he felt terribly tired —it was all over, and he wanted to sleep a hundred years. He thanked Catherine for his and Jim Too's dinner and headed for Mum's.

Junior had beat him there and was in the kitchen, cramming down food.

"Where yuh bin, Pa?" he asked around the cold drumstick he was putting down in big gulps. "Have we ever got news fer you."

Matt and Mum were waiting eagerly to tell him the big news: that he was practically a free man.

"I reckon I heard the big news." He told then where he'd been.

Mum looked at him sharply. "You be thinkin' o' robbin' the cradle with that Green gal, son?" she asked. "I figgered yuh wuz soft on that Wheat gal."

Dolf regarded her amiably and was noncommittal.

"I be *thinkin'* uv about twenty-four hours' sleep. Where yuh gonna put me up?"

"We only got about a dozen bedrooms upstairs," Matt said. "Why don't yuh just pick one?"

"Shush," Mum said. "I'll pull down a bed fer 'im."

She lit a lamp and led him up the stairs. The shot came through the front bay window as they were part way up, and shattered the lamp chimney, blowing out the lamp with the bullet's swift passage. Dolf had heard a sharp little "whitt' as it sailed past his ear, it was that close.

"Douse your light," he yelled to the pair in the kitchen, meanwhile cautiously working his way through the strange room as fast as he could go in the dark, trying to reach the front door.

"Stay there, Mum," he cautioned.

He should have known better. She was already on her way after her scatter-gun.

He opened the front door quickly, pausing in case a shot might follow, then rapidly stepped out and to one side. He listened for the sound of running footsteps or a horse. He could hear a trotting horse somewhere, he thought, but his party would have hit out on the run. Perhaps he was still skulking around to try to get another shot. He waited silently. In awhile, the front door opened stealthily.

"Dolf?" Matt hissed.

"Over here," he said in a low voice.

Both Junior and Matt came out. Pretty soon Mum followed with her scatter-gun.

"Family reunion," Dolf whispered. "Spread out; he couldn't miss this bunch if he's still around."

They all listened in silence for several minutes. Only the occasional distant sound of town could be heard. No one seemed to have been aroused by the shot. Their nearest neighbor was in the next block, and gunshots weren't an unusual sound at night where people kept chickens in a coyote country.

"Probably long gone," Dolf guessed.

"I told ya it was crazy ta let Pardeau go," Junior said disgustedly.

"Think it was him?" Matt asked Dolf.

"Unless Mum has a jilted lover on her hands," Dolf said.

Mum snorted, "Half a dozen is more like it," she said. "O' course it was that skunk Pardeau!"

They all went back inside.

"Lock up," Dolf said. "We'll look fer sign when it gits light. I can put Jim Too on the trail."

"Easier said 'n done," Mum stated. "No keys."

"Push chairs under the knobs then," Dolf said. "Thataway, at least we'll hear someone tryin' ta git in."

An unpleasant thought was plaguing Dolf as he tried to

drop off to sleep. He suspected Pardeau was actually insane. *Gone off his rocker, fer sure,* he thought as he dozed off.

Mum, who'd been getting up with the chickens for three-quarters of a century, roused them all out at the crack of dawn. They congregated in the kitchen for a cup of coffee.

Matt let Jim Too out the back door. In a little while, they heard his growl and bark almost together.

"I'll see what . . ." Matt was saying as he opened the back door and spun back into the room, falling heavily to the floor and blocking the door. The sound of a shot followed at once.

Dolf grabbed him and dragged him inside, leaving the door open to get a view of the backyard.

"Any the rest o' you Morgettes want a waltz, come on out!" Ed Pardeau's voice roared from somewhere outside.

Dolf figured the voice came from behind a tree near the barn. He whistled in Jim Too, covering the tree in case Pardeau decided to take out his maniacal revenge on the dog. Then he slammed the door.

"Stop that bleeding," he told Mum.

The whole front of Matt's shirt was crimsoned where the shotgun charge had hit him.

Dolf yelled to Junior, "Take a couple of shots out the window at the tree next ta the barn door, but duck if he steps out. I'm goin' around from the front. I want yuh ta try an' keep his attention."

Dolf swiftly passed through the house and around the outside. He peeped cautiously around the corner.

Junior was shooting now. Dolf could see a heavy bullet take effect, knocking bark off the tree. He thought he saw an elbow stick out as the shot hit. Without attempt to conceal himself, he stepped away from the house and moved swiftly to get where he'd have a clear shot. Pardeau, behind the tree was peeking around the other side of it. Junior shot again, and Ed drew back to where Dolf had a better view.

"Over here, Ed," he said.

Pardeau whirled, startled, half-raising the shotgun.

"I thought I jist shot you," he gasped.

"Go ahead, Ed, try again," Dolf invited. "I'll give yuh first shot fa'r 'n' squar'."

He saw Pardeau frantically raising the gun to aim. Dolf drew and let off his own shot just an instant before he figured Ed was ready. The shotgun went off as Ed fell.

"Fa'r 'n' squar', Ed," Dolf said softly. "Pardeau-style, that is."

The shooting must have attracted half the town. In the forefront of those rushing to the scene were Tobe Mulveen and Doc.

Doc was shortly working over Matt.

"Mostly in the shoulder, I think," Doc said. "Help me get 'im on a bed."

Dolf was relieved to hear that.

"Friend o' yours over behind that tree," he told Mulveen. "Unless my eyes 're goin' bad, he won't be needin' Doc."

Mulveen went over and looked, then stumped back to where Dolf was standing.

"It seems like," he said, "we jist git yuh outa one mess 'n' yuh git inta another. I got a letter on my desk—got it yesterday—from Mark Wheat in Washington, D.C.; a confession, I guess yuh'd call it. Said he'd got word I wanted him held. Told me I'd likely find 'im in South America or the South Sea Islands. Also said he hired Ott and Hardin ta beef yuh, among some other ancient history. It was him had that stage yuh was supposed ta come in on shot up—figgered you'd blame it on Pardeau an' go after 'im. So yer in the clear on the two deputies. But I'll hev ta hold yuh fer beefin' Ed till we hev a coroner's jury hearing."

Dolf couldn't believe his ears.

"Are you crazy, Tobe? Where'd yuh think I'd be runnin' after shootin' the skunk that shot my brother just now? I ain't goin' anywhere. An' if yuh try to lay a hand on me, they'll be needin' a new sheriff before election."

With that he stalked into the house and left Mulveen standing open-mouthed.

"Come ta think o' it," Mulveen mumbled to himself, "that makes pretty good sense, Dolf."

Dolf went in to see how Matt was making out.

"I got real bad news," Doc said with a long face. Dolf felt his hopes sink until Doc added, "He's sure ta pull through. You'll probably hev ta put up with 'im another fifty years."

CHAPTER 19

BY afternoon the excitement had died down. Matt was upstairs, asleep. Doc had quickly and deftly operated on him right on the big kitchen table, removing all the buckshot. Doc himself was doing the nursing.

Dolf was now alone on the back porch, lounging in a rocker with his feet propped up on the railing. Jim Too was stretched out beside him, contentedly asleep, occasionally breathing a huge, satisfied sigh.

A few old acquaintances who had avoided him before had been by to sheepishly pay their respects. Dolf ruefully recalled that some of them had been in that lynch mob. All of that unpleasantness seemed a lifetime ago. He simply wanted to forget—to live and let live.

Clipping off the end of a cigar and getting it evenly lit occupied his hands, but a constant new worry fully occupied his mind. He knew how Victoria Wheat must feel about killing. Now he had just had to kill again, practically under her nose. She could not help but have heard of it. The whole town had buzzed over it for hours. Before this unhappy incident, Dolf had firmly made up his mind to march over and make his case with Victoria. Remembering the former promise in her lovely eyes, he felt certain one moment what her answer would be, only to have doubts return the next. When his doubts weren't of her, they were of himself.

The question is, he thought, *will I ever be able to let someone else mean so much to me they might hurt me as bad as Theodora did?* He knew that unless he was able to give that sort of complete devotion, he would not be offering Victoria what she, or any woman, deserved.

Her face haunted his memory, the honeyed hair haloing her

great, expressive eyes. He always saw them mirroring the tender concern for his welfare that had been there so many times recently. This vision of Victoria had returned repeatedly during his long convalescence, perhaps contributing that necessary "something-to-live-for" that was the hair's breadth by which he had pulled through.

The sun had passed behind the hills while he'd smoked down his cigar, deeply engrossed in these reflections. Evening's coolness quickly followed sunset in that mountain altitude. It somehow suggested to Dolf he either had to go in where he could hear Mum starting supper or march down the street and learn his uncertain fate. Mum had looked out the window at him several times, shaking her head a little, then left him to his thoughts. She'd bet she knew what was on his mind. *I oughta go out an' point him in her direction and give 'im a kick*, she thought.

His future would most likely have been a great deal different if only she had done that.

Before Dolf could resolve to leave his comfortable perch, Doc joined him, carving the tip from a cigar

"How is he?" Dolf asked.

"Good," Doc said. Noting the stub of a cigar Dolf held, he added, "Care for a fresh one?"

"Why not," Dolf said. He felt the need to talk to someone, perhaps mainly to postpone his final decision.

"I was thinkin' we're gonna have to find some way to give Matt's railroad loot back," Dolf said, avoiding what was really on his mind. Mum had acquainted him with that situation.

"It can wait. We'll figure out a safe way," Doc said. "Maybe we kin give it ta the one o' them two detectives that looked like he had some sense. Where are they, by the way?"

"Dunno. I asked Mulveen ta drop the charges against 'em if he was keepin' 'em alive on my account. They're out on bail anyhow."

"Think he'll do it?"

"He said he would."

Doc laughed. "I shudda beefed the lippy one as a public service."

Dolf chuckled. Then he suddenly stopped. Something indistinct inside the edge of the darkening belt of nearby timber moved and caught his eye.

Doc noted Dolf's sudden alertness.

"Wadya see?" he asked.

"Not sure. Maybe a deer or elk."

Whatever it was, Jim Too, previously awakened by the conversation, noticed it too. He headed out to investigate.

"Gittin' jumpy, I guess," Dolf allowed. "With Pardeau layin' uptown on a plank, I guess we don't have anyone else to be watchin' for."

"Let's hope not."

In a short while, Jim Too returned with his tail wagging.

"If it was anything to sweat over, he'd have raised a fuss," Dolf said, rising and stretching.

Mum opened the door just then and said, "Soup's on."

Dolf welcomed this excuse to further delay his inevitable trek down to the Wheat mansion.

When he stepped out after supper to finally walk the few blocks to Wheat's, full darkness had descended. The sky was crowded with winking early stars accented by a faint, luminous hint of moonrise promising from above the hills to the east.

"Well, boy," he said to Jim Too, "faint heart never won fair lady. I reckon we oughta go up an' see this fair lady; I wouldn't want Mum ta think I was a cradle robber."

If Jim Too's eagerness to be off was a harbinger, Dolf figured he didn't have a thing to worry about.

They passed a few houses and cabins with warm lamplight shining out or reflected on the curtains. Behind some of them, shadowed figures moved, announcing family life inside. It gave Dolf a warm feeling of kinship to his fellow men; he remembered the constant quiet satisfaction and occasional joy of family life. *It all could have been so different*, he thought. *I hope it can be again.*

But there was still an apprehensive twinge of pain close to his heart at the recurring thought that his hopes were perhaps only vain imaginings.

Victoria hardly understood her feelings. One part of her kept counseling, *Run away and hide!* Another cautioned, *Don't be a coward!*

She knew that Dolf had had to kill another man that morning. The whole town was naturally pulsing with the story. Her eastern schooling made her course quite clear; one didn't associate with killers, no matter how just their cause. But she'd known before then that he'd killed.

What about wars? a part of her argued. *Our heroes are the most successful killers when it's supposedly in the cause of society. How have his killings been any different except for the twisted rules society applies? Everyone he ever killed was an enemy of this whole community.*

But suppose that he had killed her father? Would he have done that? Not likely. He had even given Pardeau an opportunity to simply go away. She was sure that Dolf no longer harbored a lust in his heart for revenge against anyone. This was a compelling consideration since someday Mark Wheat might be able to come home again. What then if Dolf were . . . her mind hesitated to even consider this possibility.

She reread the last short paragraph of her father's letter, but her mind was listening for the front gate, as it had been all day. She was seated facing the window in the bedroom above her father's office.

Wheat had written her: "I have asked myself again and again how I can ever face you, of all people. My terribly tragic mistake I can blame on no one but myself. I have betrayed my friends, my trust, myself, but above all you, because I love you above life itself. It is selfish to run away from my past, but nothing can be gained by facing the music now. Prison—and that would be my only possible fate—would kill me in a short while. I would never see you again. Perhaps you would not wish to see me—I hope otherwise. So I'm going away to live down the past, and perhaps someday can return home."

I can never bring myself to condemn him, she thought, tears very close again.

Victoria's spirits received a tremendous lift at the familiar sound of the gate latch being lifted and the hinges protesting slightly as the gate opened. She flew down the stairs, walking on air, her doubts flown.

She threw open the door and was totally unable to suppress her crestfallen look at the sight of Alby Gould. Her look and its significance did not escape his perceptive mind. He had recognized before then what was happening and had accepted it. In fact, he had come to tell her graciously that he was resigned to the inevitable. If he had arrived a scant moment later, he'd have found the man there before him to whom he was unhappily ready to yield the field.

Dolf noted Alby's arrival and recognized the familiar figure in the glow from the front hall lamp as Victoria admitted him. About to turn on his heel and retreat, something arrested him for a few seconds. He soon wished it hadn't.

Victoria, seeing the hurt expression on Alby's face, impulsively put her arms around him and gave him a placating peck on the cheek.

"You know, don't you?" she said.

"I know," Alby replied, holding her in his arms consolingly. "I understand. He's a good man."

But Dolf could not see what was really happening. He was the key person in the situation who *did not* understand. He turned swiftly and strode away, fearful that his presence might be detected, to the embarrassment of everyone. The fleeting pain that had visited his heart from time to time was now heavy and constant.

Jim Too did not understand the sudden change of course. He'd thought he knew where they were going. He sat before the gate and whined dolefully just once. Dolf turned and saw him there in the first mellow light of the rising moon. It was what he'd have liked to have done. But he knew what he actually would do now.

He's her kind, he thought. *How could I have thought anything else?*

He was almost relieved for a moment. He was even able to grin ruefully. He thought, *I guess I've been so lonesome that if a gal said good morning to me, I might have proposed.*

That was indeed a small consolation, however.

At home he checked in on Matt, who was conscious for the first time since he'd been shot. He looked good for one who'd been injured only that morning.

"You Morgettes are indestructible," Doc observed, commenting on both their recent ordeals.

Outside Dolf asked Doc, "Is he apt to have a setback?"

"Not likely," Doc guessed. "Why?"

"I'm goin' on a little *pasear* for a few days. I'll be up at the cabin."

Over the joint protests of Doc, Mum, and Junior, he packed up a few things and was gone within an hour. All three watched him from the porch as he rode Wowakan away in the moonlight, Jim Too trotting faithfully beside the big horse.

"Wadya think?" Doc shrugged the question at Mum.

"The gal must be a damnfool. She sure surprised me. I ain't often that wrong."

"What're you two talkin' about?" Junior asked.

Neither one said anything. He shrugged. Adults were a mystery to him sometimes, although he was rapidly becoming one himself.

Dolf's sixth sense was warning him he was being followed. *Who?* he wondered.

Then he recalled that indistinct motion at the edge of the timber earlier in the evening. This brought back a surge of anger over his fate to always have someone dogging his trail. *We'll arrange a little reception,* he thought, urging Wowakan to a gallop.

He knew just the spot, an arroyo with high, brushy banks

crowding the trail. But he didn't intend to wait in ambush there. Anyone following him with evil intent would surely avoid that spot, expecting him to watch his back trail there. Instead he chose the place where his follower would turn out to go around the narrow arroyo. He hid in the deep shadows of a dense clump of spruce, secure in the knowledge that he'd patiently taught Wowakan and Jim Too to be as silent and still as rocks on his command. There they waited.

Their pursuer soon arrived in view astride a pinto horse, its white spots revealed starkly in the moonlight. Dolf had his rifle ready, but the rider was making no effort at concealment. This was puzzling. Nor did rider and horse turn out to avoid the narrow trail into the dark arroyo ahead. However, when they reached the spot where Dolf had pulled Wowakan aside, it was obvious that this person had been following their tracks. Horse and rider stopped, the rider looked around as though fully aware of what had happened and why.

"Dolf?" the voice called.

He was startled to recognize a female voice. Then he knew who his follower was.

"Over here, Margaret," he answered.

She directed her pinto toward him. It was Chief Henry's daughter. As she came up to him, she was silent, pulling in her mount and looking at him.

"I came after you," she stated.

"I know," he said, not understanding yet.

"I came after you *for two days* and waited for you to do what you had to."

It was the Indian blood in her talking. Now he understood. And suspected even more. He had been, in her eyes, on the warpath. Squaws sometimes went on the warpath, but only if invited. So she had followed, staying out of sight. Her next words confirmed this.

"If the evil one, Pardeau, had killed you, I would have cut his heart out."

She did not mention Victoria, but somehow he knew she'd been an observer of tonight's tableau at the Wheats' gate. If he had gone in and stayed, he would never have seen Margaret Henry again, he suspected.

"I am going with you, Dolf. My father told me."

He thought about that, remaining silent. He did not speak until after he had mounted Wowakan and resumed his course.

"All right," he said.

She swung the pinto in behind him without further talk.

He was grinning slightly. He didn't feel half so lonely anymore. He thought, *Maybe "all right" isn't as proper as "I do" but it'll have to do for now.*

After all, he owed his life to this self-possessed, dusky beauty. He would do right by her. He did as much, as part of his innate code, by even those to whom he owed only revenge.

Later, in the flickering fire glow of his quiet cabin, she lay warmly close to him, her head on his arm, and thought, *This is the great warrior my father foretold.*

Dolf was peacefully asleep, his mind untroubled for the first time in many years.